The Tunnel of Litora Falls

Suzanne A. Smith

Dedication

I would like to dedicate this book to everyone who encouraged me to publish it. I am especially grateful to my grandson, Justin, who played a pivotal role in bringing it to fruition. Throughout the process, he motivated and supported me unwaveringly, and for that, I am deeply thankful.

Preface

Long before the modern world, there was a land of fairies, a land of castles, kings, and queens. It was home to the Gibbon Apes and the fierce Komodo Dragons, who were formidable in battle and devoted to friendship. But perhaps the most important of all were the Litoran people.

The story begins as Neree, the former King of Litora Falls, shares the tales of his lifetime with his grandchildren. And though this land may seem like a dream come true, at times, it is anything but. While many great things occur in the land of Litora Falls, the evil Draconian, Trillian, lurks in the shadows, waiting to destroy Neree and all that he holds dear. In particular, Trillian has his eye on Princess Kayla, the most powerful Litoran woman of all time, who is to be sacrificed for her powers to Trillian's son, Ciar. As Kayla is introduced to the new, simpler world and the parents she has known nothing of for the past years, she also encounters a new kind of evil unlike anything she has ever imagined.

Will King Neree be able to fend off all that threatens his land and the lives of his loved ones? Can he destroy Trillian and Ciar before it's too late? Or will the evil Draconian Trillian find a way to reach Princess Kayla and reign, destroying the world as Neree knows it?

What is the destiny of the Litorans? Be prepared to venture into the Tunnel of Litora Falls.

Special thank you to Kylie Shelton!

Acknowledgment

I would like to express my gratitude to my project manager for her patience and encouragement, as well as her amazing team and everyone who worked on my book. I am especially thankful to EzMariah for helping us create the perfect book cover.

Contents

Chapter One — The Stories Begin

For many years, I was King of the land of Amphibia. It was not something I would have chosen for my life — it was destiny.

My dream has always been to help the young of our land develop their powers to their full potential. The one most important thing to me is that our youth grow up knowing the true history of our land and our ancestors. I have always known that I was meant to train others rather than rule them. I passed my kingdom on to my daughter and her husband at a very young age.

Today, I am following my dream.

The sounds of thunder, streaks of lightning, and the pouring rain splattering on the rooftop make this a day for keeping promises. I could hear the crackling of the fire from halfway down the hall. The boys had been up for hours. I had awakened much earlier to the sounds of their excited chatter about my stories while they scuffled around with the wood.

I couldn't help but smile as I entered the doorway. Snuggled in their blankets in front of my favorite sitting place, Elliott and Koda had fallen asleep.

Young Elliott is my oldest grandson. Koda has called me Grandfather Neree since he was old enough to speak. He is not of my blood, but he couldn't be more of a grandson to me in my heart.

"Good morning, sleepyheads!" I whispered before making myself comfortable.

"Grandfather Neree, the perfect day has arrived!" Koda quickly replied.

"Oh… has it?" I teased.

"Yes, it has!" Elliott interrupted, giving me no chance to tease. "You must! You promised! Please begin where you left off!"

"And that would be…?"

"Grand…fa…ther! You were telling us about your grandfather. You must remember — the day he was attacked!"

"Ah, yes," I replied.

Still in my robe and slippers, I knew well that there would be no getting dressed today. I decided it would be fun to step it up a bit. I wanted to tell my stories in a way that would help them feel like they were there — in that time — seeing everything for themselves. I knew I must be a little more dramatic than usual. Yes, yes indeed... these two never miss a detail, I thought as I began…

***

At first, I thought I was dreaming. The strange array of events around the grounds fogged my mind — at that place somewhere between asleep and awake. The bed slowly drifted from underneath my jaded body. I struggled to pull my thoughts together.

As I slowly began to reach reality, I knew that this was no dream. Spears swished through the air, loud screams of pain, and the thunder of horses engulfed the castle with an eerie feeling of fear.

"The King! The King!" echoed from the entrance square just inside the doors. Shadows of the guards rushed about the grounds, searching the darkness for the intruder, circling the walls.

I flew down the stairs into the entrance just as Father fell to his knees. His unsettling scream pierced my soul... his body trembling at the sight of the King lying on the hard castle floor. Frozen in the doorway, I could feel my heart burst as my eyes met the staff embedded in Grandfather's burly chest. Blood from his wound slowly seeped through his robe.

"How could this have happened? Where were the guards?" Father demanded.

"My prince, we know not from where they came. I was awakened by the noise… just as you!" Lin answered, overcome with fear.

Lin was an elderly castle guard. He had been my father's good friend since he was a young boy. Father trusted him with his life. He handed Father a wooden staff with jagged edges that he had pulled from the window.

"The same as struck your father… I saw only a glimpse… I know not from where they appeared. A black flash of evil beings on horses vanished through the darkness. Large creatures beside them… a spirit like a cloud floating above their heads. It… it was not… it was unlike anything I had seen before. I know not how to say, sir!" he mumbled. "I was helpless. I did not know what was happening. I wanted this to be a dream. But… I knew that it was very real. Evil beings had invaded our home and attacked my grandfather!"

***

For many long hours, Father sat sadly at Grandfather's bedside. Sadness and distress began to consume him as he tried to figure out how this could have happened.

Father was a strong and handsome prince. Most would say he was the image of Grandfather. His dark green eyes and olive skin were a perfect match. He was very proudly blessed with the same friendly and caring personality.

Born and raised in the castle as the eldest son of King Cambious Small, he had always known that, when his time came, he would take his place as King. He never dreamed that it would come at such a young age.

I slumped quietly in the chair next to him, trying to envision who could have done this.

"Why would someone want to hurt my grandfather?"

I remember every detail as clearly as if it were yesterday. I had just turned eighteen.

As far back as I can remember, Grandfather had taught me to look for the good in all things. At the time, it was impossible to understand why anyone would cause this kind of pain to such a great man. I pulled my knees to my chest and covered my face with my hands, trying to hide the tears.

My heart was deeply saddened at the sound of my father's whispers. That day was the first time in my life that I had seen him cry. His sorrowful words broke my heart.

"This is not the time for me to take your place in our kingdom. You are the strongest man I have ever known of all the great leaders and warriors in our lands. You must fight this, my father. I have much to learn from you. It is too soon. I need your guidance… I need you… my father… my king!"

Grandfather could barely open his eyes as he listened to the painful cries. With every ounce of strength in his withering body, he slowly turned his head toward the faint sounds. He calmly looked into Father's tear-filled eyes, carefully raising his limp arm in an attempt to point to the drawer in the tiny wooden table next to his bedside. As he softly closed his eyes, his last breath left his severely wounded body.

Sounds of sorrow echoed across the lands.

"Oh, my father… my king!" Father cried.

I rushed across the room to my grandmother's arms.

Grandmother Tanya was a beautiful, strong, and powerful queen. She had fallen asleep from exhaustion in the long chair at the far end of the room. She sadly rose to comfort me.

"He is gone, Grandmother! Grandfather is gone!" I sobbed, burying my head in her chest. "I will miss him so, Grandmother! My life will not be the same without him."

"We all shall miss him, my child," she replied gently.

She gave me a final hug, raised my face with her hand, and softly wiped the tears from my eyes.

"My child," she whispered, "Grandfather taught you to be strong. You are a prince! Always remember that you must be strong, like your King!"

With the sudden authority of an army, she immediately turned to Father.

"Elliott, you are the King of Litora Falls. You must prepare your father for his departure from our lands and… from us. We must make the proper announcement to our people at once," she commanded. "You have many decisions and arrangements to make, my son."

"Come, Neree… we must wake your mother and your little brother. They must be told of the tragedy that has taken place in our home. Your father must be alone to prepare his thoughts. All of the responsibilities of our lands have now become his to bear."

Father remained at Grandfather's bedside for most of the evening.

"I will know who is responsible for this! This type of spear is unknown to our land. I must know from where it came. I must know who has done this!" he cried, holding the large, flat stick in his hand.

The thought of his father's last moments suddenly flashed before him. Opening the small drawer, he knew well the old white scroll tied with the golden ribbon that lay inside. Through his tears, he carefully opened the note tucked neatly into the edge and read:

***

My son, if you are reading my words… I have passed on from this life. You must not avenge my death. You must always remember that we are a kingdom of good in all ways. You are now the King of Litora Falls and must rule all the regions of Amphibia. I know you will serve your people proud and strong.

Make known to young Neree how much love I hold for him. He will make a great King when his time comes. The time is now at hand for his adventure to begin.

Do with your son as I did with you when you reached the proper age.

He must take the scroll with him on his journey. The time will come when he will be in need of its words. Teach him to keep it safe. It has now become his responsibility to explain these writings to future Litorans.

I love you, my son. Serve your people well.

***

Father tucked the scroll and the note under his arm and left the room, knowing well what he must do to honor Grandfather's final wish.

Chapter Two — Neree's Destiny

Moments after everyone paid their final respects to Grandfather, the ceremony for Father was completed, and Grandmother officially honored him as the new King of Litora Falls and all of Amphibia.

I kept to myself during the ceremonies, trying to fill my mind with all the good times I had spent with my grandfather. I barely noticed when Father approached me and began to speak.

"It has been a long and sad few days for you, my son," he said as he sat in the chair beside me. "I know you are strong and very brave. Your grandfather was your best friend. He taught you many things over the years. He will live on through you. Always remember all the things you learned from him."

"I miss him so much, Father!" I replied.

"You will always miss him, my son. Keep his memories in your heart. He loved you with everything in him. You were his firstborn grandson. You have always been his hope for the future of our world."

"There is one more thing he left for me to do in his honor. I hope you can endure another change in your young life."

Father paused for a moment before he could continue. He asked me to take a walk with him, heading in the direction of the backfields. I knew something serious was about to take place. Father and I had taken many such walks over the years. They always came at a time when he felt the need to explain something difficult to me.

"Just as you do… with us," Koda interrupted.

"Yes," I smiled. "Just as I do with you."

We walked in silence for a short time before he began to explain.

"The journey you are about to begin will greatly affect how you will live for some time to come."

I remember how frightened and confused I suddenly felt. It was difficult to force out the words.

"Father, wha–what journey? What has happened?" I finally mumbled.

"The time has come for you to learn of your destiny and the destiny of your firstborn child."

"My destiny? My firstborn child? I do not understand," I cried. "I thought my destiny was to learn the ways of our land and become King when my time comes. I do not have a child. I do not have a wife. I am much too young for such things, Father. Why do you speak of these things?"

"Neree, you are now a young man. You must begin to plan for your future… the future of your land… your people."

"Yes, your birthright is to take my place as leader of these lands. From my father's own words — you will make a great king when your time comes."

"As for now, an amazing journey awaits you. This journey will take you on a great adventure far away from our land. We will be apart for a very long time."

Suddenly, a swishing roar of shooting lights swarmed around us from every direction! A powerful rush of fear flowed through my veins as I spun around in circles.

"Father... What is happening?" I screamed.

Suddenly, I felt something grab my arms. I could not move. I faintly heard Father's voice as I fell to my knees.

"Neree, take a deep breath. There is nothing to fear," he explained.

As I slowly stood to my feet, I could see Father's face through the blur. Something strange... A small being with beautiful long hair, wearing a flowing white gown, was calmly floating in the air before me.

"What is it, Father?" I asked.

"I am Nalana!" a soft voice interrupted.

"My son, Nalana is the queen of all fairies. She and her followers are special to us. They have protected our secret for many years."

"Secret? Wha..." I began, but my words were cut short by the loud roaring sound of many fairies swarming in the air.

The waterfall embracing the mountain slowly began to part. As it formed a deep tunnel in the center of the mountain, Father began to explain.

"This beautiful tunnel has been well guarded by the fairies for many years. It is revealed only for the eyes of special Litorans. It is an entrance into a world many years in the future. Through our connection with this world, we have opportunities beyond our imagination. The fairies are the only link to this magical tunnel. They alone have the power to form this opening. Only the most special beings of our land have knowledge of the world you are about to enter. Our powers and abilities, along with the protection of Nalana, have made it possible for our family to keep this secret."

"The moment Grandfather passed from us, you became next in line to be King. You were born a very special being, my son."

"Just beyond the woods, at the end of the tunnel, you will find hundreds of acres of undeveloped woodland. If you follow the path around the pond, you will come upon a forty-acre farm. Your grandfather left this land for you and your firstborn child. He built the modest farm home with his own hands many years ago. This world has many new things for you to explore."

"In time, you will return to us and prepare yourself to take your place as King. You will have much wisdom to offer to all who live in our lands."

"Farm… woods… modern world… a future time… I do not know of these things, Father," I cried. "Father, I do not want to go away. I will be lost for what to do. I have never been alone. How will I know where to go… what to do… how to speak? I... I am afraid, Father!"

"Neree, there is no need to be afraid. If the time comes when you feel you are in danger, simply return home instantly. Make use of your powers. Everything will gradually fall into place. You will know what to do, my son."

"At your age, I traveled here. My father and his father and grandfathers before him also traveled here. It is our way! I am wise beyond the times in which we live because of all I learned in this world!"

"This is not something you can refuse to do, my son! It is the beginning of your life as our future King and the beginning of your destiny!"

"There are papers and maps on the table just inside the back door of the farm home. These readings will explain everything you need to know about your new way of life. You will fit in very quickly. Your mother and grandmother are from this world. They have taught you well. You speak the same language as the people you will meet."

"You will become a great and intelligent man, for the betterment of our time. You have the opportunity to learn of future healing and modern inventions."

"I was also afraid!"

"You, Father?"

"Yes, Neree!"

"Choose well how you spend your time on this adventure. There is much knowledge for you to gain in this amazing world. You owe this to yourself and to your people. You owe this to your grandfather."

Father took my hand in his. He held it softly for a moment before closing it tightly around the family scroll.

"Keep this scroll in a safe place, my son. The time will come when you need to explain to your child how your family came to be. Read and explain these writings to her, as I did to you many years ago. She will need to understand how important she is to our world. The information in our scroll will help her understand her own powers and abilities. You will know when the time is at hand."

"Your mother and I will visit you often. You can visit Litora Falls at times you feel the need. You must tell no one of this place."

"Before you go, you must read the note Grandfather left for you."

With much sadness, I opened the small, folded paper and read in amazement:

Neree,

Your destiny has now begun. You must travel through the Tunnel of Litora Falls to a world far beyond our time. Your powers and abilities will become the greatest in the three regions of our land. You will be the most successful and powerful King known to our people and discover many things useful to our lands for the hope of our future.

You will fall in love with and marry a human woman of this future world. Your firstborn will be a daughter with the greatest powers and abilities of her father, and the human blood and knowledge of her mother, and her mother's world. This combination will help to make her the most powerful woman born to our land. She will also discover many things.

She will marry the son of Sir Harold Rainie. Together, they will lead our people to a great future.

She will be in grave danger from the evil that has settled in the dark hills of the Dracara Mountains. Their leader, Trillian, has plans for her destruction and the destruction of our people and our great land. She must be hidden in this new world. She must be told nothing of our lands or our people until the day she becomes old enough to surpass this evil plan. The future of Litora Falls depends on her survival.

Remember, my prince, only use your special powers to protect your kingdom from danger. I will always be with you… inside your heart.

Grandfather

"Father, does this mean I will take a wife here, in this strange land and time? Will my child be in great danger in my own land?"

"Just follow your heart, Neree. You will be safe here! This is a wonderful world with many great advantages. Yes, you will find your future wife here. As for your child's danger… only time can tell us!"

"Go, my son… quickly!"

"You must get settled into your new place. Your mother and I will visit you soon. Read over all the papers and maps. Try to learn as much as you can of this new world before we return."

"Give this adventure a chance for your people… for your grandfather… for your firstborn child… and for yourself!"

"Our future, the future of our land and our people, depends on you and your firstborn!"

"I will do my best, Father… As Grandmother said, I am a prince. I must be strong for the people of Litora Falls and all of Amphibia, and for Grandfather's memory!"

"I will make you proud, sir," I promised.

"Neree, there is one more thing," Father said as he handed me a tiny gold key. "Behind the mirror in your sleeping room at the top of the stairs, you will find a small safe. It will open by pressing the numbers on the back of this key and turning it slightly to your left. Inside the safe, you will find a checkbook, cash, a credit card, and instructions for their usage. It is the way of life here. You will understand as time passes. In this world, things are not as simple as you have known in your young life. There is much to explain!"

"You should probably know one more family secret before you begin your life here. We are what they call… very wealthy… in the lands you are about to enter. It has to do with diamonds… very difficult to explain; no time now. You must read the instructions in the safe. Yes… then you will better understand. You must go now."

"I do not know of any of this, Father!" I said with a deep sigh. "Cash, checkbooks, wealth… I know nothing of any of these things! I am going to miss our simple way of life!"

"That is what I always missed the most, my son!"

"Father… I will do my best. Are my powers…?"

"Yes, my son, your powers work much the same here as they do in our world," Father interrupted. "Just remember to use them wisely. The people of these lands do not understand such things."

I tried to think positively as I watched Father disappear from my sight. The fairies gathered tightly, forming a lighted bridge over the fast-flowing river. I slowly walked across, in amazement at their abilities.

I was emotionally exhausted as I followed Nalana toward the opening. The fairies suddenly flew apart behind me, their glow giving me light as I sadly walked through the tunnel and entered the woods leading to my new home. I did not want to go away! I was frightened and confused! I did not know what to do… what to think.

When I reached the edge of the beautiful trees, I thanked Nalana and all the fairies. I will never forget the kind words she spoke as she flew away.

"If you are ever in need of anything, just think of me. I will appear unto you. Good luck, young prince. We will await your return!"

I watched in amazement as the tunnel disappeared into the trees, and the waterfalls flowed freely once again.

"Unbelievable," I shouted, looking ahead.

I managed a smile of pleasure while I continued. The view of the farmland and home before my eyes was much more beautiful than I expected. This was the first day of my new life. I continued to walk slowly across the grounds to the adventure awaiting me. I had no idea what lay ahead. I will never forget the feelings I had that day. My life was changed forever. This was the first time I learned of "The Tunnel of Litora Falls."

***

Koda asked, "Grandfather Neree, is this true? Is there really such a tunnel? What are diamonds?"

"Yes! It is all true!" Elliott answered. "I have been there with Mother. I have never heard of diamonds. No one bothered to tell me about that. I do know that it is a very sacred place. I could tell no one… not even you… I am so sorry, Koda!"

"Elliott is right, Koda. This is one secret that he was sworn to keep. You must also promise to speak to no one of this story. Diamonds are beautiful, clear stones we find in our tunnel. They have great worth in the modern world. It is not something we have use of… here, in our time. It is most necessary in the land of my story, however. Anyway, for many reasons, it would be very dangerous if the evil beings in our land learned of this place!"

"I promise, Grandfather. I will tell no one. It is just… it is so unbelievable!" Koda replied.

"The tunnel is very real! You have been there… you were too young to remember… It was the night your little brother was born… Your time will come, Koda… I promise you!"

Chapter Three — New Adventure

"Grandfather... How did you meet Grandmother?" Elliott asked.

I tossed him a large pillow and told him to get comfortable.

"Many adventures have crossed my path in my lifetime. It is best to continue from the beginning. When I have finished my stories, you will know everything that has taken place in my life," I assured him as I continued.

The afternoon flowed quickly into the evening as I reached the edge of the backyard of my new home. The reddish-orange sunset in the distance of the rooftop began to softly disappear into the evening. With every step, the full moon slowly rose above the thick, green grass. Beautiful oak trees, shrubs, bushes, and flowers encircled my vision from every direction.

The emptiness in my heart quickly filled with warmth and calmness as I continued across the grounds. When I reached the center of the backyard, I paused for a moment to admire an old oak tree. I envisioned a treehouse, in the likeness of the Litoran castle, near the top.

Someday, I thought.

I felt comfort like I had never known.

I entered the house through what appeared to be the cooking area. The room was large. Several strange items stood against the walls and were placed orderly on the countertops. I opened the door of the tall, gray, square box that stood against the far wall. I stepped back for a moment, stunned by the brightness inside. It was full of food and drinks, much like our cold box at home. It appeared bright, like a huge firefly lantern.

Several papers and maps were neatly stacked at the end of the large table, just as Father had said there would be. Looking around the room, I realized how much I had to learn. I quickly understood my father's enthusiasm for this world.

I gathered the papers and maps before entering the next room. The ceiling was high, creating an amazing appearance of space for such a small building. Three doors filled the area to the right. Next to the last door, a spiral staircase reached all the way to the top of the room.

To the left, the space was wide open. A long, dark seat faced the fire-burning hole in the wall. Pieces of cut tree limbs were neatly stacked against the wall. A soft cover filled the center of the floor. Reading books covered the remaining wall to the far left of the room.

Darkness began to cover the sky as I searched for lanterns or fireflies, with no success. Before checking where the steps led, I spread the papers and maps across the cover on the floor and made a fire in the fireplace to warm the chill in the air. The light from the fire and the brightness of the full moon flowing through the window gave me enough light to read the material.

I was very anxious to learn about this place and all it had to offer me. Quickly, my head swam with enthusiasm. I could not stand it any longer. I had to observe some of the unbelievable information boggling my mind. My body trembled with excitement as I walked across the room to the white switch on the wall. I could not control my smile as I flipped the switch.

Instant light… amazing… words cannot explain the feeling.

"I wonder what our fireflies would think of electricity?" I mused.

"Electricity?" Koda interrupted.

Young Elliott giggled as I continued.

I wanted to bring this new way of life to the castle. However, I knew it would be impossible to explain these wonderful things to anyone in my world so many years in the past. I was not sure I would want to disrupt my simple world in such a way.

Before continuing my studies, I quickly toured the rest of my new home. I tried very hard to remember everything I had read: stove, refrigerator, television, stairway, fireplace, bookshelf... repeating each item as I passed. I was fascinated by the miraculous inventions that surrounded me at every turn.

I spent most of the night studying the papers and maps. I was determined to learn quickly. As I studied the maps, I became very confused. I noticed all the lands were spread apart, covering all ends of the world. I searched frantically, trying to find my world as I knew it.

"Nothing!" I exclaimed. Maps of our three great regions were nowhere to be found. It was as though my world had vanished.

"How could something like this have happened to my land? What of my people... my friends... if our land no longer exists as it did in my world?"

"My family and friends must be saved!" I sighed.

I knew that I must research this matter.

"I cannot let this happen!" I declared. "I must warn my father... my friends!"

I could not imagine what could have taken place to create this change. My head spun like the twisting winds of a storm. I suddenly felt very alone and confused. I glanced sadly at all the things across the room and managed to find my way to the wall of books. I picked up an encyclopedia and quickly flipped through the pages, paying careful attention to the maps and pictures, trying to find information, if only a clue, about my world.

Finally, I spotted a map that resembled how I imagined the lands connected to my homeland would be shaped. Turning back a few pages, I knew it must be... but how?

"Pangaea... The supercontinent drifted... millions of years... what does this mean?"

I leaned against the wall as I continued to read. This theory... **"Theory!"** I yelled.

Maybe — just maybe — when my ancestors returned home to tell their parents of their adventure, the land had only moved, and they were still alive. We have never searched beyond the waters... It is not possible... I wonder... Is the land we now live on what is called an island, developed from this change that took place?

"What are you speaking of, Grandfather?" Koda asked.

"Give him time, Koda," Elliott interrupted. "We will know as he goes on."

"Yes, you will, I promise. Sometimes I get a little ahead of myself, Koda. I will get to everything in time!"

I read everything I could find on the theory of Pangaea. Then I remembered the stories my mom had read to me from her sacred book. She had taken it with her when she left this world with her father to live in ours. She had told me it was the one thing she could never leave behind. She had a lot of faith in its readings. Just maybe the same superior being had created our world, and the plan for our connection was there all along.

I found it strange that this world, with all of its modern inventions and intelligence, could not figure out how it all really began so many years ago.

A sense of pride and confidence came over me as I realized that I was much more intelligent than I had thought. I knew that I had a good chance of making it here after all. I placed the books back in place and continued studying the maps and papers Father had left for me.

Just as I finished going over the final pages, I fell asleep on the floor in front of the warm fire.

I woke feeling refreshed, just in time to view the sunrise. My mind was bursting with all the information I had attained. The early morning breeze filled the room with the smell of oak, enhancing the chirping sounds of the birds on the window ledge. After enjoying a few deep breaths, I took another quick tour of the upstairs.

I was most excited to find a closet full of clothes in the sleeping room on the left as I entered the door on the right.

"Awww yes, bathroom... an amazing invention!"

"This is unbelievable!" I thought after taking a hot shower.

In Litora Falls, bathing was done in washing stalls or ponds. In those days, we gathered water to heat in pots on the wood-burning stove when the weather was cold.

"Wow! With the turn of a silver knob — instant hot water!" This was beyond anything I could have imagined.

"Grandfather, we must take Koda to the farm. It's not fair to him, especially now that he knows of it," Elliott interrupted.

"I would love to go!" Koda butted in.

"I will take you both soon. I promise. Let me continue."

After forcing myself to finish such a wonderful experience, I tried to remember all the instructions for the day. I dressed in a nice casual outfit and lace-up shoes. When I looked in the mirror, I remembered the safe Father had mentioned. I took the key from my pouch and carefully opened the lock.

Everything was just as Father had said it would be.

I gathered my wallet, checkbook, school transcripts, and my birth certificate. After reading the instructions for their usage, I was confident that I was fully prepared for my first journey into the city.

I was excited to begin my adventure. After all that I had learned in a few short hours, I could not begin to imagine the information on medical treatment and cures that I would have the opportunity to learn. I took my father's advice and used my powers to instantly arrive at Eureka Springs University.

Chapter Four — Nadia

As I looked through the glass door of the building ahead of me, I stopped — frozen in my steps. My heart melted at the sight of the beautiful young woman before me. She had pretty long hair and the most beautiful eyes I had ever seen. She was sitting alone at a large table in front of the window.

I took a deep breath and collected my thoughts before I steeled myself to enter the building. I hoped she would not notice that I could not take my eyes off her beauty as I approached the table.

"Good morning. May I help you?" she asked, looking up at me with a pleasant smile. My heart melted inside my chest at the sweet sound of her voice.

I do not know how I managed to get the words out.

"I would like to register for these classes," I mumbled. It was very difficult not to stare while handing her my transcripts and ID. My heart continued to throb at the sound of her kindness.

"I think everything is in order," I announced with a deep swallow.

"You're in luck, sir," she said. "All the classes you need are available. You will need to fill out these forms. When you have them completed, turn them in to the lady at the first window. She will finalize your paperwork and show you to the bookstore. Once you have paid your tuition and purchased your books, you will be all set."

"Thank you for your help," I said.

I paused for a moment — powerless — gazing into her beautiful eyes.

"Is... there something else?" she asked, breaking my trance.

"Do you work here? May I ask your name?" I blurted out before I could stop myself.

"I am Nadia," she quickly answered.

"Grandmother," Koda interrupted.

"Yes," Elliott whispered.

"I hope to work here soon. I will actually be one of your classmates. I am a student teacher at Eureka Springs High School. I am taking a few classes here at the college to get my master's degree. Once I have completed my courses, I will apply for a job here teaching chemistry and anatomy."

"You look much too young to be a teacher," I interrupted.

"I entered college at fourteen… just one of those geniuses… mostly in science and math… you know… too smart for my own good," she laughed. "I am actually only eighteen."

"Anyway, Professor Dunn is retiring in a year or so. I hope to replace him at that time."

"I guess I will see you in class then," I said.

"It was nice to meet you," she replied.

"I am very pleased to meet you too, Nadia," I assured her.

I sadly walked away. I wanted nothing more than to stay and get to know everything about her.

It was late when I finished the last bit of paperwork and collected my books. I took a detailed tour of the facility before I left for home.

I could not get Nadia off my mind. She was the most beautiful, interesting, and sweetest woman I had ever met. I could not wait for my classes to begin.

When I returned home, Father was quietly sitting by the warm fire. Mother was straightening the papers I had left scattered across the floor. She had picked up my clothes and other things about the house.

I was embarrassed that I had left such a mess for her to see. She had a delicious meal warming on the stove for my return. I knew that I, without a doubt, had the best mom ever.

"How was your day, my son?" she asked as I entered the room.

"It was very good," I replied. "I have learned many things since I arrived. This is the most amazing place I have ever seen."

"I registered for school, purchased my books and supplies, and..." I paused for a moment. "Oh, I... I met the most beautiful, interesting, and intelligent woman I have ever seen. You should see her, Mother. She is so... um..." I mumbled, realizing suddenly that I was speaking to my mother.

"She teaches high school here in town. She is taking classes at the college to get her master's degree. She is only eighteen. She has completed four years of college. She is a genius of this time. I have some classes with her. I hope to get to know her better very quickly. She is..."

"Slow down a bit, Neree," Father said. "There are many beautiful women here. The right woman will find her way to you. It is your destiny. When you meet her, you will know."

"I think I met her today, Father!" I replied.

"Perhaps I should stay for a while to guide our son!" Mother interrupted.

"He will be fine on his own, dear!" Father replied. "You must remember he is a prince... an adult... no longer your little boy."

"He will do the right thing when the time comes."

"He will always be my little boy," she replied.

"We must return home before Aron discovers we have gone away. Take care of yourself, my son. If you need us, you know what to do," she said with a big hug.

"I will miss all of you so much. You must bring Aron with you on your next visit," I said sadly.

"He is too young. He must not be told of this world," Mother said.

"We will miss you, my son," Father interrupted. "We will see you often. Be very careful and try to get the most from your adventure here, as I did," he added, as they vanished from my sight.

I spent the next few days getting to know the farm. I planted a small garden beyond the backyard, practiced cooking on the stove, and looked over my schoolwork.

I missed my family and friends even more than I had thought possible.

"Maybe I will make some friends at school today," I thought as I prepared to leave for my first class.

I arrived at the university somewhat early in hopes of seeing Nadia.

"She must be in a different room," I thought as I took a seat — just as the bell rang.

I had always been a very bright child. Early in my third class of the day, I knew I was going to enjoy my training. I found the professors serious but interesting, the material fascinating, and my classmates very different from my friends at home.

I could not understand why I had not seen Nadia. She had mentioned that she was going to be one of my classmates, but I had not seen her since I had arrived.

At the end of my last class, as I was preparing my notes, I glanced out the window just in time to catch a glimpse of Nadia sitting on a wooden bench. I rushed out the door in hopes of catching up with her.

"I missed you in class today, Nadia," I said as I sat on the bench next to her. She looked very sad… as though she had been crying.

"Are you all right?" I asked.

"Neree," she said. "I'm sorry. I didn't realize it showed. I am a little sad."

"My grandmother passed away last night. I stopped by to pick up my homework. I don't wish to get behind in my classes. I won't be attending school for a few days."

"I am very sorry," I said. "I understand how you must feel. My grandfather passed away a few days before I came here. He was a great man. I miss him very much. It is so hard to lose someone you love."

"If you need help, I could help you catch up before you return. I live outside the city on the Small's farm."

"I know the place," she said. "I didn't know that anyone was living there."

"My grandfather left it to me when he passed away. I am just getting settled in," I explained.

"We do have some of the same classes. I might take you up on your offer. I'll try to stop by over the weekend," she said. "I'll see you then. I have to go now. I need to spend time with my mother. She isn't taking my grandmother's passing very well."

Early Sunday morning, Nadia stopped by the farm to look over my notes. Together, we spent most of the day going over my material, walking about the farm, and getting to know each other.

"I did not want the day to end!"

"Thank you so much for your help, Neree. I should get going. I would like to get home before it gets dark. I'll see you in class tomorrow."

"Thank you again. I really enjoyed getting to know you," she said. I was stunned but happy when she gave me a hug.

As she drove away, I knew, deep down inside, fate had brought us together. I felt in my heart that she was the woman I was destined to marry.

We spent the first semester of the school year learning many things, dating, and getting to know everything about each other. We quickly fell deeply in love, knowing in our hearts that we belonged together.

I told her everything I thought she should know about my home and my people. I knew I must be honest about how my family came to be if we were going to have a solid future together. She curiously read the scrolls and notes of my family, my home, and my destiny, increasing her love for me even more. Not once did she show any signs of fear or disbelief about anything I explained about my life.

In October, I invited her to my home. I cooked her a nice dinner and asked her to be my wife.

She happily agreed to give up her world and make her new home with me in Litora Falls.

We spent weeks discussing our plans for our future together. Nadia traveled with me through the tunnel for a tour of Amphibia in November of the following year. She met my parents, family, and many of my friends. She quickly fell in love with my simple way of life. Nadia knew she had made the perfect choice — to be our Princess and Queen.

Mother instantly knew that Nadia was the woman for me. She felt a special love for her the moment their eyes met for the first time. She knew, without any doubt, that she was the perfect choice for our Princess and future Queen.

We were married on that Sunday afternoon in a beautiful flower garden ceremony in the backfields of the castle.

Just before we were to begin, I surprised Nadia with her mother Lori's arrival to the lands. I knew how much it would mean for her to have her mother there with her. I also knew how important it was for Lori to meet my family and become a part of her daughter's new world.

A few hours after the ceremony, Nadia, Lori, and I returned to the farm and school. We were more compatible and comfortable together than I could have hoped. We were truly happy.

We finished our third year of school together, knowing that it would be our last. We had both advanced well ahead of the rest of the class, graduating in a much shorter time.

Nadia told me just before our graduation that she was going to have a baby in late August. I agreed to her wishes to give birth at the Eureka Springs Women's Center before we returned to Litora Falls. She felt a sense of comfort knowing our child would be born in her world with all the advantages of modern facilities and medical care.

She was content with the fact that soon after the birth, she would be leaving her mother and her friends. She knew our future would be to reign as the King and Queen of Litora Falls.

"Grandfather, do you still have the family scroll?" Koda asked.

"Yes, he does," Elliott interrupted. "I have seen it."

"Grandfather, would you read it to us?"

"Yes! The time has come for you to learn how we came to be."

Chapter Five — The Litoran Family Scroll The Beginning

In the beginning, our world was simple. All the creatures of our land lived together in peace. We thought nothing of the differences in our appearance from other species.

I was the leader and protector of the young frogs in my family. I will never forget the day that changed all of our lives forever. I led my siblings and all of the young frogs in our homeland on an overnight adventure.

The sunrise sparkled through the trees as we set out on our journey. We traveled far beyond our home to the land of springs and waterfalls.

About an hour into our travels, we came to the edge of an unusually high cliff. Through the fog, we could faintly see what appeared to be a cluster of springs seeping through a small section of rolling hills.

Suddenly, a dark cloud covered the sky. Flashes of sharp light, loud thunder, and strong twisting winds shifted the lands. Without warning, we were thrown into the waters below. I vaguely remember the strong current, the screams of my friends, the feeling of helplessness, and the horrifying sensation of fear as we were swept downstream into the rugged hillsides.

I will never forget the painful feeling of my body being trapped inside a dark cave. Every inch of me was stuck deep inside the walls of hot clay, with hot water of many colors and unusual smells gushing through the creases from every direction.

I was helpless and terrified for the first time in my life.

The burning sensation and the screams of pain cut through me like nothing I had ever known. I could feel my body expanding with every move. I did not know what was happening or how to free myself.

I could faintly hear voices and the shuffling of brush in the distance.

I knew them.

Yes, it was them. My Komodo dragon and Gibbon Ape friends had followed us; they must have heard our cries.

I felt hope for the first time. I knew that they would help us.

Suddenly, the river slowly calmed enough for them to swim closer to us safely.

They dug and dug through the thick clay to free us.

After washing the clay from our bodies, we slowly stepped out of the water. We were grateful that our friends had followed us and saved our lives.

As we reached the land, we realized something very strange. We were no longer the same. We were tall anthropoid creatures, walking upright, strong and powerful. We did not know what was happening.

We knew that our parents were the only ones who could help us understand.

We began our journey home.

As I slowly walked away, I turned for one last look at the caves.

To my surprise, crystal-clear waterfalls were flowing down the hillside once more.

When we came upon the entrance to our homeland, everything was very different. There were no signs of our families or homes. It was as though everything had vanished.

Water from the ocean covered the land that had once been ours.

Something unexplainable had truly happened across our land.

Our world, as we knew it, was no longer.

It was a very sad day for all of us, indeed.

We were left alone to grow up on our own — without our parents, without our homes.

Over the next few weeks, we worked hard to build shelter and gather food.

We were forced by fate to become adults well before our time.

We began to notice many strange changes taking place in the appearance of our young bodies.

We had transformed into amazing upright creatures with the strange ability to metamorphose into frogs at any time for protection. We were strong and handsome, with great intelligence and many powers.

We named the beautiful world we had settled in Amphibia in honor of our heritage.

As we grew and trained to perfect our powers, we began to pair up and reproduce.

As the eldest and leader, I helped each species choose names and sections of land to make their homes and raise their families.

We divided Amphibia into three great regions.

Our species would remain in the southern and central regions of Litora Falls.

We chose Litoran for our family name.

Litora Falls was the most beautiful of the three regions of Amphibia.

It was covered with thick green grass and trees. Beautiful flowers covered many rolling hills, while rivers, streams, and breathtaking waterfalls lined the southern ends.

We were blessed with great strength and many powers.

We had perfected the ability to travel from one place to another with the simple power of thought. Some had the ability to communicate with the animals and the trees across the land.

We attained many magical powers that could prove to be very useful once developed properly.

We devoted our lives to accepting our place with pride and honor.

Many of the Litorans traveled outside the boundaries of our land from time to time.

Some of the males paired up with women from the Cherokee Indian tribes across the lands.

It was known that the Cherokee Indians were the first to settle in this place. A Litoran woman named Vida Mae married a Cherokee Indian chief's son called Bear-Cloud Rainie. They produced a son that began the Cherokee Indian bloodline in our world.

The Gibbon Apes developed the ability to metamorphose from their larger, less creature-like form to their naturally smaller gibbon ape species. They retained the least powers and were the most creature-like in appearance among the three species. Some preferred to remain as apes and live in the trees. They found it difficult to accept the change.

They chose the region to the east, naming it Salientra Springs. Gathering in the thickest section of the trees, they named their homeland Gibbon Forest. Salientra Springs was covered with beautiful trees and many springs flowing from the rivers and ponds.

A panoramic mountain, adorned with beautiful trees and flowers, covered the far east side of the lands, connecting to the large ocean.

They called themselves Ceairans. Raised with the bow and arrow for recreation and competition, archery became a major part of their training. They became well-known for their amazing archery abilities. Although vegetarians by nature and nonhunters, this special talent could prove to be most useful in the event of an invasion or battle.

The Komodos chose the western region, naming it Trundra Hills. Its beautiful combinations of rolling hills, desert, and streams were perfect to meet their needs. They settled in the desert section of the region, calling their new home Varanus Desert.

They were strong and powerful. The leaders of the species lived as upright beings with creature-like features. Many of their species also found it difficult to live in their new form and remained as true Komodo dragons.

All in the lands considered them the most prepared and greatest of warriors. Each one was a swordsman of great perfection. They alone had the ability to shoot poison from their mouths, so powerful it could paralyze or even kill their prey within seconds. This ability allowed some to forget they had many other powers of even greater use when needed. They would be most feared by an intruder if an invasion should arise.

They kept their family name, Komodo Dragons, in honor of the families they had lost.

For the next few years, we lived closely together as a group of a few survivors from an unusual species of friends. We did not know how to explain all the powers and gifts that we had been given. We did not fully understand why this had all happened to us.

Above all the vows we had made, the most important was to remain the best of friends and to help and protect each other in times of need.

Soon after we settled in our new homes and our young were born, an unknown evil settled in the lands. Strange darkness formed on the far side of the north hills of the Dracara Mountains. The evil beings, seen only from a distance, wore dark cloaks with hoods, hiding their true appearance from all not of their own kind. They rode black horses as they crept around in the darkness, keeping all knowledge of them hidden deep in the mountains.

Soon, stories of their evil ways swept the lands, causing fear for all.

Trillian made known his plan to destroy our lives and our land. The events that would unfold at the hands of Trillian are unclear in the writings of this time.

We are a strong unit, bound together by fate.

Our destiny is to protect our world and the Tunnel of Litora Falls from the evil Draconians.

The future of our world is in our hands.

Chapter Six — Nadia's Pregnancy

It took a bit for the boys to absorb everything that they had learned. After a short break to clear their minds, they were ready to hear more. They were anxious to learn about the wars and many amazing adventures of my life. Above all, I felt that it was important for them to understand how we all came to be such amazing living beings.

All of the stories will come in time.

"Grandfather, I am confused," Elliott blurted out as he took a seat in front of me. "You said the letter your grandfather left you read that the son of Sir Harold Rainie (who is my dad) was destined to marry the Litoran Princess (who is my mom)."

"Yes, that is true. And he did. I do not understand the problem," I answered.

"My father has always told me that our name, Rainie, is of the Cherokee Indians. How can that be if we are frogs? Are we Cherokee Indians, or are we frogs? I do not understand, Grandfather."

"As it said in the scroll in the beginning, many of the Litorans traveled outside the boundaries of our land from time to time. Some of the males paired up with females of the Cherokee Indian tribes across the lands. The Cherokee Indians were the first to settle in these lands. A Litoran woman named Vida Mae married a Cherokee Indian chief's son called Bear-Cloud Rainie. Together, they produced a son. Their son was the beginning of the Cherokee Indian bloodline in our world. You are part of that bloodline," I explained as I continued.

Nadia enjoyed her pregnancy. She spoke often of how quickly the time seemed to be passing. Before we knew it, August had arrived.

A couple of weeks before our baby was to be born, we attended an award dinner at the local high school. To our pleasant surprise, the dinner was in honor of Nadia.

A loud roar of applause echoed through the ballroom as she made her way to the podium.

"Teacher of the decade!" "What an honor!"

It was at that moment when I realized how much she would soon be giving up. I could not help but wonder if she really understood the simple way of life that she was about to begin with my family.

I could feel the warmth of joy and love in the hearts of her friends and colleagues. I knew that she must love me more than I could have dreamed possible.

The excitement and attention exhausted Nadia very quickly. We left the ceremony a few moments after she graciously accepted her award.

Lori felt concerned that we had arrived home much earlier than we had anticipated.

Nadia proudly placed her award on the mantel of the fireplace, gave her mother a quick review of the ceremony, and retired for the evening.

Lori told me to get some rest while I had the chance because she had a feeling the baby might be coming sooner than we had been informed.

Nadia was restless and uncomfortable until around midnight. Unable to fall asleep, she quietly eased out of bed, trying not to wake me. She took a nice warm shower, quickly dressed, and gathered her things for the hospital. She knew there was no time to waste.

She smiled as she stood over the bed watching me sleep, knowing I was unaware my firstborn child was about to make her appearance in the world.

She carefully sat down on the edge of the bed and softly touched my shoulder.

"Wake up, sleepyhead!" she whispered. "It is time to go to the hospital!"

I was startled at the sound of the most anticipated words I had ever heard spoken. I jumped out of bed so quickly that I stumbled over my own feet, flipping halfway across the floor and landing flat on my back.

The boys thought my making a fool of myself was quite funny.

Nadia could not stop laughing, much like the two of you. I commented with a smile, "This is not exactly a good time to make me laugh!"

"She giggled! You are such a clown!"

"I wonder what your people would think of their powerful future leader if they could see you now!"

"Try to pull yourself together quickly. We need to get going. I am afraid our firstborn is not going to wait much longer to arrive!"

"I will wait for you downstairs," she laughed.

Nadia stepped into the hall just in time to see Lori waiting at the top of the stairway.

"I'm ready," Lori announced. "I could hear all the commotion coming from your room and knew your time had come!"

"Let's go slow, poke," Nadia yelled as she and Lori headed for the front door.

"I am coming," I answered, hurrying down the stairs so quickly that I tripped on the bottom step. I grabbed the railing to stop myself from falling for the second time in fifteen minutes.

"You would think you were having this baby," Lori laughed.

"I do not know what is wrong with me this morning," I said. "I have never been so clumsy!"

"Give me the keys," Lori insisted. "I think it would be a good idea for me to drive. I would really like to get my daughter to the hospital in one piece before my grandchild is born!"

"I've never seen you so nervous," Nadia whispered.

"You would think you were a normal human being," she laughed.

"I have never seen a baby born. I am going to be a father," I said. "This is a most exciting day for me… This is a most special day for my kingdom… my people!"

Chapter Seven — Princess Kayla

I calmed down quickly the moment we arrived at the hospital. Dazed by the rushing around of nurses and doctors, the modern machines and monitors with wires and IV tubes numbed my body. I had studied all of these things in medical books and practiced with them in the classroom clinical, but… my child was about to be born.

"All of this was for my family!"

Seeing all the equipment in use at one time under the bright light above Nadia's bed was much more intense than the photos and demo machines.

"I watched my brave wife in amazement as our baby daughter entered the world!"

"You made it just in time," the doctor said as he handed our baby to the nurse. "You have a strong baby girl!"

I could not believe all the attention and care that my family was getting from the hospital staff.

"This is a wonderful place to have a child born," I said as the nurse wrapped my princess tightly in her soft, pink receiving blanket. She placed a tiny matching cap on her head to help her feel safe and warm.

Nadia's heart filled with pride as the nurse laid Kayla in her arms for the first time.

"Kayla is my mother," Elliott said.

"She sure is, Elliott."

"She was a most beautiful baby!"

I could feel so much love and joy when Mother, Father, and Lori entered the room. I knew that I must be the most fortunate man alive to have such a wonderful family.

"Have you ever seen a more beautiful little girl?" Nadia asked.

"Never," I spoke softly as I quietly sat beside her on the hospital bed. Tears rolled down my face as I tried to imagine how this wonderfully perfect baby — with the biggest deep-blue eyes I had ever seen — could possibly be my very own little princess.

After everyone left, I cuddled beside Nadia and Kayla for a while longer. I wanted to hold my family as close as possible... forever. We quickly fell sound asleep.

When the nurse came in to check on Nadia and Kayla early in the morning, she told us that she didn't have the heart to wake us.

The doctor checked in at about… She told us that they were doing remarkably well, and I could take them home.

The aide brought us both breakfast after checking Kayla over thoroughly.

We had not talked much since we had arrived at the hospital. Everything happened so fast, and Nadia was too exhausted for much conversation.

I knew we had some important decisions to make and could not wait any longer.

I laid down my fork and looked at Nadia for a moment before I broke the silence.

"How long before we can leave for Litora Falls?" I blurted out. "I must plan her presentation to my world."

Nadia looked at Kayla for a moment before she spoke.

"You know we can't take her with us," she replied. "As much as it breaks my heart, we both know it's much too dangerous for her in your world."

"She is your firstborn child."

"I fear the words written in the scrolls of the evil Draconians!"

"We have talked about this many times; we agreed!" she insisted. "How is it that you cannot understand?" I demanded.

"The stories that you have heard were written by Trillian, the Draconian leader. They were his plans for his firstborn son!"

"I am sure he wishes his words were indeed his son's destiny. I have explained this to you many times before. They have no power over me — or my people. They are evil beings with a goal to destroy all that is good in our land!"

"I alone have the powers to keep my daughter safe."

"You have not yet seen the things my people can make happen when we need to protect ourselves. We have powers and strengths beyond our imagination. I have shown you very little of the powers which I possess. We only use these special gifts for good and to defend our own from danger. However, we are capable of things you know nothing about."

"I do not know why you cannot understand the things I try to explain to you."

"They are not like us. They are evil… ruthless… destructive beings. They are trying to scare us with this talk!"

"They do not have the power to make anything they speak of happen!"

"You don't know that for sure!" she insisted.

"The first part of their… talk, if you will, has already come to pass!"

"Your father told me himself, on the day of our wedding, that the scroll reads: 'the firstborn son of King Elliott and Queen Angelique will marry a woman — not of their own kind. His firstborn will be a daughter with the blood of an… unknown world and time.'"

"If there is no reason for concern, how do you explain… us?"

"My father!"

"I am soon to be the leader of my world. I will protect my people and my daughter."

"We have many scrolls passed down for generations that explain the destiny of my firstborn child. The words of our elders also read: 'I will have a daughter of a different world and time.' It goes on to read that she will grow to be the most powerful and intelligent female leader the land has ever known."

"Our generations hold the power for this destiny to be fulfilled!"

"This is what will come to be!"

"Trillian could have received word of Kayla's destiny and written his own to try and shake up our world a bit. My people have waited many years for this birth!"

"They are preparing for our arrival as we speak! We control our destiny by our own actions!"

"Neree, your father told me himself of Trillian. He also told me of his evil ways and the words he has written!"

"Your father is the leader of your world at this time!"

"You are leaving out the final words of the passage you quoted… It states: 'If she is kept from the hands of the Draconian leader and all his evil.' Your father read it to me himself."

"Do not think you can make light of this and change my mind!"

"He made me promise to keep our firstborn safe from this evil. He is the wisest man I have ever known. I put my trust completely in his word!"

"My mind is made up!"

"As much as I will miss her in my life until this dark time passes, she will remain in my world with my mother!"

"She is safe here! Besides, I want her to know of my world and our modern way of life before she learns of her heritage and her destiny."

"The Draconians know nothing of this time… this world. You said it yourself; they do not have the power to come here."

"You can come for her and tell her everything once it is safe for her to take her place in your kingdom."

"And you?" I asked.

"I will go with you and take my place in your land as her mother, your wife, and the Litoran queen!"

"This is the best thing for everyone!"

"I would rather know she is safe — here — and miss her for a time than…" She paused, unable to speak the words. "I can't think what could happen if we take a chance like this with her life!"

"Think of your people and what could become of them if she is sacrificed unto this evil man!"

"I cannot imagine!" I said, lowering my head. "You must know I'm right!"

Nadia continued, "You must! You must!" she cried.

"Yes, I know!" I whispered.

"She will understand when the time is right!" Nadia said.

She suddenly became silent, sitting quietly and smiling at her beautiful little baby, whom she must leave behind.

"Please understand and forgive me," she whispered, kissing her cheek. "I must do this because I love you more than my own life!"

Suddenly, Lori walked into the room, the carrier seat and diaper bag in her arms.

"I'm sorry, am I interrupting?" she asked, noticing the serious look on Nadia's face and the sternness of her voice.

"Mother!" Nadia exclaimed with much happiness.

"You're not interrupting… we were just discussing… we are finished… I'll explain later."

"It's time for us to take this little bundle of joy home!" Lori announced happily, trying to calm the air a bit. "I hope I remembered everything you told me to bring."

"She is so beautiful!" Lori said, unloading her arms to pick up her first grandchild for a closer look. "I have never seen such beautiful eyes on a newborn baby! I think she grew overnight," she added with a big smile.

Lori gathered their things while I arranged for Kayla and Nadia to leave the hospital.

Before I returned, Nadia explained the decision they had made to her mother.

Understanding the seriousness of the conversation she had interrupted, Lori listened carefully to her daughter's words.

As much as she was surprised and very concerned that her granddaughter could be in danger in my land, she knew she must do as her daughter asked.

She had known since the wedding that I was not of her world but of the future king and leader of another. She had seen enough during her short time at the castle to know my home was a very special place.

She felt in her heart that I had become a wonderful human being and knew how much I had come to love her daughter.

She agreed to raise Kayla with the loving kindness she had always shown her daughter and to keep her safe until the day we returned for her.

She was very sad to think Nadia would be leaving without her but respected our concern to protect her from this evil.

"I am really going to miss you both!" she cried.

"At a quiet time after you return home, read this carefully. It will explain how my family came to be and will help you understand we are only of good," I said.

"Nadia will be very happy and well taken care of," I promised as I handed her the Litoran family scroll.

I placed a small, deep green stone in the palm of her hand, closing it tightly.

"At any time you wish to see your daughter, hold this next to your heart and simply think of her, wishing to be with her. It will happen in an instant!" I whispered.

"You must never let anyone see this stone or know of its power. Keep it in a very safe place, always," I explained.

"There is one thing you must remember: you can never tell Kayla about any of this. You must never bring her with you when you visit our world!"

"You can never tell anyone who we are or where we come from!" I demanded. "You must promise! Kayla must not be told anything of us until she is no longer in danger!"

"I understand, Neree," she replied.

"I will always keep her safe!"

"I will raise her strong and proud! Do not worry!" she assured me.

"I know! It… it is just… I am really going to miss her," I said.

I took Lori's other hand, placed the deed to the Small's farm in her palm, and folded her fingers tightly around it.

"When you feel the time is right, take her here and give her this deed," I said.

It broke Nadia's heart when she placed the carrier seat — with her little baby snuggled in tight — into the taxi.

She sobbed as they drove away, knowing this was the right thing for everyone.

"You will always be in a special place in my heart, my beautiful blue eyes!" she cried as the taxi disappeared from sight.

When Lori arrived home, she fed and changed Kayla as she fought back the tears. She laid her quietly in her cradle, rocking it gently, as she took the scroll from her bag.

She held it in her hand for a few moments, wondering if she really wanted to know more about this strange land and time her daughter was about to call home.

After Kayla fell deep asleep for the night, she made herself a strong cup of coffee and sat down on the couch to prepare her thoughts.

Desperately needing to understand how my family came to be, she slowly untied the ribbon, carefully rolled out the scroll, and began to read…

Lori took a deep breath. She sat quietly for a few moments, trying to absorb the words she had just read.

She slowly rolled the scroll up and tied the ribbon back in place. She felt a new peace about all she had learned about my family and my homeland.

She put the scroll safely away, as I had asked, knowing someday she would share it with her granddaughter.

She stood by Kayla's cradle, watching her sleep as the thoughts of the past few days flashed before her.

"You are a very special little girl," she whispered.

She now knew one thing for sure: she must spend the rest of her life keeping her little princess safe from harm.

With her granddaughter next to her bedside, she made herself comfortable, wondering why the scrolls mentioned nothing of her and how she fits into all of this.

As she dozed, she was certain she had been put on the earth to raise her granddaughter and prepare her for her destiny.

The darkness grew near as Nadia and I prepared for our adventure. We held each other close, giving one last look over the beautiful farm that I had called home for the most amazing three-and-a-half years of my life.

"I am really going to miss this place," I whispered as I gave the woods one last look before we vanished, leaving our precious Kayla behind in another world and time, safe from the Draconians and all their evil.

"I knew that you did not raise Mother. I always wondered why. I was afraid to ask. Now I know."

Elliott stood to his feet and threw his arms around me. He was big on giving hugs, but this was special. He held me tight as tears rolled down his cheeks.

Before letting go, he whispered, "Thank you, Grandfather. I love you!"

Chapter Eight — Kayla's Birthday

Twenty Years Later…

The years passed peacefully while Kayla evolved into a beautiful, intelligent, and very independent young woman. Although she knew nothing of me or her mother, I had not missed a moment of her life. I proudly attended every special event at school, church, and home from the moment of her birth. Of course, she had no idea that the little frog hanging around was her father.

Lori visited Litora Falls as often as possible until she became too ill to travel. Nadia and I visited her many times during her illness. We carefully managed our time around Kayla's work and activities to ensure we would not run into her. We forbade the hospital staff to inform them of our visits or the fact that we were taking care of her extra expenses.

The years seemed to have flown since Lori had passed away. Kayla was turning twenty. The time had come for her to learn of her family and her destiny. The time had come for me to bring her home.

I arrived at the farm just in time to witness all the commotion.

"Dang it!" Kayla screamed as she stepped off the front porch, realizing she had locked her keys inside the house behind her.

The weather was unusually cold for a late August morning. A light mist of rain covered the grounds as a strong breeze swept across Kayla's face. The chill in the air felt more intense due to the dampness of her clothes. She quickly checked the doors and windows, trying to find a way inside.

Finally, she noticed a slight opening in her upstairs bedroom window. "So unlike her, but not today." She carried her ladder from the backyard and quickly crawled through to her warm, dry room.

She changed her wet clothes and grabbed her sweater and umbrella from the closet. Suddenly, a strange feeling swept over her. Odd sounds seemed to be coming from the woods beyond her backyard.

"It must be the wind and rain; I'm late!"

"I do not have time for this!" she screamed.

She ran down the stairs, grabbed her keys from the table, and flew out the front door. She was finally on her way.

When she reached the car, she stopped for a second to catch her breath before opening the car door.

"There… again… what is that?" she whispered. "It must be my imagination… I'm going to be late… I wish I knew what is making those strange sounds!"

"Later. I have to leave, or I'm going to be late."

She was so flustered that she did not notice me sitting on the porch swing, watching her every move. I hopped into the back seat of the car the second she opened the door. I did not intend to miss one second of her birthday.

Kayla was well known around the office for arriving to work much earlier than her co-workers and usually being the last to leave. "Not today!"

"I'm going to be late!" she screamed as she drove around the parking lot behind the office building for what seemed like the hundredth time.

"I am never going to find a place to park!" she yelled in frustration.

Eureka Springs is a very unique city. Cars are not allowed to park on the streets. Parking lots are located outside the city limits. Red trolleys escort all tourists to the shops and sights of the city, running from the parking lots to the main street every twenty minutes, seven days a week.

Kayla happened to work at one of the few buildings that had a small parking lot located in the back.

"Finally, a car is leaving!" she mumbled with a sigh of relief as she pulled into the first empty parking place she had seen in the last fifteen minutes.

"I will make it if I hurry! Five minutes to clock in on time... What else can possibly go wrong this morning?" she shouted as she ran to catch the open elevator door.

"One... Two... Three..."

"Come on! Open!"

Kayla had a habit of talking to herself when she was frustrated or when things were not going exactly the way she wanted.

"She still does," Koda laughed, bringing a grin to Elliott's face.

"Four... yes!"

"I'm here!" she announced as she rushed through the opening doors into the office suite, where she had worked far too many hours for the past two years. She couldn't remember the last time she had taken a vacation or a personal day off.

Her deep blue eyes sparkled as she walked into her office; flowers and balloons were everywhere she turned.

"Happy Birthday, Kayla!" yelled Sarah, peeking out of her office door.

"Thanks!" Kayla replied.

I quickly hopped into her office and made myself comfortable inside a little gift box I had prepared for her big day.

"Happy Birthday!" Jim shouted, stepping into her office.

"Sleep in on your birthday?" he joked, giving her a big hug.

"Oh, thank you so much!" she replied, adding her own squeeze.

"It's been one of those mornings that you would not believe," she said.

Jim was the type of person who was always there for his friends. Such a nice man… If she were interested in having a relationship, he would be a good catch. But a relationship of any kind was the last thing on her mind.

The only thing Kayla seemed to care about was advancing in the company.

"I'd forgotten. It… is my birthday. I guess I put it in the back of my mind somewhere," she said with a quick smile. She was surprised yet pleased that everyone had remembered. "Twenty years old!"

"How could that be?"

"No longer a teen!"

"An adult?"

She couldn't stop the thoughts going through her head. She tossed her purse on her desk and checked her messages.

"I have been an adult way beyond my years since I was ten years old," she thought.

Her grandmother had always said she was ten going on twenty… and seemed twice her age. Mature, yes.

"Age? Age doesn't mean much," she thought.

Kayla is a very special soul. She had always had a strange feeling that someday she would endure an adventure of some kind. She knew she was destined for a special life. She didn't know when or how it would happen, but she knew for sure that someday something very special was going to take place in her life. As odd as it seemed, she could feel it deep in her soul. She had never been able to let go of the dream of something or someone special turning her world upside down.

She had always felt that she would never grow old. She had always had special abilities she didn't understand. Afraid of what her friends would think if they knew, she quietly kept all her thoughts and secrets bottled up inside. She was afraid that all of her co-workers and friends would think she was nuts if they knew the thoughts and dreams always rushing through her head. She knew they would probably freak out if they found out just how special she really was.

"Twenty!" hum…

No time for nonsense… Just another busy day… A major layout to finish and only twelve hours until the deadline. She knew if she did her usual great job with this advertising layout, the promotion would be hers.

"Imagine! Kayla Marie Gordon, Junior Partner of one of the largest advertising and design firms in the country! Perfection Advertising and Design!"

A dream come true (for anyone) just hours from her reach.

"I can do this! I know I can! I need to concentrate!"

"Chill, Kayla!" Jim laughed.

"Sorry!" she replied.

As she sat down at the drafting table, she noticed a beautiful little box on the corner of the chair next to her. A note was hanging from a tiny gold ribbon, "At Last" written in red.

"Probably a prank gift from someone. Why no name?" she wondered. "No time to open it now. Too much to do," she thought.

"I have to clear my head."

"Stop thinking! Stop thinking!"

This was a very important day for the future of the company. It was the largest advertising campaign they had been offered since it opened ten years before. It was such a big deal. It would mean a very important career move for the advertising designer who presented the best ideas and layouts for the campaign.

Everyone in the office was on edge. For the next few hours, they all, especially Kayla, were very busy privately working on their own ideas and design layouts.

Kayla was the first to finish. She presented her work to the board with her usual enthusiasm and confidence. As usual, every member of the board was very pleased with her presentation.

She gathered up her things and quietly went back to her office. She was confident that she had done her best.

"I feel certain… I nailed it! It could be years before I have a chance like this again, if ever! I did the best work I have ever done!"

"I can't wait to hear the results," she thought.

Her mind was working double overtime. Well-educated, self-confident, and very well-raised, she was special in her own way. You could say she was definitely one of a kind. She had become very respected and loved around the office. Everyone knew there was something very different about her that made her a unique young woman indeed.

Little did anyone know what was soon to come into her life.

"At least three days!"

"I can still hear the words!"

"I don't know how I will stand the wait, but there's no way to speed up this process," she kept thinking.

"Hey Kayla, let us take you out for a birthday dinner!" yelled a voice from the front of the office.

Jim, Kaci, and Dana were standing together with their crazy grins. They were quite the group. They hung out a lot in college and became great friends.

Dana and Kaci are identical twins. Kaci, the oldest, is a wonderful designer. Dana is best at coming up with advertising ideas. They have serious plans of opening their own firm someday after they gain some good experience and make a name for themselves in this crazy business.

"Come on, we never get to spend any time with you!" Kaci insisted. "All you do is work, work, and work!"

Knowing she had no excuse this time, as the work for this century was on the waiting table, she knew she couldn't say no.

"Sure!" she answered. "I could use some fun! Yeah… let's do it!"

"Finally!" Jim blurted out, giving Kaci and Dana a high five.

"We better go before she changes her mind!"

Chapter Nine — The Strange Gift

Kayla arrived at the restaurant before everyone else. El Torres was a nice place, with the best Mexican food in the world, in her opinion. It was actually the only Mexican restaurant in Eureka Springs, Arkansas. Just as she finished explaining her request for a table for four by a window to the host, everyone else walked in.

"This way!" Dana announced, talking on her cell phone while walking toward the back room.

In the very back of the café, by the window, there was a nice table with flowers, balloons, and a big "HAPPY BIRTHDAY KAYLA" sign surrounded by gifts in the center. Kayla was not an emotional person. She was determined not to cry, but that didn't last long.

Sarah was sitting at the end of the long table with a big smile on her face. "Surprise, my friend!" she whispered. Sarah had secretly left the office early. She wanted to set everything up before Kayla arrived. Kayla couldn't believe that she hadn't noticed when Sarah left the office.

"What a nice surprise!" Kayla said, trying to stop the tears from pouring down her face. "This is the first birthday party I have ever had with friends! I can't thank you enough." No one could possibly know how special this was for her. It was a wonderful ending to a very busy, stressful day.

Sitting in a daze, unable to speak, Kayla was excited to open the nice gifts everyone had gotten her: a new set of sketch pencils (Jim was always teasing her about her old ones), a nice sketchpad for traveling from Dana, and a neat little lamp that hooks to the corner of the drawing table to pinpoint any little spot on the layout from Kaci.

"I don't deserve this!" she said as she set everything on the seat beside her, out of the way. "I have never had friends like this. You guys are the best!" she cried.

The waiter brought their food very quickly. Sarah knew what everyone liked and ordered ahead of time.

"She knows us better than we know ourselves!" Dana said.

The waiter smiled as he walked up, overhearing the conversation. "The plates are very hot!" he said. "Be careful not to burn yourself."

"I will," Sarah said thankfully as he placed her plate in front of her.

The time seemed to fly by as Kayla sat quietly, listening to everyone talk. She was enjoying the time away from the office rush, along with her best friends.

"Life is good," she thought.

Just before everyone finished, the waiter brought out a little white cake topped with a red sparkler. He set it on the table in front of Kayla. She sat quietly, trying not to cry again, as they all joined in singing "Happy Birthday" to her.

"Everything is wonderful!" Kayla said. "I can't thank you guys enough! This means so much to me! Thank you! I will never forget this!"

"Thank you, everyone," she said as tears continued to roll down her cheeks.

"We all love you very much, Kayla," Dana said.

"Yes, we do," Sarah added, handing her a card. "Open it later," she whispered. "It's late, and I have a lot to do. I have to be in the office by six. Better go." She hugged everyone before grabbing the ticket and heading for the front.

Noticing the clock, Kayla realized she hadn't realized the time had passed so quickly. "I must leave too; it has been fun!" Jim announced.

"Dana, I will give you a ride home," Kaci said as she stood from her chair. "We will have to get together more often, Kayla," Kaci said. "There's an office meeting early in the morning, and we need to get going. Some of us have to work the rest of the week."

"Kayla, I will help you get everything to the car," Jim whispered.

Jim was tall, dark, and very handsome. He had just turned twenty-one and had never been married. Actually, he had never had a serious relationship. He had been a wonderful friend to Kayla since her first day at the office. She knew he would make a great husband for some lucky woman, but at this point in his life, the only thing on his mind was work, just like the rest of them.

As they walked out, Jim looked at Kayla with his nice smile. "You have a peaceful vacation, and do not think about work," he insisted.

"It's only two days, plus the weekend. I will be back in time for the results of the presentations on Monday," she replied with a laugh.

"Now, why would I not have guessed that?" he laughed.

Everyone was certain that Kayla would be the one chosen for partner of the firm.

"Thanks, Jim. Looks like that's everything," she said, setting the last of the flowers in her car.

Walking toward his car, he looked back over his shoulder with a wink. "See ya next week," he said with a wave.

"If I did not know better, I would think you were flirting with me, Jim Thomas."

"Me? Flirt? Never!"

Blowing off the remark, Kayla opened Sarah's card before starting the car. The card and envelope were handmade, with "best friends" written on the front.

"Inside this note, you will find a gift card for you (my best friend) and me to go to the Water Springs Bath House for the day. We will have the works. What fun! Just let me know the day..."

Love, your best friend, Sarah.

"How sweet," she thought as she put the card in her purse and started her car. She had never been happier than she was at that moment. She realized for the first time what wonderful friends she had in her life. She could not help but smile as she began her long drive home.

Kayla had always been a loner, especially now. She lived miles from the city. Her beautiful forty-acre farmland, peacefully secluded from the outside world, was surrounded by hundreds of acres of thick woods. She loved her job but loved her privacy more. Her passion was living well beyond the fast pace of city life.

Driving home, she thought about how nice everyone in the office had been to her over the past two years. She felt like she was getting more comfortable outside of her secluded life. "So many good friends; almost home," she kept thinking.

She had never been one to let anyone get close to her and had never known why. Everyone had always thought she buried herself in school and work because she thought she was better than everyone else. She appeared to be much happier when she was alone. The truth was, she never felt like she fit in anywhere outside of her own home.

Now that she had friends, she had become more confident and a little more outgoing. She had never allowed herself time to have a boyfriend or any kind of personal relationship. When it happens, and it will… it will be a whole new experience.

One of my many powers is the ability to know what others are thinking. I am not so sure that I should have known what was on her mind.

"Jim is very nice-looking," she thought with a soft smile. "I could be a little attracted to him."

"No… we need not go there," she thought. "He is just a wonderful friend. I would never want to spoil that. This is the way it should be between us. Yes, the way it needs to stay."

"I do love the way he teases, though!"

"Romance?"

"No, not interested… well."

"Not yet."

The drive to her place was always peaceful once out of the city limits. She smiled as she couldn't stop thinking of how special her birthday had been as she pulled into her driveway.

Stepping out of the car, she took a deep breath and stretched her arms as far as she could reach. "Ah! Fresh air, wide-open space, beautiful view, trees as far as I can see. So good to finally be home, my favorite place in the whole world," she yelled as she walked up the sidewalk, miles from everywhere and everyone. This was how she wanted life to be.

When she reached for the front door, she remembered the box she had laid in the front seat. On her way back to the car, she noticed the same noise coming from the woods that she had heard earlier. She picked up her box and headed back to the house.

She couldn't help wondering where the strange noises were coming from as she locked the door behind her. Finally, she would have time to see what was inside her surprise gift, which had been waiting all day to be opened.

"I can't wait to open you," she said as she gave the box a good shake. "Why would someone just leave this? What could it be? Who could it be from? Everyone I know gave me gifts at dinner! It's so odd!"

She stopped at the table next to the front door and quickly read a note her housekeeper, Shea, had left on the table. Questions rushed through her head as she sat down on the couch.

Thanks to the warm fire Shea had made for her, the room was warm and cozy. Kayla carefully untied the ribbon and read the card.

"How strange," she thought, now reluctant to open the box. "I had never told anyone about my thoughts or feelings… of an adventure… or anything else personal about my life. Who could have sent this to me? Birth… ten… twenty… at hand? What could this mean? Is this some kind of a joke? Your adventure will begin!"

Kayla dozed off, staring at the box next to her.

"What the!" she yelled as she suddenly awoke with the box in her hand, not knowing for sure when she had picked it up. She slowly peeled off the stickers and carefully removed the lid. At first, she didn't see anything inside. Suddenly, I jumped out of the box and landed beside her.

She hopped to her feet, startled for a second. She calmed down quickly once she realized that I was just a little frog. She giggled, thinking back to her tenth birthday.

It was early morning registration at school. She was in the fourth or fifth grade, so proud. She stepped out of the back door of her grandmother's house just as I jumped up on the bottom step. She had loved frogs her entire life. She picked me up, put me in a little square box, and took me to school with her. She announced to everyone that I came to see her for her birthday.

Kayla had never had a party of her own. She knew in her own mind that I had come to her grandmother's home just to see her on that special day. Little did she know that I, a frog, was actually her very own father.

She was ten. "TEN!"

When she showed me to her grandmother, she told her the story of an experience that she had ten years before, on the day Kayla was born. Just as her mom stepped outside on her front porch on her way to the hospital, a little frog jumped up on the bottom step. Her grandmother said she noticed it and told her mom to be careful not to trip over it. She said she wondered, at the time, if it was a sign that her baby would love the outdoors and frogs.

"The thing was," she told her, "it stayed around the steps until we brought you home from the hospital! The next day, it was gone as quickly as it had appeared. We thought it was a little strange."

"Funny… I have never thought of it again until today," she said. She told her one more very important thing: the little frog had one dark green eye and one slightly lighter green eye.

She held my little frog up for a closer look. "Now that is strange. Kayla, look for yourself," she whispered, holding his little face toward her. "So does your little guy."

She said she wondered if he was watching over her like a guardian angel.

"Oh my, no!" Kayla screamed aloud. "I had forgotten about all of this. It all fits! A frog at birth… Another at ten… Now, twenty… No way! No way! This cannot be real! This must be a prank! But… whom?"

"No one knows… I have no other family! Grandmother is gone. Who else could there be?"

"Oh no, this is not possible!" she blurted aloud, taking a deep breath as she leaned over, looking as closely as possible into my eyes. "It is you," she thought, noticing that I had one dark green eye and one slightly lighter one, just like the other frog.

"I knew it! I knew it was you!"

"But… it can't be. Frogs don't live that long! What does this mean?"

She froze, staring at me, assured she must be dreaming or crazy or something that would explain this. "It just couldn't be possible! This can't be real!" she screamed aloud in a panic.

She quickly picked me up from the couch, ran to the back door, opened it, walked to the end of the patio, and set me in the grass. "Bye, little one. There is a nice woods and a pond for you to live in. It is just ahead, there," she pointed as she turned to go inside to forget this had taken place.

She looked over her shoulder to see how far I had gone as she stepped onto the patio, but to her surprise, I was just sitting there on the edge of the step, looking up at her. I was not going anywhere. I had longed for this day for twenty years.

"Shoo! Shoo!" she shouted. "Go on. It is very nice out there. The pond is beautiful. You will love it!" she shouted as she turned to open the door.

"What the!" she screamed. "The door would not open; it must have locked behind me when I went out," she thought, trying desperately to open it. "How could this be? I know I didn't lock it! What is going on?" she yelled as she tried all the doors and windows. Nothing… nothing would open. "Oh my… not now!" she cried. "My cell phone, keys, everything I need is inside!"

She walked around the house to the door that led to the laundry room. She knew that it would probably be locked, but she thought there might be a chance she could have accidentally left it open.

"No luck! What am I going to do?" she yelled, feeling helpless.

"She must have been really confused," Grandfather said.

"Koda," Elliott whispered, interrupting, "let Grandfather finish."

"Would you guys like a break?" I asked.

"No, Grandfather," they both replied.

I continued with a smile, realizing they were really into my stories.

Chapter Ten — Kayla's Adventure Begins

Kayla turned from the south side of the house just in time to catch a glimpse of my shadow as I dashed behind the old oak tree. It had become my favorite spot on the property, over a hundred years old, with thick limbs, beautiful leaves, and twisting vines reaching from just above the ground, topping off at over thirty feet in height. A sturdy tire swing hung from a large limb on the right side, while a ladder led halfway to the top, ending just below the door of a beautiful treehouse.

She had inherited the place a year ago when her grandmother passed away. She had no idea that she owned it until the reading of her will. All she knew was that she would give anything to have grown up here in such a wonderfully secluded home. There could not possibly be a more perfect place in this world to complete her lifestyle.

She fell in love with the beauty of the land, the view of the woods surrounding her from every piece of the property, and the wonderful, older home. The big pond beyond the back woods, glimmering in the sunlight of the day and the moonlight of the night, was her special place to relax and create her designs.

It felt like home to her from the moment she arrived. She was absolutely certain that this was where she belonged. Deep in her soul, she felt that something connected her to this place.

She slowly walked across the backyard toward my shadow. My body blended well with the limbs and leaves, shining from the beams of the small moon just overhead. As she moved closer, I slowly stepped out into the light.

She took a big step back as she screamed, "Who?"

"Do not be afraid," I interrupted. "It is I!"

Something about my voice lifted her fear instantly. I was much taller than she, with greenish-brown rough skin, slightly web-like feet, rough hands, and a round face. I had big green eyes and a mouth almost covering the width of my face, and strangely, no hair. I was in that odd place between a frog and the human specimen I had become.

She could not tell the color of my eyes in the moonlight, but she was certain, in her heart, that one would be dark green and one lighter green.

"I don't know why, but I'm not afraid of you," she said. "You're him, aren't you?"

"How?"

"Why?"

"How is this possible?"

I appeared as a cross between an oversized frog and a human being. She was excited, afraid, curious, and confused, all at the same time. She couldn't wait to know where I came from and why I was there.

All these years, in the back of her mind… "Does this have anything to do with…? Impossible!"

Many thoughts were rushing through her mind. After all these years, the time for explanations had arrived.

"Happy birthday, Kayla," I said softly.

"My name is Neree! Finally, we meet!"

"How do you know my name, and how do you know it is my birthday?" she anxiously asked.

"I have been waiting twenty years for this moment, my dear," I replied. "I have known of you since the day of your birth! I have come for you!"

"I have always known you were coming, or someone, or something! I just knew it!"

"I'm not afraid of you!" she said calmly.

"I can't wait to hear everything you have to tell me!"

"Who sent you?"

"How do you know me?"

"Where do you think you are going to take me? You have to tell me everything!"

"I am so relieved!" I interrupted. "Let us go inside, and I will tell you what we need to do first. We will prepare for our journey!"

"Journey!" she shouted. "Wow… I knew it! I wasn't dreaming… all these years. It's really going to happen! I feel like I am ten again!" she said.

As she reached the back door, it was no longer locked.

"You!" she said, looking over her shoulder at me.

"Me!" I answered with a nod and a grin.

"I would like to change and freshen up a bit before you begin to fill me in, Neree. I have a feeling this is going to take a while, and it is late," she said as she grabbed fresh towels from the linen closet on her way up the stairs.

"I am not going anywhere," I answered. "Take your time!"

"I won't be long," she said, closing the door to her room. She needed a chance to catch her breath and pull herself together. This was a lot, even for Kayla, to absorb in one day.

I quickly walked about the house, very pleased with Kayla's personal touches. I admired her design talents. It had been twenty years since Nadia and I had lived there. I had returned to check on Kayla many times over the years but had not seen her since the day of her grandmother's funeral.

I followed her to the farm after the reading of the will. Once I saw she was settling in, I left for Litora Falls. I knew she was safe and happy and that I would be returning on this day to take her home.

As Kayla was taking her shower, she became anxious and excited in a way she had never known. "I am unusually comfortable with Neree. It's as though I've known him forever. I don't understand why, but I'm so excited that I don't care," she thought.

"I feel like this is my destiny... or something. I don't know. All I do know is... I can't wait to find out. I have waited my whole life for an adventure. I trust him."

"I hope I'm home for the results of my presentation," she thought as she finished putting on her shoes. "Three days… actually four… if you count today and the weekend."

"Well, I can't worry about that now," she told herself as she ran downstairs.

She sat across from me at the table. She could not help but notice my eyes. Just as she thought, one of my eyes was light green, and the other was slightly darker green.

"You are truly the tiny frog I saw on my tenth birthday! I knew it!"

"Yes," I whispered.

She felt deep inside her heart that this was how it was supposed to be. Kayla seemed to have a gift for knowing when things were right.

"So, tell me everything…" she blurted out.

"The first thing you should know is that I have been watching over and protecting you since before you were born."

"I know," she whispered as I was talking. "I've always known someone special was watching over me."

"Something very important you must understand, Kayla," I continued, "your grandmother knew all about me!" (Now the little white lies begin… I knew I could not tell the exact truth without explaining more than I should so soon.)

"She did not want me to make myself known to you as long as she was alive to take care of you," I continued. "I have always respected her wishes. Just before she passed away last year, she asked me to promise to protect you after she was gone. She said it was up to me if I took you on this adventure as long as I protected you with my life. She made me promise to let you make the decision on how you live the rest of your life. I can only tell you of this adventure waiting for you!" I said.

"I will not force you to go with me. Adventure or not, I will protect you always! What you do with the knowledge you receive is up to you!" I added.

"Before I continue, on your tenth birthday, did your grandmother give you a gift in the beautiful sterling silver box?"

"When you saw me on the step, I was leaving for home. I had given the box to her as a gift for you. You delayed my departure when you took me to school for the day. I did not have the heart to hop away and ruin your happy plan. I calmly went along with your fun."

Kayla giggled. "Sorry," she said as chills ran down her back.

Anyway, the box contained a pendant of a silver tree with a house built into the top, much like your treehouse, on a thick silver chain. In the center of the tree, just below the door, was a large, deep green stone.

"Grandfather, Mother has the pendant. It will be Eliza's. Eliza and I both have the same stone on a rope," Elliott said as he pulled his out from beneath his robe.

"Always keep it with you, my child," I insisted.

"I have one, too," Koda added.

"Never take it off. It is very important."

"We know, Grandfather. Please continue," Elliott replied.

"There was an inscription:

Princess Kayla

'Our Future!'

Love, Mother & Father"

"I didn't notice the inscription on the back. It was so big and strange that I never took it out of the box."

"I'd never known my parents. I grew up as an only child with my wonderful grandmother. She wouldn't talk about them with me. Actually, she didn't talk about them at all."

"The only thing I knew about my mother was she was her only child, and as Grandmother put it, she was gone before her time. I've never seen a photo of her… nothing. She wouldn't tell me how she had died. She would get upset if I asked about my dad. She wouldn't talk to me for hours."

"If I asked, her answer was always the same: I never knew him. She wouldn't even tell me his name, where he was from, or anything about his family."

"I grew up loved but lonely. I always wondered what it would be like to have parents, cousins, aunts, or uncles. It was just me and my grandmother as far back as I can remember. I loved her, and she took good care of me. I was always led to believe that we had no other family."

"She got very upset if I asked questions or brought the subject up in any way. Yes, I remember. It's the only thing she did that had anything to do with my past. She wouldn't tell me what it meant or how she got it."

"She just handed me the box and said, 'This was your mother's. I never want to see or hear of this again. Please keep it safe always,' and walked away."

"I never understood why she even bothered to give it to me. I always thought it was gaudy and not exactly in style or my taste."

"No, definitely not my taste!"

"Do you still have it?"

"Sure I do!" she said. "It's the only thing I have ever seen or heard of that had any connection to my parents!"

"Would you get it out for me, please?" I asked. "I left it for you… for this day. You are going to need it from now on!"

As she was running upstairs to her room, I struggled to hold back the tears. It made me very sad to realize how much Kayla had longed to know of us. I could not help but wonder how she was going to react when she learned the truth. How would she feel when she found out her grandmother had been visiting us? Would she forgive us when she found out we kept the truth from her all these years?

"Yes, I remember where I put you!" she said excitedly as she opened the bottom drawer of her jewelry box and took the pretty box out of the drawer.

She ran down the stairs as fast as her feet would carry her. "Here it is!" she said, handing me the box.

I held it in my hand, glaring at it for a few minutes before I opened it.

"Ah, yes! Such a beautiful thing! Magnificent!"

"If you say so," she replied.

"What is so beautiful about it, Neree?"

"It is a big, gaudy silver tree with a house on it!"

"It is beautiful silver! It has a dark green stone in the center of the house."

"Is that it?"

"Look closely at the house, Kayla."

"Wow! It is my tree house. How could that be?" she asked.

"All I can tell you right now is that this green stone in the center of your tree house is going to help you more than you will ever know on our journey. You must wear it at all times and never take it off!" I said, with a very stern and sharp tone to my voice.

"Do you understand?" I yelled.

"Once we begin this journey, you can never take it off!" I continued. I did not like being so firm with her, but I knew that I must make her understand.

"Yes, I get it, Neree!" she answered.

"But what?"

"Not now!" I interrupted. "The time will come for all questions and all answers!"

"O.K., O.K., I get it!" she said. "Where are we going? What do I need? When do we leave? When will we be back?"

I just sat there, looking at her as she went on… and on… and on… with her questions.

"That was an awful lot of questions," I interrupted. "Do you always talk this much?"

"Sorry," she answered. "I am a very curious woman."

"All you need to know is this: your journey will be long. It will be full of excitement, travel, a lot of work, strange and fearful encounters, and wonderful surprises."

"Oh, yes, also a bit of danger," I added. "Last but not least, you will see things beyond your imagination. You will also learn many things you have wanted." I paused for a moment before I could continue. "You will learn things that you have needed to know for a very long time. You must be stronger than you have ever been in your life to endure these things."

"Before we begin, I need to know if you sincerely want to do this. It is your choice."

"You do not have to come with me. I can assure you that everything will make sense. If you trust me, everything will fall into place very soon."

"Are you kidding me?" she screamed. "I wouldn't miss this for anything in this world!"

"Neree, you must know how I have dreamed of this adventure since as far back as I can remember. I didn't know how or when this was going to take place, but deep down inside, I have always known something wonderful and amazing like this was going to happen to me. I have to go; do you not see? I would never forgive myself if I let you leave, and I didn't go with you."

"Good, then!" I said. "We are off!"

She picked up her backpack and headed for the front door.

"This way!" I said as I opened the back door leading to the woods and the pond beyond the farm.

"Aren't you forgetting something?" I asked, waving my hand toward the silver box. "You must put it on before we can begin!" I demanded. "Remember?"

"I know, never take it off!" she rudely interrupted. "I got it! You worry too much!"

Kayla took the silver chain out of the box and put it around her neck. It was a little heavy, but she thought she should wear it, as I had insisted. She knew it must mean something very special, or I would not have known about it.

When we walked out of the door to the patio overlooking the woods, she assumed we were about to begin our journey. She was a little afraid… not of me, but of all that was about to take place. There was something about me. She seemed to have a natural trust in me. I knew everything about her, and she wanted to know how. She felt like I had always known her, almost as if I were part of her in some way.

At this point, I felt very fortunate that I had the gift of knowing what others were thinking. Kayla was full of curiosity. However, she was short on patience. I realized that this was not going to be as simple as I had thought.

How is this pendant going to help me? What does it mean? Why…

"Kayla!"

"O.K., I will wait, and I will trust you. I got it."

"Sorry!"

Walking across the backyard, I stopped under the huge limbs of the old oak tree in the center, looking up at the treehouse.

"Twenty years ago, on the day of your birth, I came to this tree and built that," I said as I looked down sadly. "For you!" I added with a deep sigh.

"Why?" Kayla asked.

I hesitated for a few moments before I could answer.

"Your parents were supposed to raise you here. Things did not work out the way they had planned. Sometimes things happen that we cannot explain," I answered as the lies continued. "Your father inherited this place from his grandfather before you were born. He left the deed with your grandmother, Lori, to give you at the right time."

"Tell me what happened to them!" she said. "Please, I need to know!"

"In time, Kayla, in time!" I replied. "Enough questions! As time goes by, you will know everything you need to know. This is not the time!" I said.

"That explains why I was so drawn to this home!" she said. "I knew I was supposed to live here. I felt it deep in my heart!"

"You knew them?" she asked. "You know everything that happened to them! You do; I know you do!"

"Enough questions, Kayla!" I shouted. "We must be on our way! Enough for now!"

"But…"

"Enough!" I interrupted loudly. "This is not the time!" I insisted, knowing the more questions I had to answer, the more lies I would have to explain later.

"O.K., O.K.," she said, with frustration.

Now, very angry, she didn't say another word. All of her life, she had wondered what happened to her parents.

"He knows what happened to them and won't tell me," she thought. "It's not fair. I need answers, and he has them all! Why won't he just tell me? This is not the time… how dare he! It's many years past the time! How dare him!"

After having her fit, she decided to let it go for now.

"He did say that I would know everything as time goes by. I'll just have to wait until he feels it's the right time. I just want him to tell me everything he knows about my family. I have waited this long; I guess I can wait a little longer. Anyway, what choice do I have?" she thought.

With those thoughts, I felt she was finally going to calm down a bit and enjoy her journey.

Chapter Eleven — Kayla's Father

As we reached the edge of the woods, she took one last look across her backyard, wondering if she would ever see it again.

"I love this place so much," she whispered as she turned to follow me deep into the woods.

Glimmers of moonlight sparkled in the crystal-clear water of a small pond at the edge of the woods. The rustling of brush, fish jumping in the pond, and frogs croaking in the distance set a mood of calmness that was comforting to Kayla. There was nothing she loved more.

Two deer bedding down in the bushes just beyond the small trees brought a much-needed smile to her face as we passed. It had always been so peaceful and quiet here, but on this night, something seemed a little strange to Kayla. The animals were a little more restless and noisier than usual.

We sat down on the bank together, watching the sun slowly begin to rise over the trees.

"Beautiful!" I whispered.

The moment the sky grew lighter, she saw them — at least twenty of them on the far side of the pond. Bright beams of morning sun streaked through the trees, bouncing off the water in front of them and enhancing their odd appearance.

"Neree!" a voice yelled from the right side of the pond, where the thickest area of trees stood tall and beautiful.

"There you are!" Neree replied. "We have been sitting here taking in the peace and quiet for most of the night, waiting for you to appear."

"Come, Kayla, meet Ikan," I said as I stood and began to walk to the other side.

"Ah, you must be Kayla!" the strange man said.

"I am Ikan Rainie. It is such a pleasure to finally meet you," he announced, gently shaking her hand. "I hope you had a nice birthday, ma'am."

He was of our kind. They all were.

"You are?" she asked. "And… how do you know who I am?"

"How do you know about my birthday?"

"I answered quickly," giving Ikan no chance to speak. "He is a defender… what you call an army here," I announced. "They have been waiting for us to help us on our journey. This is something we would not want to do on our own. As I told you, it may be dangerous."

"You are the strange noise I have been hearing!" Kayla said.

"You did not tell her, did you?" Ikan asked.

"No, in time!" I answered.

"Tell me what?" she insisted.

"King Neree has to answer your questions, I am afraid!"

"King!" she screamed.

"You did not even tell her that?" Ikan replied, looking at me sternly. "Do you not think if she knew, it would help her understand things more clearly as we go along?"

"Ikan, this is not the time," I said sharply.

"Do you not think she has waited long enough? She has the right to know!" Ikan said.

"I like him!" she said. "Listen to him, Neree!"

I stood there glaring at Kayla, then at Ikan.

"Sorry, sir," Ikan said. "I was out of line."

"No, you weren't," Kayla said.

"What is he talking about, Neree?"

I put my head down, shaking it in dismay.

"We need to talk, Kayla," I said, pausing sadly. "There are a lot of things you need to be told."

"I had planned to explain everything when we arrived home, but thanks to someone who needs to learn to keep his mouth shut, now I must explain a few things before we can begin this journey! I am... just... not sure where to begin."

"At the beginning," she whispered. "Start at the beginning! Don't leave out a single thing!"

"This must be really good!" she added, giving Ikan a big smile. I stood there looking at her, shaking my head quietly.

"I will deal with you later," I told Ikan as we walked away.

"I am afraid it is much too soon for you to know some things… but yes… the beginning will be a good place to start."

Kayla followed me to a private area of woods under a big weeping willow tree.

"Sit down, Kayla," I said. "I am uncertain how you are going to react to what I have to tell you. Ikan is right. If you know more about what is going on, it will help you endure the journey we are about to begin."

"I knew your father and your mother! They were very much in love and wanted to be married. Your grandmother was very hurt by the thought of losing her daughter, as well as her being with — um… anyway, she was her only child, and she would not allow it." (The lies continued in a different direction.)

"She had your father sent far away. He was in danger of being seen with your mother. She made it very clear; she would make much trouble for him if he did not stay away from her."

"Why was he in danger?" she asked.

"Because, Kayla, he was one of us!" I answered.

"When people saw him, they thought of danger! They were afraid. They did not understand his appearance."

"I am…!" she blurted aloud, a little confused.

"Yes, half!" I said.

"Anyway… Without your grandmother knowing, he and your mother continued to see each other and were secretly married. They settled in the family home. Your home. They had acquired it while planning a perfect life with you."

"She was very hurt when she realized he was the father of the baby your mom was carrying. When she found out they had secretly married and that she was going to have a child, she continued to object to the relationship but gave up the idea of causing trouble for your father. She accepted what had happened but never approved of her being with him."

"You became her life after your mom was gone. Although she always blamed your father for everything, she allowed him to look after you all these years from a distance. In spite of everything that had happened, she could not change one very important fact… He was your father! He was always close by, watching over you! He loves you very much," I assured her.

"Where is he now?"

"What is his name?"

"When can I meet him?"

"How…?"

"Too many questions, Kayla," I said.

"Answer one then," she insisted, "just tell me… Where is he now?"

I turned my back to her. I could no longer control my emotions.

I paused for a few moments, took a deep breath, and collected my thoughts before I finally answered.

"Here, Kayla," I said, turning to face her. "I am your father!"

"I am… your father!" I repeated as I sobbed.

"I knew there was some connection between us!"

"How could you?" she screamed as she ran into the woods with tears streaming down her face. "How could this be? How could you have left me like that? How could I be like them and never have known? So close all these years! Why didn't you tell me? Why?"

She stopped running, threw herself over a big log, and sobbed.

"Why did you wait so many years to tell me?" she screamed. "Why?"

"Because I loved you and your mother," I whispered, kneeling beside her while putting my hand on her back. "And… out of respect for your grandmother."

"Kayla, I thought you would understand!"

"Your grandmother and your mother wanted you to live a normal life as long as possible. I did not want to take that away from her… nor from you."

"Have you not had it good since you were born?"

"We did what we thought was best for you to be as happy as possible."

"Your mother was all Lori had. It would have killed her if she had lost both you and her only daughter. She needed you," I said as I stood up, wiping my tears away.

"I understand all of that," she said as she slowly stood up, facing me.

"I needed you," she whispered as she walked toward me. She wrapped her arms around me, holding me as tightly as she possibly could.

As we held each other, twenty years of emotion poured from our souls.

"I am so happy to have a father, but for it to be you… How much better can it get than this?"

"You are absolutely wonderful," she whispered.

With a final squeeze, she said, "I can't say I'm happy to realize that I'm a frog... but I am pleased and proud to be your daughter, Father!"

"Oh, Kayla, I have watched you grow over the years into this beautiful and successful woman. I am very proud and honored to be your father!"

"Your grandmother did a wonderful job raising you! I could not bring myself to take you from her as long as she was alive!"

"I hope you will be able to forgive me someday," I said.

"I do!"

"I know I was her whole life!"

"I just wish I could have known you all these years, also. But I realize you were respecting her needs, and I love you for that!" she said.

"We missed so much!"

"I have had a good life, but now... wow... now! It is even better! I have my father!"

"We have a lot of time to make up for!" she said. "I want to know everything about you and my mother!"

"In time, Kayla, we must get going!" I said.

As she finally let go of me, she could not believe her eyes. She could tell it was me, but the webbed feet and rough skin were gone. I had changed into my human form.

She took a step back to stare at how handsome I had suddenly become. With a big smile, I added, "One more thing, Kayla!"

"Yes, Father?" she answered.

"We are frogs, with the ability to change form to human and back to frogs at any time. We can go one step further than any other metamorphosis types in our lands. We can change our appearance to any stage of the metamorphosis process."

"We live our lives in human form," I assured her. "We only use our metamorphosis ability to protect us from danger, travel quickly, or sometimes just play around. We are a very special breed indeed," I explained with a smile. "You have no idea."

"We have many special powers, Kayla. You will find, as time goes on, that you have many powers of your own!"

"What?" she said, with little surprise, considering the strange abilities she had kept hidden all her life.

"Oh yes, one more thing!"

"You are a princess in our land!" I said.

"Wow!" she thought as we walked toward the others. As if everything else wasn't enough… "A princess! Powers!"

We walked hand in hand through the woods to where the others were waiting without saying a word. I knew she understood and had forgiven me in her heart. I was amazed at how much love she truly felt for me.

When Ikan saw us coming out of the trees, he yelled at us, "We were getting worried about you two," as he walked around the pond to meet us.

I told Kayla to wait with the others.

"I need a word with you alone, Ikan!" I said in a very stern voice.

"How did she take the news, sir?" Ikan asked.

"I told her that we are descendants of frogs. I also told her that I was her father and she was a princess. Oh, also, that in time, she will find she has many powers of her own."

I paused, then sternly continued, "It is far too soon for her to know this, much less everything else she needs to be told! I wanted the time to be right!"

"Do not ever put me in that position again!" I ordered.

"Yes, sir!" Ikan answered, looking at the ground.

"I am very sorry, sir!"

"Let us get one thing straight! How much she is told and when is my decision, and mine alone. No exceptions!" I demanded, looking Ikan square in the eye.

"No exceptions!"

"Do you understand me?" I yelled.

"Yes, sir!"

"I understand, Neree," Ikan answered. "It will not happen again, sir! You have my word."

I noticed Kayla waiting a few feet ahead.

Giving Ikan's shoulder a soft squeeze, I whispered, "Um, you are probably her hero."

As the Litoran Defenders leader, I trusted Ikan with my life. Handsome, brave, strong, and loyal to his king and his people, I respected him in a way that I respect no one else. Ikan would not want to do anything to ruin our special relationship.

He made a vow to me to keep his distance from Kayla and his thoughts to himself.

"She is a very strong soul, a lot like her mother." He knew that he could not take a chance on messing up again. Next time, I would not be so forgiving. He would not want to face those kinds of consequences.

As we gathered up our things, put out the campfire, and started on our way, Kayla could not help but notice that all of the defenders had taken human form.

"I really have powers. This explains so much," she thought. "I am only half… I am like my mother… Impossible… I would have known, wouldn't I?" she thought as she followed me on her long-awaited journey.

"Time for a break," Kayla announced as she and Nadia entered the room, carrying breakfast trays for us.

"Your grandfather needs to keep up his strength, if only for storytelling," Nadia announced.

"It smells delicious. I am starving," I whispered.

"So, what is my father filling your heads with this time?" Kayla asked.

"Mother, he is telling us all about your adventures," Elliott announced. "Just remember, your grandfather tends to exaggerate a bit."

"Yeah, we know, but it is so interesting," Koda laughed.

The boys gobbled down their food quickly. I barely had time to finish my coffee before they were begging me to continue.

Chapter Twelve — The Journey

And the long-awaited journey began, I said as I set my tray on the floor and continued my story.

"There, through the trees to the north!" La-too yelled. La-too was the head guide. His gift of direction and knowledge of the land set him apart from the rest of the defenders as a young boy. Everyone trusted him completely.

Looking through the trees at the edge of the woods, the beauty was more than Kayla could have imagined.

"Where are we?" she asked.

"No longer in your world," Miki answered as he passed, overhearing her mumbling. Miki was short and chubby in size, strong and loyal by nature, and knowledgeable beyond his years. He had looked forward to meeting his princess since the announcement of her birth and was most anxious to help guide her on her journey home, dedicated to keeping her safe.

Kayla's mind was captivated by the lustrous beams of sunlight showering through the creases of the thick green trees while enhancing the breathtaking beauty of the waterfall.

Startled by a loud roaring sound, she quickly turned in the direction of an odd swinging bridge that appeared from what seemed like… nowhere. It hung in — what looked like — midair, stretching the full width of the river and ending smack in the center of the waterfall.

"How is that bridge…? There are no beams or boulders supporting it. That is not possible… What is going on?" she asked.

"Ikan, please tell me that this is not the direction we are taking to cross this river," she said very sternly as she pointed to the bridge.

"This would be the way," he answered.

"Actually, we are going straight into that," he added, pointing in the direction of the waterfall.

"No way!" Kayla yelled. "I'm not going across that odd-looking bridge or going anywhere near that waterfall!"

"You are a frog!"

"You love water!"

"I don't even go swimming!"

"The closest I get to water is my shower, and when I can't avoid it, the rain!"

"Besides, that bridge looks too dangerous. It is… It is in midair. It could fall. There is nothing holding it up. How is this possible?"

Kayla took a deep breath, paused for a moment, then glared at Ikan.

"I won't cross it. It doesn't look safe. I won't. Show me the way, and I will walk around. I will meet you on the other side of the river. Unless you're afraid, I will beat you there."

"Sorry, Kayla," Ikan replied. "The only thing I am afraid of is that this is the only way possible to cross this river and reach the other side safely. It is our special bridge. You do not have a choice if you want to continue on this journey with your father. The tunnel is the only entrance to Litora Falls. The opening will only appear once we cross the bridge. I am certain this all seems very strange to you."

"You must trust me; it is the safest option."

"Besides, you have forgotten. You also possess frog blood. It is of the royal kind — the very best!"

For the first time in her life, Kayla was speechless. She stood for a few moments, frozen and unable to argue with Ikan. She realized that if she wanted to go on this journey and begin the adventure she had always dreamed of, she must cross the bridge.

I could not believe what I was overhearing as I listened from a distance. Kayla did not have an answer or a smart remark. Not one word came out of her mouth as she calmly followed La-too across the bridge above the river.

"That is one for your side!" I said as I caught up to Ikan at the edge of the bridge.

"My daughter has a lot to learn," I added with a grin. "This may prove to be the greatest challenge of your life!"

"What?" Ikan replied. "What do you mean by 'my greatest challenge'?"

"Did I not tell you?" I asked.

"Tell me what?" Ikan replied, afraid to hear my answer.

"You have been chosen as Kayla's trainer. You will be personally responsible for her learning everything she needs to know to help her develop her powers and take her place in our land."

"King Neree… no! She is so… stubborn!"

"There's no room for discussion," I interrupted. "It has been decided!"

"Yes, sir," Ikan said. "You are the king!"

"Ah… sometimes you do remember," I whispered as we continued across the bridge.

I love Ikan like my own son. I was deeply proud of the fine leader and friend he had become. I trusted him completely and secretly hoped he and Kayla would someday fall in love and marry. I knew for certain what a wonderful husband, father, and future king he would be.

Yes, I would then truly have the son that I never had.

I can never let Ikan know how I feel. I do not want him to think it is his responsibility to marry Kayla. I want Kayla to find the same true love that Nadia and I have come to know. I could only hope it would be their choice someday, as I had always planned.

"Neree, where are you? You seem deep in thought," Miki said as he passed.

"Oh, just thinking," I said as I continued.

The loud flow of water pouring down the hills, splashing into the waters below, overwhelmed Kayla as she reached the end of the bridge.

"Watch your first step, Kayla!" La-too yelled. The ground below was soft from the dampness in the air. Kayla carefully took a few steps to the side to get out of the way, letting the others pass as she glared into the beauty before her, taking it all in.

"It's so exquisite!" she said as Ikan and I reached the edge. "I have never seen anything like this before!"

"It's so amazing!"

"Where do we go now?" she asked. "Where are we?"

"Beyond this pass is a place not known by your world. It is too difficult to explain. Just follow us," La-too answered, heading right into the waterfall.

"You can't be serious!" she said, watching the others follow the trail leading directly into the stream of water.

"What do you mean, 'Not of my world?' I am so confused!"

"You keep saying, 'Not of my world!' What does that mean?"

"It's only been a few moments. We are just beyond the woods of my home, aren't we? Where are we and how…?"

"Just trust us, Kayla!" Ikan replied. "This is the only way to the tunnel! You can do this! Stay close behind and follow me!"

"What is happening?" Kayla screamed as she glanced over her shoulder for one last look at the world she was leaving behind. Suddenly, the bridge burst into flashing streaks of light shooting across the river, disappearing into the mountain through the waterfall.

"Do not be afraid, Kayla. You have many things to see that you will not understand. No harm will come to you. Remember, we have powers not known in your world. You can trust your father, and you can trust me. You are safe with us. Many things will become apparent that you will not understand. No harm will come to you.

Know this: There are many strange and wonderful things in our world. You must give this a chance. You must open your thoughts and your heart to all the good and wonderful things that are about to come into your life. You should enjoy every moment possible of the many new things you are going to come to know."

"The streaks of light are fairies. They lock themselves together to form the bridge, which allows only Litorans to reach our tunnel," Ikan said.

"Tunnel?" she asked.

"Trust me, you will soon see. We must go at once, Kayla."

Feeling as though she had no other choice, she slowly walked toward the waterfall. Her eyes sparkled with excitement when she saw the waterfall open up to form a large tunnel in the center of the small mountain, covered with green trees, shrubs, and flowers.

"Wow!" she thought. "I could never have imagined this kind of beauty! Where are we?" she asked again.

"This is the Tunnel of Litora Falls," Ikan said.

"Where does this go? How deep is it? Does it…?"

"Kayla…" Ikan cut her off before she could speak another word. "I need you to do something for me!"

"Sure, anything," she replied.

"Trust me… Follow us… and please stop asking so many questions! You will be told everything you need to know when the time comes," he insisted.

"Fine!" she said with animosity, stomping her foot as she turned to join the others ahead.

"Ooooh… He is so… so infuriating!" she continued, sneaking up next to me.

"You are so much like your mother," I said as I shook my head, giving her a smile.

"This friendship is not going the way I planned. Hopefully, things will improve along the way," I thought, shaking my head as I continued through the entrance of the tunnel.

"Mother did not like Father very much at first, did she?" Koda snipped.

"Not really," I replied as I continued.

A shiver of fear swept over Kayla as she stepped into the dark tunnel. The faint light from fireflies swarming about the air formed the appearance of huge shadows crawling up the walls. The sounds of the flowing water and the shuffling of footsteps, combined with an odd roaring sound that seemed to be moving in her direction, gave the tunnel an eerie feeling she had never known. Bright streaks of light suddenly shot through the Defenders toward Kayla. A strong breeze swept through her hair as the roaring sounds quickly grew closer… then closer.

"What is it?" Kayla screamed. "It is like the streaks of light from the bridge!"

Suddenly, one of the bright lights landed on her shoulder, startling her. She knocked it to the ground, quickly raising her foot in an attempt to stomp it into the tunnel floor.

"No, Kayla!" I yelled, jumping in front of her to rescue my friend. "It is Nalana!"

"It is Na, who?" she questioned, quickly stopping her attack. I reached down and picked up the glowing light.

"Look very closely," I said as I held my beautiful little friend close to Kayla.

"What is that?" she said as she stared into my hand.

"Nalana, the Queen of the Fairies."

She was not much taller than a small bird, beautifully dressed in a flowing white gown, accenting her soft wings, long curly hair, and large blue eyes. Her hand clenched what looked like a small lantern in the shape of a box. It was neatly woven with branches of a weeping willow tree and filled with fireflies, creating a nice light.

"Tiny as she is, she has as many powers as anyone you will meet in all the lands," I explained.

"I am so sorry, Nalana. I was frightened. I have never seen anything like you, a fairy, before. I'm really sorry."

"I hope I didn't harm you," Kayla said.

Nalana lifted herself in the air in front of Kayla's eyes. "No harm done," whispered her soft voice. "I was shaken up a bit but still in one piece."

My little glowing friend seems to have survived.

"Ah, Princess Kayla, I have heard of you for many years. Nice to finally meet you. We will be seeing a lot of each other now that you have come home. It has been many years since we first saw each other."

"I'm sorry. I don't mean to be rude, but I believe you are mistaken. I have never seen you before. I know that if I had, I would certainly remember," Kayla insisted.

"Oh, yes, you were about seven."

"Your friend had spent the night with you in your grandmother's home. There was a big white box at the end of your sleeping room. A full moon, I believe. You woke in the darkness, very frightened."

"On the white box…"

"Freezer," Kayla rudely interrupted.

"Oh, is that what it is called?"

"On the freezer at the end of your sleeping room, you thought you saw a light shining in the image of a white angel with long curly hair."

"By the time you woke up your friend to show her, I was gone. She told you to go back to sleep and stop dreaming."

"It was you!" Kayla replied. "I knew I wasn't dreaming. I really saw you, didn't I? I knew it!"

"Yes, I have checked up on you many times over the years. That was the only time you actually saw me. I visited you often. I was extremely careful not to be seen. People from your world do not seem to accept things that they do not understand."

"I must be going. If you ever need me for any reason, all you have to do is hold your green stone over your heart, close your eyes, and wish for me to appear. I will always hear you."

"This tree can do that?"

"Yes!" Nalana said, very surprised that Kayla did not know of its use. "Did your father not tell you how to use the stone?"

"No, Nalana, he didn't! He only told me that it would protect me and to never take it off!"

"Listen carefully; the green stone in the center is very powerful. Place it in your hand close to your heart. When you close your eyes, anything you wish for will come to be. It will keep you safe, always. You will have the power to appear anywhere you wish. You should have known this before you began this journey."

"At any time you feel you are in danger, just wish to be in a safe place, and it will happen in an instant."

"No way!" Kayla said. "What if I wanted to go home?"

"Just wish it, and you will be there as quickly as you wish to be home. You can also return the same way."

"However, you must remember one thing."

"What is that?" she asked.

"It only works if you wish for something you truly want in your heart!"

Nalana had been Kayla's guardian since the day of her birth. She knew of the many powers Kayla had been born with. She understood, more than anyone, how powerful she had the ability to become. Once she arrived in Litora Falls and developed these special gifts, she would no longer have use of the pendant. She would have the power to do many things from within herself. She chose not to mention any of this to Kayla until she received my orders.

"Thank you, Nalana! I will remember. I'm so glad to have had this chance to meet you," Kayla said. "You are so amazing!"

"I have been waiting a long time for you to arrive at the tunnel. I am glad to have finally met you, too," Nalana replied.

"What happened at the bridge?" Kayla asked.

"We lock ourselves together to form a safe pass for the Litorans. It is the only way to cross the rushing waters of the deep river, and we alone have the ability to form the opening of the Tunnel of Litora Falls. Our tunnel is the only pass from our world to yours," Nalana said. "It is a very sacred and important part of your family's heritage."

"Remember, place the stone next to your heart!" she smiled as she flew ahead of the others to speak with Neree.

Kayla watched Nalana as she disappeared from her sight.

"I can't wait to see her again," she thought. "Maybe you aren't so ugly and gaudy after all," she said, placing her hand over the pendant. "Hmm, anything I wish! Unbelievable!"

When Kayla caught up to me, Nalana had gone. I was deep in conversation with Ikan, La-too, and Miki. I instantly became silent as soon as we realized she was approaching us.

"What is wrong?" she asked.

"Kayla, we are having a meeting. I need you to join the others until we are finished," I said sternly.

"You don't want me to hear?"

"Please, it is business. Just do as you are told, and do not take it personally. It is very important to me."

"O.K., Father," she said as she sadly walked away.

Nalana had come to warn us of troubles in our homeland. She had received news of an invasion. Several of the Litoran family members had been taken captive, and several guards had been killed.

All she knew for sure was that all the captives were women and children from the castle grounds. She did not know who or how many. Deeply troubled by this news, I knew that we must return home as quickly as possible.

I quickly called a meeting with the Defenders to explain the situation and plan the best way to proceed.

I felt that I had been a little harsh with Kayla. I asked Ikan to explain everything to her in private while I addressed the Defenders.

"How much do I tell her, sir?"

"As much as you feel the need, Ikan! She must understand how serious this matter is!" I answered. "I will leave that decision up to you!"

As I gathered the Defenders, Ikan began to look for Kayla. After a short time, he found her sitting alone. She was leaning against the side of a large boulder, wiping tears from her eyes.

"Your father sent me to explain some things to you," he said as he knelt down beside her.

She looked up into his eyes before looking away without saying a word. She was sad — hurt that her father had sent her away.

"Our land is a beautiful, peaceful place, Kayla. However, many lands beyond ours are not so peaceful. Some are very evil."

"Nalana has brought news of trouble in our homes. An invasion has taken place while we have been away. Some of our women have been taken captive, and guards have been killed."

"We will not know more until we return home. One thing we do know is that this is a very serious matter. Your father is making plans to return immediately. We have no time to waste. We must save our people."

"It is very important for you to be as strong as possible. You must do whatever you are told to do without argument."

"You must understand that this is most serious, Kayla," Ikan said. "Your father is very concerned. He is a very powerful being with a tremendous amount of responsibilities. He must concentrate on saving his people at this most stressful time. There will be no time for questions. Everyone must work together and do their part. We must go in haste!"

"Has this happened because you left to bring me home? Is this my fault?"

"If you had been there, this would not have happened. I'm right. I know I am. It's all my fault!"

"Kayla, this is not your fault! The kind of evil beings that have done this live to cause harm in any way they can. They hurt others and disrupt their lives simply for pleasure. It is their way of life."

"They are evil beings!"

"We are going to need you to be most cooperative as we prepare for home, Kayla. You need to be strong and pay attention to everything going on around you. You must learn as much as you can, quickly!"

"Will you help me learn?" she asked. "I feel so lost."

"Yes, Kayla, I will help you as we go!" he answered, holding out his hand to help her up.

"Thank you!" she said, giving him a big hug.

Ikan was not sure what to make of the hug. All he knew was that he really liked the feeling it gave him. Kayla kept her eyes on Ikan as he joined the other Defenders.

"Hmm, I just might learn to like him after all," she thought. "Not bad for a frog. I guess it's time for me to think of him as a person!"

"He is handsome in human form. I have Litoran blood as well," she thought with a pleasing smile.

I called for everyone to immediately gather in a circle. "It is time for our journey to end!"

"Before we started on this journey, we all agreed to travel the distance without using our powers. I wanted to give Kayla a chance to see the beautiful lands and pathways to our home through her own eyes. We knew she would learn much about our ways and the ways of the land as the journey continued."

"However, this emergency has forced us to change those plans. It has been decided we must wish ourselves home immediately. Time is of the essence! Our loved ones are in trouble and in need of our help.

The faster we arrive, the sooner we can get started! You all know what to do.”

Everyone instantly joined hands in the circle, gathered in as snugly as possible, and closed their eyes. Kayla stood next to Ikan.

I took her hand in mine and placed it over the green stone next to her heart. “Close your eyes and think of following me home. Clear your head and think of nothing else,” I said.

Kayla did as she was told without hesitation. Remembering what Nalana and Ikan had told her, she knew this was a very serious situation. She didn’t want to be left behind. She didn’t want to take a chance on messing things up for anyone else, especially her father.

As instantly as Kayla closed her eyes and wished to be where I needed her to be, she felt my hand touch her shoulder.

“You can open your eyes, Kayla. We are home,” I whispered softly in her ear.

She thought she must be dreaming as she opened her eyes and looked around at the beauty of the surroundings that I called home. The structure of the castle and the beauty of the land were like nothing she had ever seen or heard of before. The beauty of the colorful flowers, thick green grass, and the homes built of trees — each unique and beautiful in its own way — brought her more pleasure than her own property in Eureka Springs. Everything was very simple, yet very beautiful.

“This is the most amazing place that I have ever seen in my entire life!”

"I can't believe the magnificent beauty and structure. It's wonderful, Father! All this time, you could have wished us home instantly! Why did you make me...?"

"There are things you need to see and learn. I regret we did not have the time to travel. There is much for you to learn about this world."

"I understand," she said. "Did you have a chance to bring my mother here when she was alive?"

"Yes," I replied. "She had much the same reaction as you are having. Her eyes just were not quite as big."

"It's like a tropical island — only better. It's more beautiful and well-planned."

"It's... it's so amazing!"

"Is that a hotel?" she asked, pointing at the beautiful, enormous structure directly in front of them.

"Kayla, hotels are not yet known in our time. That is our home — a castle fit for a princess!"

"Wow!" she whispered. "I can't wait to see the inside!"

Chapter Thirteen — Invasion Of Litora Falls

"Mother was amazing, grandfather. It was not her fault… was it?" Elliott asked.

"No, it was not her fault. It was the evil beings," I assured him as I continued.

Dubkan rushed down the steps of the lookout tower to meet us at the front gates. "So glad you are here, sir!" he said. "We have had an invasion. The Draconians — I fear!"

"Seven guards have been killed. Eleven women and two children have been taken captive, sir! They slipped in and out in the middle of the night before we knew what hit us, sir! Nothing else was taken!"

"It appears they were after our women and children! Somehow, they must have known that you and the others were away."

"How is that possible?" I interrupted. "We have told no one outside our kingdom! We were very careful!"

"Sir," Dubkan replied, "Lin was killed, sir!"

Lin was a longtime friend and leader in the kingdom. He was old and ill, no longer able to travel outside of Litora Falls.

"He was the guard that found your grandfather when he was attacked," Koda interrupted.

"Yes… yes, he was. His older son, also named Lin, is with us today."

"I know him," Elliott said.

"I do, too," Koda added.

"Just before he died, he was able to speak one word. He told us who killed him, sir."

"Give me the name?" I demanded.

"Trillian! The evil one himself, sir."

Trillian, the ruthless ruler of the evil Draconians, was better known as the evilest being of all evil tribes and kingdoms. He lived in the land that is located deep in the dark, un-forbidden hills of the north — the Dracara Mountains.

"How rude of me, sir! Is this... is it her?"

"You are more beautiful than I had imagined!"

"Dubkan, this is Kayla," I introduced.

"Oh, my dear, I have waited all these years to meet you!"

"Welcome! I wish the circumstances were better," he said, taking her hand in his. "You will love it here. It is usually quiet and most peaceful."

"Where is Nadia?" I interrupted.

"Nadia!" Kayla thought. "Did he say Nadia? It couldn't be... Oh, it couldn't be!"

"She is safe in the caves to the south with Sly, Silas, Aaron, Talisha, Ren, Yara, and Misty," Dubkan answered. "They left early yesterday for the two-night adventure you had planned for them before you left. Have you forgotten, sir? They are at the caves of Ka'ron. They are to return this evening. However, you were not expected home for two more days."

"Ah, yes!" I remembered. "I am so relieved!"

"Hold on," he said. "Ikan, Miki, La-too, split up and gather every able warrior and leader in our land! Bring them all to the castle for a meeting within the hour!"

"We decided to wait upon Nadia's return to inform her of the invasion. We were hoping that you would arrive first. I thought you would want to be here and tell her, sir."

"I knew that it would be best to have plans for our approach to save our women and children in place before the queen was informed of any of this!" Dubkan said.

"This could not have been a better time for Queen Nadia to have been gone from the castle, sir! I am grateful you have returned before she had to be told of the captives. She will be most upset. She will blame herself for being gone, sir. You know how she is about these things!"

Sly and Silas are two strong guides, brave Defenders, and Nadia's personal guards. Aaron is my younger brother, the Prince of the land. His wife, Talisha, is Queen Nadia's best friend, and Yara is her only daughter. Yara was born on the same day as Princess Kayla. Her father was a very close friend of Aaron's from childhood. He was killed in an accident a few years ago, leaving Talisha and Yara alone.

Aaron was in love with Talisha for many years after the accident. He did not let his feelings be known to her until after Yara and Ren were married and Talisha was alone. Talisha has always spoken to Yara about the memories of her father. It was important to her that she grew up knowing what a great man he was. She made a promise to her on the day her father was laid to rest that she would never be raised by a stepfather.

Yara was very spoiled and demanded that Talisha keep her promise. Once a year, they all traveled together for an overnight adventure to the caves of Ka'ron.

Nadia created a secret shrine of Kayla deep inside the cave. It was filled with photos, clippings, and other memories that Lori had saved for Nadia. She followed Kayla's successful life; however, she had cut off any details of her world's location. Her identity was removed from the clippings for her safety. The cave was kept very well-hidden and well-guarded at all times.

Nadia kept it from me, fearing that I would object. She longed for our daughter and needed this place to help her feel her in her life. They awaited her arrival with excitement and much love. Through the special memories, she had been with them in their hearts since the day of her birth.

"Queen Nadia!" Kayla shouted, no longer able to keep silent. "Father… Father…!"

"Nadia is my mother's name!"

"Father!"

I could not speak. I just looked at her. Dubkan did not know what to do. Had he spoken out of line? He could not believe I had not told her!

"Say something!" she insisted, grabbing me by the arm.

"I wanted to surprise you, Kayla."

"Yes, Nadia! Your mother is here! She has always been here with me! She did not die as your grandmother led you to believe!"

"When she told you that she was gone before her time, she wanted you to believe that she was dead."

"She could not let you know that she was alive because she chose to marry me and make a life with me… here."

"She was so devastated by her choice that Nadia could not bear to take you from her. She knew how badly she had hurt her, and she loved her very much. You were all she had left! It would have killed her to lose you! Your mother cannot wait to see you! She loves you more than you will ever know! Please, Kayla, hold on to that thought!"

Kayla stood there with tears running down her cheeks. She did not know how to feel. "Her mother was alive! Why had she never told her?"

She fell to her knees, sobbing. "Too many feelings, Father," she cried. "How could this be?"

I picked her up in my arms and carried her inside the castle. She hugged me tightly as she wept, unable to control the tears.

"I had a family… a mother and a father… all these years! How could everyone have kept this from me?"

"Left alone in another world while you made this wonderful life — here — without me! Why? Don't you love me? Were you ashamed of me?"

"Kayla, I have always loved you more than life itself. Please believe me. I must rescue my people. We will talk when I return. I will explain everything to you, I promise," I said as I laid her on the couch in front of the huge fireplace in the living room.

"Try to get some rest while I help gather all the Defenders, elders, and workmen of their lands. I must make plans for the rescue of the captured women and children. You will be safe here until I return."

"Try to get some sleep, my beautiful daughter," I whispered as I walked away.

Kayla was very hurt but excited at the same time. She sadly lay there, alone, trying to sort out her thoughts. She knew for sure her grandmother loved her very much. She also knew she was all she had. She had the best life, although somewhat lonely for her family.

Her entire life, she had a family she knew nothing about. On the other hand, she had given her grandmother the happiness she deserved for raising her.

"Now, while still young, I have been given a chance to have the love of my mother, father, aunts, uncles, cousins, and who knows how many others."

"I can do one of two things," she thought. "I can be bitter and ruin this, or I can get over myself and be thankful for the family I am about to meet for the very first time."

"I missed out on this for the first twenty years of my life, but now… now I can have them to love and enjoy forever."

"My mother is alive! I am going to meet her any moment!"

"I can spend the rest of my life getting to know everyone and have a wonderful, long, happy life here, in this amazing place — with all of them!"

"What about home, my friends, my job?" she thought. "How can I give that up?"

"One thing at a time," she decided. "I have to get to know everyone first! I can't spoil this! One step at a time!"

"I can't wait to see my mother!" she thought as she fell deep asleep.

I gave my beautiful daughter one last look over my shoulder as I headed down the hall, hoping that she would forgive me someday.

Chapter Fourteen — Trillian's Letter

Written in Blood...

When I opened the door to the chamber of the council, I could overhear the discussions already in progress. All able Defenders of the kingdom had gathered. Everyone was shouting at once, with no sense of order. They all had their own opinions on how to approach this most serious situation with the least amount of danger to the women and children.

"We have always been known for our great virtue!" I loudly interrupted. "This will undoubtedly prove to be our greatest challenge of all time! Trillian and his Draconians are the evil… above evil in all the lands! It fills my heart with animosity like I have never known, trying to imagine the ordeal our people are enduring as we speak!"

"We all feel deep anguish for them, but we must force our minds to think in proper perspective to ensure safety for them, as well as for ourselves! Enough lives have been lost! The lands we must enter are virtually unknown to each and every one of us. All we know of these evil beings comes from stories handed down through generations."

"We must consider many things before we decide how to approach this delicate and dangerous matter. The kingdom cannot be left unguarded, open to another attack while we are gone. We must ensure protection for our families and friends above all. Our peaceful lands have never endured such turmoil. We may need to ask for help from our friends, the Ceairans and Komodo Dragons."

"Sorry to interrupt, sir!"

Every head turned toward the left doors as they flew open.

"Ah, Sir Meinkard," Neree said. "To what do we owe this interruption, sir?"

Meinkard, the mighty leader of the Ceairans of the eastern lands of Amphibia, is a very strong member of the Litoran council. The Ceairans are kind-spirited and peaceful by nature, much like the Litorans. They have many great strengths and powerful abilities to defend their own when threatened. They also have the power to change form and to possess human-like abilities, albeit with a more creature-like appearance.

"Sorry to intrude, but I have news of the utmost urgency," he replied.

"May I, sir?"

"Speak, my friend; the floor is yours!"

"My wife, Kindall, was traveling here to see Queen Nadia with a personal invitation to our daughter Layla's wedding. We had received word of Kayla's coming home, and she wanted to honor her arrival. Just as they reached the entrance to your land, the evil Draconians were on their way out of the gates."

"Kendall's guards were attacked, and she was taken captive — with your women and children!"

"This is Col, Layla's betrothed! He was the only guard to survive the attack! We have come personally to offer all able Ceairan men to join the Defenders in this rescue! If we combine forces, we will be much more powerful, sir!"

"Cheers roared through the castle!"

"Sir Meinkard, until this day, the Draconians have had no quarrel with you. Now, they have invaded your family."

Shaking Meinkard's hand, I shouted with hope, "There is your answer, sir! I cannot thank you enough! Please join our meeting! We must plan our approach and be on our way as quickly as possible!"

"Thank you, King Neree!"

"No, Meinkard, the thanks go to you!" I replied.

Turning to face the Defenders, with me by his side, Meinkard shouted, "We all have much at stake here. May we all come together as one!" (Shaking his fist into the air) "Victory! Victory!" echoed throughout. Each of the castle's Defenders and Ceairans raised their fists together, shouting, "One!"

Suddenly, there was a loud hiss. A spear sliced through the window from outside, landing in the center of the floor, just missing both Sir Meinkard and me.

I carefully pulled off a paper tied to the end. Meinkard and I read it together, with much distress in our eyes.

"Sir, I do not know what to say!" Meinkard spoke with sadness and fear. "I do not understand how he knew she was coming!"

"Do not worry; we will do the right thing for everyone!" I replied, turning to my people.

"Listen to me, everyone," I yelled.

The silence was instant as I began to read the note, written in blood, for all to hear, with sadness in my voice.

"If it is the last thing I ever do, I will find out how Trillian knew of Kayla's arrival to our land! Listen carefully to these words!"

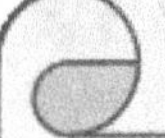

King Nereel Once the bond is tied (Ciar's
destiny), the completion ceremony will begin! Her

Literan blood and powers will be sacrificed to him
Oh, what a ceremony it will be.!

"Our greatest evil will be complete! Our next
generation...Let your imagination go...!"

"The most powerful, endless evil will emerge
through this sacrifice! Bring her to me in three days!

If you refuse my demands. The consequences Ah
yes... The Ceairan Queen.

"Your women and children. Only the beginning!"
As ever, the one and only.

King Trillian

Remember, "THREE DAYS!

"Kayla is in great danger here! She must leave at once!" Ikan yelled loudly for all to hear. A loud roar of anger arose across the floor.

"Silence!" I demanded. "Meinkard, this horrific news means one thing! We are truly bound together as one in this unforgivable matter! Please, I must excuse myself for a short time to speak with my daughter. She knows nothing of this."

"I trust you to begin the plans, my friend! Give Meinkard the same respect and attention you would me!" I insisted.

"Sir," Meinkard replied, "with all due respect, send your daughter home to her world until this is settled! She will be safest there! We will avenge this and rescue our loved ones! Kayla must be safe from this destiny of Ciar's! All our futures are at stake here! This must not come to be! She must...!"

"I know!" I interrupted, shaking my head sadly. "I am afraid you do not know my daughter, sir."

With a nod of his head, Meinkard divided the room into three groups. Each group tried to come up with the perfect plan.

"I cannot believe I brought her here! If I had only known Ciar's birth date! I thought she could come, spend time getting to know her family, and return home without danger. How was he informed of our being gone? And of her arrival? How?"

I just could not help myself once her grandmother was gone. I needed to bring her home. Her place is here with her family.

"I wanted her with us so badly! Now! Now I have put her in much danger and my people! How could I have done this? I must tell her everything. The true reason she was left in her mom's world was to be raised by her grandmother. How can I tell her any of this?"

"Lori... she was supposed to live and raise her until this black time was over! She was taken away from her... from all of us... too soon."

"I now know true hate and the feelings of wanting revenge," I thought. As I entered the den, Kayla was sound asleep on the couch before me.

"Wake up, my daughter," I said as I pushed her beautiful hair from her large bright blue eyes. "You are so much your mother," I thought. "I almost wish you were like her in every way. Yes, with no powers or Litoran blood."

"Wake up, my daughter," I repeated.

"Father, is my mother home?"

"No, Kayla. She has not yet arrived."

"I need to speak with you."

"I need you to listen to everything I am going to tell you before you speak a word. This is the most important thing I will ever ask of you, Kayla," I said. I did not know exactly how to explain this to her. The one thing that I did know was that I had to convince her she must go back to her world — immediately.

"I have not been truthful with you, Kayla," I began. "I need to explain everything and only hope you will understand. You must do as I ask of you as soon as I have finished."

Knowing the time had come for me to be completely truthful with my daughter, I began to explain.

"The story I told you concerning your grandmother was not completely the true story. It is what your grandmother, your mother, and I decided you should be told. We felt the need to keep you from learning the truth about the danger you are in."

"Father, what is going on?" she said, fear creeping into her voice. "You sound so serious! You are scaring me!"

"Kayla, your grandmother, Lori, did not disown Nadia, and she did not disown me. She visited us as often as possible here, with the assistance of a dark green stone similar to the one in your pendant. She would come for the day while you were at school or on trips. She would leave in time to arrive home before you. She continued to make these visits until she became ill and could no longer endure the journey. She was very proud of your mother and loved her very much."

"There is a good reason we had her raise you and why she could never speak of us. This was all necessary to protect you and to keep you safe."

"I don't understand, Father!" she cried.

"She could not have any memories of your mother or me! No photos... no letters or clippings, nothing! It was far too dangerous for anyone to know who your parents were! You are a very important part of this world, very special to our future. This is not the time for you to be here. It is much too soon!"

"Here," I said as I took Trillian's note out of my robe and reluctantly handed it to Kayla. "Read this carefully! Its words will help you understand! I had hoped you would never have to learn of any of this! This note will explain what I am trying to tell you in a way that should help you realize that our decision was the best thing for everyone. It will also assure you of the danger you are in! It is not safe for you here... at this time! You must return to your world immediately!"

"But Father... I want to see my mother!"

"I will not leave without meeting her first!"

"You can't ask that of me!"

"Please!" she cried.

"Read the note, Kayla," I interrupted.

Kayla quickly opened the note and read through a flood of tears. "Ciar! Sacrifice! Evil! Father, this is my fault! The dead guards, the invasion, that man that captured your people! It is because of me! What powers? I have no powers!"

"I don't understand, Father!" she said, sobbing into her hands. "Everyone must hate me!"

"No!"

"This can't be! It can't be!"

"Kayla," I said, wrapping my arms around her, "this is not your fault. This is the doings of an evil man — above any evil you could possibly imagine! If this destiny is allowed to take place, it will be the end of these lands and everyone who lives outside the realm of the dark hills of the Dracara mountains! The evil Draconians, Trillian, and Ciar… I cannot begin to imagine the outcome of evil that will come to pass!"

"The destiny is to take place the second Ciar turns twenty-one. The marriage must be bound at that moment! One hour later, you are to be slain, and all the powers of both of your worlds will pass through you… into him! He — this oh-so-evil young man — will become the most powerful, dangerous, evil being ever known to our lands! Our only hope, and yours, is for you to leave and not return to us until this is finished once and for all! I will come for you again when it is safe."

"You must never speak of our lands to anyone in your homeland. You must go on with your life as you were before you knew of any of this. No one must know who you are!"

"This is most serious, Kayla. Please understand!" I insisted, holding her face in my hands as I looked into her sad eyes.

Kayla looked back into my eyes for a few silent moments.

"Father, I fear the danger this note reads of, but at the same time, I am so relieved," she spoke softly. "For the first time in my life, I understand everything. This is my home, where I am supposed to finish my life. I have a family that I have never known! This is the reason I have always felt I did not fit in with anyone, anywhere. Why I have always been teased that I am one of a kind. I am! And I am proud!"

"You had to keep me from this land to protect — not only your kingdom — but also all the lands around you that are good from this evil. It feels so good to know you love me that much!"

"I am a very intelligent woman, Father. I understand completely. I know you are right! I must go home until this is settled! I could not bear being the cause of this evil consuming your world — that you love so much! I certainly don't want to be sacrificed unto this evil man! I have so much to live for, especially now. I really do understand! I do! I just don't want to leave now!"

"I need to see my mother before I go! I want to hold her and tell her how much I love her! I want to look into her eyes and save her imoage in my mind and my heart! You can't make me aware of all of this — then take it away from me — before I get the chance to see her! Please give me at least that much to hold on to!"

"Please…! Please, Father," she begged as they held each other peacefully.

Chapter Fifteen — Kayla's Mother

The noise of horses approaching, along with voices and laughter, brought us to our feet as the front doors of the castle flew open. Rushing to the entranceway to see who had arrived, I smiled with joy as I saw her in the doorway.

"Nadia, my dear, you are home at last!" I said with great relief.

"Neree, what a pleasant surprise!" she replied, her eyes freezing as they caught sight of her beautiful daughter standing in my shadow.

"Kayla!" she cried, overwhelmed with excitement at the mere sight of her. "Oh, my beautiful daughter! I have so longed to see you!"

"Mother!" Kayla cried, with all the love one young woman could possibly feel at one time. "Mother," was all she could say as they rushed across the floor into each other's arms.

"Oh, Mother! I am so glad you are alive!" she whispered through the tears flowing down her face. "It is really you, isn't it?"

"Yes, my beautiful blue eyes! It is. It is really me! I am never going to let you go again! It will take us many moons and suns to catch up on the time we have lost together!" Nadia said as she noticed shouting coming from the council room.

"Neree," she said, fear in her voice. "What has happened? Why have you arrived home early? What is going on in the council room? Something is wrong; I can feel it!"

"Now, do you see, Kayla? You are so much like your mother! Not only do you look alike, but she asks more questions than you do," I teased. "Come, Nadia!" I replied. "I will explain everything!"

I carefully and quickly explained all that had taken place while she was on her trip to Ka'ron. She listened sadly as the events I spoke of unfolded in her mind. She remained calm until I showed her Trillian's note.

As she read the cruel words, she sobbed. "There is no time to waste!" she cried. Quickly excusing her guards, Sly and Silas, to leave her and rest from their trip, she turned to me.

"You need to return to the council meeting, Neree; we will be fine."

"I need to talk to my daughter before she leaves for home."

"Kayla, it breaks my heart that we will have no time to get to know each other, but you must return home at once!"

"But Mother!" Kayla screamed.

"I cannot lose you now, Kayla, after all these years of waiting to finally have you in my life!" Nadia interrupted. "You must be kept safe! This destiny cannot be allowed to be fulfilled! This is the only way!"

"But, Mother," Kayla cried, "I want to stay here with you! Please, just a little while!"

"We don't have a second to waste, Kayla! I did not give up our life together for all these years to bring you here and lose you now! The time will come for us to be together. After this is over, and it is safe for you here, we will come for you again! You must consider not only yourself but our people and friends of all of these lands! Everyone and everything here is in danger!"

"I know! I just need to be with you so much!" Kayla replied. "Are you not in danger as well?" she added.

"Yes!" Nadia answered. "I will not lie to you!"

"Then come with me, Mother! Come with me… so you can be safe too!"

"I need to be here, Kayla!" Nadia replied. "You sent me away for twenty years to keep me safe. You kept the fact that I had you and my father and all our family from me. Now I have a chance at a wonderful life with my parents and family I have never known. Give me back part of what you took from me. Come home with me and spend this time getting to know the daughter that you have never touched, or talked to for hours with, or had a chance to cook for or take shopping."

"Father, the Defenders, and all those joining them will take care of the situation here. Please come home with me! I can't leave without you! I can't! I won't! I… I need you now, Mother! Me… your daughter!"

Tears rolled down Nadia's face as she held Kayla tightly in her arms. She thought how nice it would be if they could have this time together. She had not been home, to her own world, for twenty years.

"I would be safe there," she thought. "It is a world beyond the powers and evil here in our land. Trillian has no power to travel there. It is the only place to be safe from him and his kind."

"I am the queen. My people need me here in the castle. But you are my daughter, and you need me now more than ever."

"How can I turn my back on you again?"

"You will hate me!"

"I will talk with your father," she whispered.

"Oh, thank you!" Kayla cried as her mother held her tightly in her arms. "He will let you go," she whispered.

"Yes, I will!" I agreed as I entered the room, overhearing the conversation.

"Nadia, my beautiful wife, I must prepare to leave immediately for this most dangerous rescue of our captives. It is feared by all that Trillian may have planned to capture you in the invasion, not knowing you were away from the castle, in hopes of forcing our hand with Kayla — in time for his plans to be fulfilled!"

"He may try again while we are away! We must not take any chances with either of your lives! The only way to keep you both safe is for you to go back to your world with our daughter. You must both stay until this is finished once and for all."

"You must leave immediately! There will be no discussion!" I demanded. "Take Ciara with you. She will be of much comfort for you both."

Ciara, Nadia's personal maid, was also her dear trusted friend. She had been very disturbed by the nature of conversations she had overheard between Talisha and an unknown man in the shadows of the garden the evening she left with the queen on their journey to Ka'ron.

She had been unable to get those thoughts out of her mind for the past two days. Determined to protect her wonderful queen, she decided to take a dangerous chance and search Talisha's personal room before they returned. Deeply hidden at the bottom of a locked drawer, she found a curious-looking black pad folded in half and tied with a dark red ribbon.

Flipping through it quickly, she skimmed enough to realize she might not be the loyal friend Nadia had trusted her to be all these years. Startled by the sound of many footsteps and voices coming from just outside the window, she quickly tucked the pad in her pocket under her apron and hurried to her own quarters to read the words Talisha had written.

"Misty would like to meet Princess Kayla before she leaves, sir, with your permission," Dubkan said as he and Misty entered the room.

Nadia had found Misty, as an infant, wandering about the caves of Ka'ron during one of her visits. Now seven, she had grown up in the castle. When she was an infant, Dubkan and his wife cared for her. She quickly fit into their world. Everyone in the kingdom loved her. She was a quiet, very intelligent, mature, and obedient child. She took to Dubkan instantly and called him "Pa Paw." He loved her as if she were his own daughter and spent as much of his spare time as he possibly could with her.

"Don't worry, little one; I will return soon. I promise," Kayla said, very impressed with the manners and maturity of the young child.

"I will come for you when it is safe," I insisted. "Now, inform Ciara, and be off at once," I said, holding them both tightly in my arms for one last moment.

Pleased with the news she would be leaving with Kayla, Ciara took Talisha's black pad with her. This would give her time to read it carefully before she informed the queen of her concern.

I could still feel their touch and hear Kayla whisper, "Be careful, father. I need you in my life!" as they vanished from my sight to safety at last.

I noticed that the boys had not spoken for a while. "You must be getting very tired of listening to me go on and on. We should stop for now."

"No, grandfather, you are just getting to the wars. Please continue. I am not tired," Elliott insisted.

"I agree," Koda added.

"Please, grandfather, you cannot stop now."

Chapter Sixteen — The War

Ikan gathered all defenders and able men of Litora Falls to prepare for their journey to the rugged Dracara Mountains. Small groups of guards were sent west to the region of Trundra Hills to request help from the Komodo Dragons that lived in the Varanus Desert area of the land. The power and strength of these great warriors would greatly increase the chance of victory over Trillian and his warriors.

Malachi traveled north to the Dracara Mountains with a small group of the most trusted warriors. They transformed into the smallest of frogs to look over the situation inside the dark caves and find the exact location of the captives and guards. They were to return as quickly as possible. The information they were to obtain was much needed to help finalize the rescue plan with the least amount of danger to all.

Meinkard traveled east to the region of Salentra Springs, to his home in the Gibbon Forest. He gathered his warriors with great haste and returned immediately to join the defenders and the Komodo Dragons in our rescue. Each having special powers of their own unique kind, they became an army of great talent, all in hopes of overpowering Trillian and his warriors. Together, the warriors waited with excitement for my command to begin the war.

"King Neree, would it not be simple for you, with your power, to appear at any location with only a wish, simply to remove them with the help of only a few men? You could gather them together quickly, the guards unaware, my king," Eckhard said.

"Yes, it could be done, but this would be a most dangerous approach. For this plan to be successful, without danger to our women and children, they must be gathered together in one place, unguarded, and prepared for our plan. If one is held alone, at any other location in the caves, away from the other captives, Trillian could have enough time to harm them before we have a chance to save them. If our plan was successful and they discovered we had rescued even one of them, Trillian would be most angry."

"You must know he would spread endless evil across our lands for revenge. Many more lives could be lost very quickly. Enough harm has been done! We must stop Trillian and all of the Draconians once and for all!" I demanded. "As long as they survive, a shadow of fear hangs over our lands. We must save our world from this evil that threatens our future. We must do this with the least amount of danger for all of our women and children. These evil beings must be destroyed."

"Sir Eckhard, I speak for myself and Sir Meinkard. We owe you deeply for your dedication to us over the years. You must know that by joining us against the Draconians, you bring war and revenge upon your lands and your families if the evil beings survive our attack. Trillian knows little of you at this time. Please, my friend, know the danger you may bring upon yourself and your people before we begin. Be sure in your heart you want to join us and bring this possibility of tragedy upon yourself."

"Yes! With all our power, we are in. We will always honor the bond of our three families. We must not let this evil take over our lands or our people. The peace of our land means everything to every one of us!"

"We are all in as one!" Eckhard yelled with much excitement for all to hear. "If this destiny comes to pass, the sweep of evil will come in a much more powerful and destructive way than we could possibly imagine for all in the lands of Amphibia. Trillian must be stopped..."

Malachi suddenly interrupted. "The captives have been separated, sir. The women are in a room just above the basement, and the children are in a connecting room, alone, in the darkest section of the caves. We could not locate Kindall, sir! We searched everywhere! Sorry, sir!"

"There is good news. They are guarding only the outside doors. We can easily flash in with two men at each location and flash out quickly without being seen. I have informed all the captives of our plan, with your permission, my king. We need only your order, sir!"

Before he could finish, Ranjetti burst through the doors. "I found her, sir!" he shouted. "She is being held alone in a dark room in the lower basement just below the location of the others. She is in the same black cave, sir. The plan can easily work. Pardon me for interrupting… with your permission, sir. She is only guarded by the outside door."

"It is almost too easy, sir."

"It could be trickery."

"Our plan can work. They know nothing of our ability to suddenly appear at any place we wish, as we do, sir. They know nothing of our ability to change our appearance. They are expecting us as we are now, sir."

"Thank you, Malachi, Ranjetti. You have done a great job. We will make the final decisions of our plan. Please, join the others. Inform the warriors we will leave shortly. We have a hard journey at hand."

"Sir Meinkard, the queen said not to worry!" Ranjetti said as he stepped out the door.

"We must all agree. Do we follow the plan?" I asked.

"The war will begin!" Eckhard and Meinkard shouted as they quickly joined their armies.

"We must not waste another light of day," I announced. "We will use all of our powers and abilities, bound together as one, to appear in the safest spot possible in the forest that covers the outskirts of the Dracara Mountains. We will assess the overall situation before we begin our attack. We must take this journey in our strongest and most powerful forms. We will need every ounce of strength and power we have for victory over this evil."

"Malachi, prepare your men and take your places with the captives instantly. Prepare to leave for Dracara immediately."

"Our warriors must gather quickly. Remember one and all; this victory is for the future of our land and our families. We declare war on the evil Trillian and his Draconians in this effort to rescue our people!" My words echoed through the trees, bouncing off the mountains with sounds of loud thunder and flashes of lightning across the lands. "This rescue will shake up much trouble for our peaceful lands for a time to come if this evil is not destroyed. Hear me one and all! War is at hand!" I yelled.

Shouts and screams of approval rolled across the thousands of warriors outside the castle gates as they prepared to begin.

"We must not travel on the winged horses. We must appear at once," I demanded.

"My friends, gather into a large circle as tightly as possible. Join hands and think only of following me where I travel!" I yelled loudly once again for all to hear.

Instantly, we were at the closest point possible. We quickly scattered across the thickest area of the forest outside the Dracara Mountains. The warriors hid themselves in the trees with a perfect view of the Draconians' caves.

"It is much too quiet and calm!" Ikan said.

"Something must be up."

"It could be a trap, sir."

Suddenly, Draconians appeared in herds from every direction. The ground shook with clouds of dust bouncing off the trampling of feet as they forcefully moved from the grounds before the mountain toward the forest, in full force with swords, knives, and spears held high in the air.

The war had begun. At the first sounds of fighting, Malachi had given his order. He and his men appeared home successfully with all the women and children. Eckhard and I, side by side with all our men, fearlessly fought the strongest of the Draconians. Many were wounded quickly by the strong, evil beings.

Appearing at the edge of their hiding place in the trees, Meinkard led the Ceairans, releasing arrows from every direction for added power.

Loud squeaks of whipping vines swished through the wind as many arrows flew out from the midst of the trees, dropping to the ground. Bows drawn with deadly aim, they quickly overpowered the weakest of the Draconians, driving the survivors back against the mountain. Their combined power gave the Draconians little chance to cause the damage they had planned.

A sword against the blade, arrow after arrow, Eckhard, Meinkard, and I proudly fought the remaining evil beings beside our brave men. Dust and arrows, men on horses, flying through the air… Fists and whips loudly landing with mighty power… The fierce battle continued until darkness began to cover the forest and caves.

Fearing the Komodos' great strength and swiftness with their swords, the fighting power of the Litorans, and the Ceairans' deadly aim with arrows, the few remaining evil ones brave enough to continue the battle, disappeared into the deep dark caves, blocking the only entrance.

As the moon began to appear over the mountain, Ikan yelled, "What do we do, my king?"

"So much darkness — this land is unknown to us. We are at a great disadvantage, sir. Must we wait until light? Can we use our powers?"

"Malachi and his men will come to us when their mission is accomplished. Only then will we use our great powers to enter the dark caves and finish this. We must know the women and children are all safe. Until then, we must continue to fight as we are. We must not put their lives in danger."

Suddenly, I heard a loud roar from the right side of the forest. Bright flashing lights appeared to rise over the top of the lands, headed in our direction. The lands lit up like fire in the skies.

"The Fairies!" I announced. "They come to bring us light. We must unblock the entrance to the caves."

"Take cover!" Eckhard yelled. Seven Komodos burst through rocks and dust, unblocking the entrance into the mountains.

Confused by the brightness of the lands and the shattering sounds of what had taken place, Draconians quickly rushed to the opening. Col was the first to rush down the hills, every warrior close behind. He was the greatest with the bow, each arrow a perfect shot.

Running full force into the battle — drawing his bow with arrow after arrow — Col successfully dropped many Draconians in their tracks within an instant.

Suddenly, from nowhere, seven Draconians appeared. Many heavy spears flew into the air in Col's direction.

"No! Col!" screamed Meinkard as he saw him rise for a shot. Instantly, he screamed in pain from a deadly hit.

Meinkard's heart tightened as he saw him fall to the ground in terrifying pain. Quickly changing form for his own protection, Meinkard rushed behind the shrubs next to him just as he forced the words from his mouth.

"Tell Layla I love her, sir," he whispered with his last breath.

"Jadar!" I yelled. "On the hill!"

Jadar was known throughout all the lands as Trillian's most feared warrior. He was banned from his land years ago by the leader of the Taltons. It was he — under Trillian's orders — who had actually murdered my grandfather. He and his few followers disgusted Neckatosh. He had overheard them proudly bragging about the evil they had spread across the lands, killing many of his innocent friends.

Hearing of Jadar's banishment, Trillian welcomed him to join the Draconians. The evil doings of this huge, eight-foot-tall creature and his followers impressed Trillian. He was pleased to name him one of his most feared warriors.

Jadar's first act of violence under Trillian's power had been to slaughter an entire village of harmless men, women, and children for recreation. He followed the order with more destruction and evil than Trillian could have planned himself. He appeared impossible to stop. He instantly became the most feared creature across the lands.

Ikan and I made our way around the backside of the hill from both sides, backing him close to the edge of the cliff.

Here's the revised version of your content with corrections in punctuation, grammar, paragraphing, spelling, dialogue separation, and consistent use of tense, while keeping the original context intact:

***

Ikan drew his sword for the attack. Many arrows from the warriors hidden in the trees pierced Jadar's heart. He fell heavily from the high cliff like a large rock. His enormous size landed in a cloud of dust below, accompanied by the loud sounds of crashing thunder. The image of his enormous form creased the ground as his screams echoed through the lands with earth-shattering power.

Nash, followed by a dozen warriors, appeared from the bushes, bows held high above their heads. They were proud of their victory.

"That was for my friend!" Nash cried.

"And for my grandfather!" I screamed.

"Draconians, hear me now! Your evil will not take over our land!" Nash yelled.

Nash had been Col's best friend since the day they were old enough to speak. Col was to be the best man at his wedding. Vengeance on behalf of Col was imminent.

Together, Ikan and I made our way back down the hill to Meinkard and Col.

"I am so sorry, sir," I said.

"I will send you home with Col immediately. His family will want to prepare him for his departure."

"Again, I am sorry for your loss, sir."

"Your daughter needs her mother's presence at this sad time."

"Thank you, sir, but it is too late for Col now."

"We must stay and finish this… for him," he insisted.

"Now this is most personal!" he screamed for all to hear as he laid Col's body safely under the bush.

"Many more are coming!" shouted Aaron, stepping from his lookout position outside the cave entrance to warn his army.

Suddenly, dozens of Draconians rushed from the cave entrance. At least ten were huge, fearless black creatures of Jadar's kind.

As he turned back for cover, he fell to the ground with a loud scream, a spear piercing his chest next to his heart.

"Aaron!" Ikan cried, knowing it was a deadly hit.

"Neree, Aaron has been hit with a spear, and it appears near the heart, sir!" Ikan shouted.

"Noooooooooooooooo!" I screamed.

Ikan immediately changed into a frog, rushing to Aaron to assess the damage. "Oh, Aaron, my best friend," Ikan whispered, knowing he was gone.

"He is gone!" he screamed loudly. "I am so sorry," he whispered. "I am going to miss you, my brave friend."

Aaron and Ikan had been best friends their entire lives. Aaron, being a few years older, had taken Ikan under his wing and taught him much about everything he needed to learn to be a great Litoran. He taught him well.

"I wish I could have known your brother," Grandfather, my uncle Elliott said, a tear rolling down his cheek.

"He would have loved you," I replied.

Ikan joined me as quickly as he could. "No more lives," he insisted.

"That is it!" I cried. "We must finish this now. We must stop these evil beings for good."

"I am so sorry, sir!" Eckhard said. "We have lost two of our greatest men, sir."

"Enough lives have been senselessly taken from us. Let's finish this with much haste."

Saddened by the loss of Col and Aaron, all the warriors gained a powerful new strength as they fiercely fought their way into the center of the battle with full force. Dust filled the air in the likeness of a thick cloud of smoke, with loud sounds of war roaring across the mountains.

"There! From the West!" Eckhard yelled. "My friends, the Taltons! They have come to help us!"

Winged horses filled the sky, carrying many Taltons armed with sharp stone spears and three-pointed blades.

Taltons are powerful creatures, much like Komodo Dragons by nature. Huge, upright beings with tough dark skin, many have shaggy black hair covering their bodies. They lived just outside the far mountains near the lands connecting to the Varanus Desert.

They befriended the Komodo Dragons many years ago, accidentally meeting along their travels across the Varanus Desert.

The leader and great friend of Eckhard, called Neckatosh, heard of the evil that had come to us. He prepared his army for war and proudly led them to the center of the battle at their greatest time of need.

The giant Draconians, an evil family of Taltons that had been banned from their land by Nekatosh's father many years ago, were no match for the powerful Nekatosh and his army.

Within minutes, everything became still and quiet.

Proudly, from the front of the dark cave, Ranjetti stood with his sword in the air. "We have defeated them all!" he shouted.

All the warriors gathered to hear what their leaders had to say.

"We must find Trillian and Ciar!" Meinkard demanded. "They are not here on the grounds with their men."

"They are not in the caves," Ranjetti announced, coming from the entrance. "I checked the entire area inside, sir."

"Ezra was killed. She never left the caves, sir."

"Ranjetti, are the women and children safe?"

"I personally took Kindall to be with her daughter in the Gibbon Forest. She is safe, sir."

"Malachi, Firmin, and Gida took the others to the castle. I am concerned they have not returned as we planned. I fear something may have gone wrong, sir."

"We will split up and search through the morning for Trillian. If we do not find him, we will return home."

"Ranjetti, return to the castle. See for yourself if they are safe. Return quickly with information."

"Nekatosh, it has been much time since we last crossed paths. Thank you deeply for your help," I said. "You have played a big part in saving us from this evil."

"How can I repay you, my friend?"

"Knowing you are all safe is payment enough," he replied.

"My King," Nalana said as she flew down from the sky above the trees, "we must leave for home now that the light has returned to the land."

"Nalana, I owe you greatly. The Draconians were most confused by the brightness you spread for us. You alone allowed us to continue our battle into the darkness."

"I am happy we could help. I am sorry for your loss, sir. We will see you the next time you pass the Tunnel," she said as she flew away.

The army spent hours searching the hills, caves, and woods beyond. Everything was too peaceful. There was no sign of Trillian, Ciar, or any other Draconian. It appeared as if they had vanished.

"Meinkard, Eckhard, something very strange is going on here," Neree said quietly. "I have an odd feeling about this."

"Something is not right."

"We must return home immediately."

"Thank you, Nekatosh," Meinkard said as they all shook hands.

"Thank you, my dear friend," Eckhard said. "If you ever need us, we are deeply indebted to you and your men."

"Neree, if you need us again for anything, just call on us," Nekatosh said as they mounted their horses and flew away.

We gathered our dead and wounded, along with the two great lives that had been lost, with much sadness. Our three great armies returned to the castle in Litora Falls.

"Take all the wounded to the safe house and wait for us there," Ikan demanded.

Meinkard, Eckhard, and I entered the castle quietly, fearing something was very wrong among us. The outside guards were missing from their posts. There were no guards wandering about the grounds or inside the castle at their usual locations. There were also no guards in the lookout tower. Yet, there was an eerie calm in the air — like never before.

Aaron and Col were laid on the tables in the small visiting room off the east hall for the final preparations and last viewings.

"Something is not right here," I whispered.

"Where is everyone?" Meinkard asked.

"I hear a strange muffling coming from the basement, below the stairway toward the west hall!" interrupted Eckhard, walking carefully toward the strange sounds.

"There! At the top of the stairs!" I said as I saw the shadow of a man.

"Ah, at last, my friends have returned!" shouted the voice of the shadow. "This must mean my army lost the battle!"

"Trillian!" Eckhard yelled, as they all feared what had taken place in the castle while they had been away at battle for the past two days.

"Indeed, I have won the war!" he yelled back with much pride.

Ikan, listening from the background where he had hidden to check out the situation, instantly rushed back to the army waiting by the safe house to follow a plan of his own. There was no time to follow orders.

As Malachi snuck into the basement to assess the location of any intruders, Ikan chose forty of the strongest men to join each of the messengers in groups of ten.

"My plan now!" he announced. "We will capture the Draconians and stop this evil once and for all! I take full responsibility for this! I am doing this my way!"

He personally led the group, following his own plan to capture Trillian.

The attack was such a surprise to the Draconians that they were restrained instantly, with no chance of resistance. Quickly, they were heavily chained together to the back walls of the basement.

Ikan, followed by four Komodo Dragons, appeared at the top of the stairs, surrounding Trillian. The struggle was fierce, but he was quickly overpowered by their great strength.

Meinkard, Eckhard, and I stood together, most proud of our warriors, as the events unfolded quickly before our eyes.

"Sorry to disobey orders, sir," Ikan said.

"I have never been so proud," I replied.

"You are a true leader, Ikan. I have always known that when the time came for you to make your own choices, you would be successful."

"Well done, my son. It is time I told you of your destiny. The day you were born, your parents and I announced to the kingdom that you would be my successor when the time was at hand. It is your destiny to marry my firstborn daughter, Kayla."

Ikan gave me a smile. "I was afraid to tell you that I have feelings for her, sir. I was in fear you would be angry with me. She really does not like me very much, I am afraid, sir."

"I think... it is she you should fear, my son, not your king. In time, she will come around, Ikan. Just let things unfold on their own. She needs not to be told. Follow your heart, Ikan. Trust me. She will come around in the end."

"Thank you, sir, for believing in me all these years," Ikan said.

"You have earned my trust, respect, and much more," I said as I embraced Ikan in my arms and gave him a big hug.

"Always remember, I love you as my own son," I whispered as we joined the others. "You will make a great king someday."

Ikan was very proud to learn that I thought so much of him. He had always known we were close but had no idea, until now, how strong our bond had become.

"I must always make my king proud," he thought. "Kayla... wow... I wonder... never happen... she is so stubborn, independent, and so, so absolutely wonderful," he sighed.

"Where are you?" Malachi asked, interrupting Ikan's thoughts. "They called you to the front of the meeting."

"Sorry," Ikan smiled, heading to the front of the room to join Sir Meinkard, Sir Eckhard, and me.

"Go to your families, my friends. You are well deserving of much rest."

"To peace!" he yelled, raising his spear high in the air.

"Peace!" echoed across the castle grounds as all the warriors proudly raised their spears above their heads.

"Peace! Peace! Peace!" the warriors shouted as they proudly left for their homes and families.

Chapter Seventeen — Talisha's Black Pad

"Were Kayla and Grandmother Nadia at the Small's Farm all of this time?" Koda asked.

"Yes, they were. And do not forget that Ciara was with them."

Born in Litora Falls, Ciara had never traveled outside the lands of Amphibia. She stood speechless in the center of the den of the farmhouse; her body was paralyzed with disbelief at the amazing surroundings before her.

Kayla could not help being amused, although she tried very hard not to laugh.

"Ciara! Ciara!" she said, with no response.

"Ciara!" she shouted as she shook her shoulder. "Are you all right?"

"Yes! I am more than all right! I have never seen… I cannot believe… This is amazing! How did you? Where? I do not understand. How could this be?" she mumbled.

"Mother, perhaps we should have explained all of this to Ciara before we brought her here. She is a bit beside herself. I think she is in shock," Kayla insisted.

"She will be fine. Just show her around and explain things to her. Once she gets used to everything, she will love it here."

"I am going to wander about the house for a bit," Nadia replied.

Nadia's expressions and the tone of her voice made it quite clear how many things had changed over the twenty years she had been away.

Kayla spent a few hours showing Ciara the house and the farm. Ciara's excitement brought Kayla much pleasure and a deeper understanding of just how simple a life she had lived. Her reaction to the simplest things was fascinating to Kayla. Things that Kayla had always taken for granted were an amazing adventure for Ciara.

Ciara flipped the light switches on and off for at least five minutes.

When Kayla turned on the water faucet at the kitchen sink to get a drink, Ciara quickly jumped back in surprise at the water flowing from the steel stick that was coming out of the wall. Trying to understand where it was flowing from, she stepped outside the back door to look at the wall below the window.

She could not understand why there was no barrel or pump anywhere outside the house, close to the wall below the sink.

Having grown up in Eureka Springs with all the modern advantages, Kayla could not begin to imagine how amazing these simple pleasures of her life must be to Ciara.

"You must really love it here," Ciara said.

"How could you ever give this all up to live in our land? Our life is very simple."

"The things you have here and the ways of your world are more amazing than I had imagined."

Watching her as she wandered about the house, Kayla realized Ciara was like a little kid in a toy store for the first time.

"I cannot wait to go there," Koda whispered.

I paused for a second, wondering if we had been unfair to him before I continued.

"I love it! I love it!" Ciara yelled. "Nadia, can we stay?" she laughed. "This is too good to be real!"

"Ciara, over here," Nadia said as she explained the cooking range and refrigerator to her.

"I am cooking breakfast," Ciara demanded.

"How long can we stay, ma'am?" she asked once again.

"Only as long as it takes for Litora Falls to be safe for us once again," Nadia answered.

"I know… I know," Ciara whispered with a deep sigh. "I can dream for a time. I love your world," she said, giving Kayla a big hug.

"I am going to rest now until morning. I am most tired from the trip. This is much to take in all at once."

"When the sun rises, ma'am," she said as she started up the stairs.

Kayla and Nadia stayed up most of the night, catching up on the twenty years they had lost. Nadia explained many things about Litora Falls and their very different way of life to Kayla.

"Kayla, be very sure you want to do this before we leave. You will be giving up everything you know at this time for a very simple way of life. We have no conveniences of this world in Litora Falls."

"Even the simple advantage of running hot water does not exist."

"During that time, we could pump our water to the castle, but hot water came only from a large pot heated over the wood stove. Much of the bathing outside the castle continues to be done in the ponds and waterfalls to the east of the castle grounds."

"I know, Mother. I'm sure I will miss all of this. Your world has something my world can never give me."

"Litora Falls has my mother and my father. You're more important than anyone or anything I will be leaving behind here in this world. Besides, if I get homesick, we can always come back for a visit, right?"

"My mother did a good job raising you, my beautiful blue eyes," Nadia cried.

"We must get some rest now," she said as they both headed off to their rooms for the night.

"Mother, before we go, I… I just wanted to say… I am so happy you are alive and here with me in my home. I feel so lucky to have this chance to spend the rest of my life with you and Father. I met you for the first time today, yet I feel as though I have always known you in some way. I have never felt the kind of love I have at this moment in my heart for you and Father."

"Kayla, I cannot tell you how your words fill my heart with joy and peace. I have always wondered if you would forgive us for leaving you behind."

"I wouldn't take anything for the life I had with Grandmother. I've had a good life, Mother. Now… now I get to experience a new way of life… with you and Father."

Hugging her tightly, Kayla whispered, "I love you so much, Mother."

"Geeeze, I have a family!" she shouted.

"I love you, my beautiful blue eyes. I have always loved you," Nadia said, tears of happiness pouring down her cheeks.

"We must get some rest now. Tomorrow, I want to show Ciara more of my world," Kayla said as she rushed up the stairs.

Ciara was up at the crack of dawn. She could not wait to try out the modern stove. She had only cooked on open campfires and a wood-burning stove. This was going to be a new experience for her.

"Good morning, ma'am; breakfast is almost ready," she said as Nadia entered the room.

"It smells wonderful," she replied as she made a pot of coffee in the coffee maker.

"Most amazing!" Ciara said, paying close attention to Nadia's every move.

"Good morning, Mother — Ciara," Kayla whispered, only a few steps behind, half asleep.

"I thought I heard someone talking down here. It's soooooo early. Um, it smells so good. I'm starving."

"Let us eat," Nadia said as she pulled out a chair for Ciara. "Things are much different here, my friend. This is the modern world. There are no servants here."

"You will eat with us, and we will all share the cooking and cleaning. Consider me your friend and family, not your queen."

"Are you sure we cannot stay?" she giggled. "I could get most comfortable here in this world."

They all laughed as they enjoyed their wonderful breakfast.

"Mother, I have a great idea!" Kayla said. "Let's go into the city and do some serious shopping. The two of you could use some... modern outfits."

"Sounds like fun!" she cried. "My first shopping trip with my daughter… ever. I cannot believe you are twenty years old, and I have never taken you shopping."

"Oh, Mother," Kayla said, hugging her tightly. "We're going to have a lot of firsts while we are here. Let's enjoy the time we have together. We can't change the past, but we can enjoy the future that lies before us."

"How do you think Ciara will react to the car ride?" Kayla asked.

Ciara continued to be amazed by the light switches, running water, cooking stove, and the big refrigerator that keeps things so very cold.

"What is a car?" Ciara asked.

"You'll see," Kayla said.

"She will be fine. It is all just new to her. She is actually having the time of her life. This is one journey she will never forget," Nadia insisted.

As they drove down the highway leading into the city, Kayla caught a glimpse of Ciara in the rearview mirror.

"Mom, she looks a little pale. Is she okay?" she asked.

"She is probably a little carsick," Nadia laughed.

"You forget, Kayla. We ride horses or travel on foot everywhere we go in our land. I am sure she is a little frightened and nervous, as well as overwhelmed by the sights of the city."

"This is unbelievable," Ciara interrupted with her soft voice. "Unbelievable!" She was very overwhelmed and a little afraid of all the traffic on the highway. She was fascinated with the trolley.

It was early enough that the stores were not too busy. Kayla had a blast explaining modern underwear and other clothes to Ciara while Nadia looked around the clothes racks on her own.

They all tried on many outfits, having a great time laughing and clowning around as the time passed quickly.

Heading to the register with their arms full of lovely outfits, they continued to laugh and talk.

"I can't remember the last time I had this much fun," Kayla said.

"Thank you, Mother! I am so glad you are here. I want to enjoy every second of this."

"Kayla, I am so glad I ran into you," Sarah interrupted.

"Sarah, aren't you supposed to be at work?"

"I'm taking a quick break. Did I hear you say, Mother?" she asked, looking at Nadia with a little confusion.

"Sarah, this is my mother and her best friend, Ciara," Kayla quickly interjected. "Sarah is my best friend."

"It is so nice to meet you, Sarah," Nadia said. "Why don't you join us for dinner this evening at Kayla's house?"

"I'd love to," she answered.

"I have a surprise for you, Kayla. I'll save it for then. See you about six," she said as she rushed back to the office.

"Mother, what are you thinking?" Kayla asked.

"Kayla, I may be here for a while. I want to meet your friends."

"Alright, but we must be very careful around her. We can't let her know about anything… You do understand, don't you?"

"Of course I do. Do not worry, Kayla; everything will be fine. Have a little faith in me. You will see."

"I know," Kayla said with a reluctant smile. "I'm sorry, Mother. You're right. I'd love for you to meet my friends. In fact, I will give Sarah a call and have her bring Kaci, Dana, and Jim if they don't have plans. We hang out as a group a lot. You may as well meet them all at once."

"They will really love you, Mother."

The drive home was quiet. Nadia was dozing off from the excitement and very little sleep she had gotten. Ciara quietly sat in the back seat, taking in everything around her and wanting to enjoy every second of her adventure.

Kayla was very nervous and concerned about dinner with her friends. She spent most of the trip home trying to decide the best way to explain to her best friend about her mother suddenly being alive after all these years.

As quickly as Kayla could unlock the door, Nadia and Ciara headed for the stairs to put away their new clothes. Kayla had never seen anyone more excited about the city and new clothes than Ciara. She went into the kitchen to plan the dinner she had no way of canceling.

As she opened the refrigerator, she heard a strange noise coming from the patio just outside the back door. Seeing him as she looked out the window, she opened the door swiftly.

"Ikan, what are you doing here?"

"What has happened?" she asked quietly, not wanting to alarm her mother. She did not want him to know how thrilled she was to see him. She had not been able to get him off her mind since she had come home. She spent most of the night dreaming about how it would be to get to know him better. She did not understand her feelings; she only knew she could not get him out of her thoughts.

"Sir Neree sent me. It is very important I speak with the Queen," he answered in a very official manner.

"I'm so glad to see you are safe, Ikan," she said. "I'll get Mother for you."

"Kayla!"

"Yes?"

"Ikan."

"When this is all over…" he paused for a moment. "When this is all over, I would really like to start over. If it is good with you, ma'am, I would like to get to know you!" he said, looking down shyly.

"I'd love that, Ikan!" she smiled. "Um, you have to stop calling me ma'am!"

"Yes, ma'am," he replied. "Oh, sorry! It is out of respect, ma'am. This will take some work!"

Kayla laughed, taking his hand. "Come inside; I'll call Mother for you."

"Very nice place, Kayla," he said, looking around the house.

"My Queen," he said as Nadia entered the room, "I have news from Sir Neree." He told her the news of all that had happened and of Aaron's death.

"I should be with Talisha," she cried. "She has been my best friend for years. I should be there for her."

"It is not yet safe, ma'am. You cannot go home until Sir Neree comes for you personally."

"I know," she said. "I just know I should be there to help her through this sad time, and my poor husband, Aaron, is his brother. I hate this," she said, sobbing.

Suddenly, I appeared before her.

"Sir, has something happened?" Ikan asked. Nadia ran to my arms.

"Oh, Neree, I am so sorry about Aaron!"

Giving Nadia a loving hug, I sat her back down and turned to Ikan. "We must return with haste!" I demanded. "Someone has set the Draconians free! We do not know how this could have happened! All we know for sure is they have vanished, and they must have taken Talisha and Yara captive because they are nowhere to be found."

Ciara interrupted, walking up to me with the black pad.

"Here, sir, read this," she said as she placed it in my hand. "I overheard Talisha talking with a shadow of a strange man about secret things just before she left for the trip to the caves of Ka'ron with my Queen. I took it from her things only moments before we left for here."

"I know it was wrong, my King. I had to know. I have suspected something strange about her from the beginning."

"I knew she pretended to be a friend to my Queen only to harm her and Kayla, but I had no proof. I just knew!"

"She was jealous, sir, because she wanted Yara to be the next Queen."

"This pad proves she is an informant, sir. I just finished reading it. I did not know for sure until a few moments ago, myself. It must have been Trillian in the shadows, sir."

"To save you time, it reads that after Kayla is to be slain, Yara will receive her strength and powers. Trillian's son, Ciar, is to marry Yara. With Kayla's pure blood and powers mixed with his evil and Yara's few powers, they will produce the most powerfully evil world above all others."

"All that exists in our lands now will be tortured, killed, or kept as slaves! All that is good will be destroyed if this all comes to be."

"I am so sorry, sir, but it also reads that Aaron will be killed and that Talisha will go to live with Trillian. It goes on to read that from her, they will learn of all our secrets and powers."

"I am sorry, ma'am, but this is what is written on her pad. It is signed, 'Talisha' and 'Trillian!'"

"I cannot believe this! Talisha!"

"How could she have been a part of any of this?"

"I thought she was my friend! I told her everything for many years. She knows all of my secrets and all our powers. She knows of the Tunnel of Litora Falls and the fairies that protect our secret."

"I trusted her. I thought she was my friend."

"No, ma'am!" Ciara replied. "She is your worst enemy, I am afraid!"

With the black pad in hand, I gave both of my girls a big hug. I thanked Ciara and assured her she would be rewarded for her great work.

"The good news is that only a few of us have the power to appear at any place or time. Talisha and Yara have very few powers. As for the Tunnel of Litora Falls and our most trusted fairies, they only appear to the eyes of the most special Litorans. Trillian has no power over them. Nalana will keep the tunnel and her people safe. Do not worry about these things. Enjoy your stay here."

"We must leave at once with this news!" I demanded.

"Please, be safe!" Nadia said.

"I am going to send Sly and Silas back immediately to protect you, just in case."

"Kayla, please prepare a room for them," I insisted.

"Please, be careful, Ikan!" Kayla said as she gave him a very loving hug and kiss. She stepped back, surprised by her action, with a big smile.

"Thank you, Kayla, I will!" he said with a smile as his big eyes sparkled like the stars. They stared into each other's eyes, realizing how much they cared for each other, as he vanished.

"Thank you, Ciara," Nadia said. "What you have done today will make a big difference in the way this all turns out. The information you have given Neree means everything to our world. We owe you greatly."

"I would have told you much sooner, ma'am, but I wanted to be sure of all the facts. I wanted to read Talisha's pad before I accused her."

"It is O.K., Ciara. I understand. You did the right thing. I am very proud of you."

"Know this, as Neree said: you will be greatly rewarded when we return to our kingdom."

"Thank you, ma'am," she answered as she started to make plans for dinner.

"Mom, we forgot about dinner. What are we going to do?"

"It is getting late. We need to get started quickly."

"Will you be O.K.?" Kayla asked. "I can call and tell them something unexpected came up."

"No," Nadia replied. "As your father said, we must put this aside for now. It is out of our hands. He and Ikan will know what to do."

"Kayla, after everyone leaves tonight, remind me to tell you about Ikan."

"I'm sorry, Mom!" Kayla cried. "I don't know what came over me!"

"It is not a bad thing, although I was surprised!" Nadia replied. "I am sure your father was quite pleased!"

"Let us prepare dinner, and I will explain everything later," she smiled.

Before Nadia could turn around, Sly and Silas appeared with a large box full of all the clippings and memories of Kayla. They had stopped at her secret cave in the hills of Ka'ron to gather them for her.

"My Queen, I took it upon myself to assume you would rather have these here with you. There is word the evil ones know of the caves. It is said that they vowed to travel there and gather the memories of the princess. I know not when. I only knew they were no longer safe as they were. I removed them without permission, ma'am. I wanted no chance for them to get in the hands of the evil ones," Sly said, sitting the box on the floor in front of her.

"Sly, I cannot thank you enough," Nadia said.

"It appears we will be your guests for your protection, ma'am. What are your orders for us?"

"Oh my!" cried Kayla, rudely butting in. "This is never going to work. How are we going to explain them to my friends in one hour? We will never be able to explain these two! There is not enough time to even begin to prepare them!"

"Kayla, go into the kitchen and help Ciara finish up!" Nadia said sternly. "Leave everything to me. Everything will be fine, do not worry."

"Wait, do you have anything that would pass for men's clothing?" she asked.

Kayla ran to the laundry room and quickly came out with two pairs of her large overalls and shirts she used for helpers when she worked about the farm. She liked them big and baggy so that even she could wear them over warm clothing.

"Hmm, perhaps you can turn them into farmers in forty-five minutes," she said, shaking her head with a giggle as she flipped the clothes to Sly. "I am so glad you at least look like human beings."

"We are in so much trouble," Kayla worried as she walked away to help Ciara.

"This has to work," Nadia whispered as she picked up her box of clippings and hurried her guest off to her room in hopes that she could quickly get them suitable for dinner.

"You are very intelligent men," she said with hope. "Listen very carefully to every word I say, and just go along with everything. This is very important to Kayla, and I would not want to be in your shoes if you mess this up for her," she said as she quickly filled them in.

Chapter Eighteen — Dinner For Friends

"They are here!" Kayla shouted, opening the front door.

Seeing her friends outside with their wonderful smiles made Kayla relax and calm down about the situation.

"They are my friends," she thought. "They will totally understand whatever happens here tonight," she assured herself.

"Come in!" she smiled with excitement. "We have been looking forward to you coming all afternoon!"

"Mother will be right out. She is just finishing up a few things. Come into the kitchen. I will introduce you to her best friend. She is going to visit for a short time."

"Ciara, these are my friends: Jim, Kaci, Dana, and Sarah, whom you met at the mall today."

"Everyone, this is Ciara, my mother's best friend."

"It is so good to meet you," Ciara said as she shook everyone's hand.

"Welcome," Nadia said as she entered the room. "I am Kayla's mother, and these are my friends, Sly and Silas. They volunteered to come with me on my visit and help Kayla with a few things around the farm before summer ends."

After all the introductions were made, Kayla thought there might be hope after all. Things seemed to be going very well.

"Let's all go into the den for a drink before dinner," Sarah insisted, pulling out the bottles of wine they had brought for this very special occasion.

While Jim poured everyone a glass of wine, Sarah banged on her empty glass with a spoon as she made her announcement. "Here's to Kayla, the new Junior Partner of 'Perfection Advertising and Design' of downtown Eureka Springs, Arkansas!"

"Congratulations, Kayla, from all of us!" she cheered.

"It will officially be announced on Monday, but we couldn't wait," Jim added. "You will just have to act surprised!"

Kayla was speechless. So many things had changed in her life in the past few days. She had no idea where her life was headed.

A week ago, this was all she wanted. Now... everything about her life had completely changed. She was different. Her thoughts and dreams were different in a way that her friends would never be able to understand.

"Kayla, are you O.K.?" Kaci asked.

"Yeah, I just didn't expect this!" she said.

"What is a Junior Partner?" Sly asked.

"Thanks, you guys! This is a great surprise. I promise I won't know a thing on Monday. Let's eat before Ciara's wonderful meal gets cold."

Kayla was very nervous as they all sat down together for dinner. It was good that Ciara had prepared the meal. Sly and Silas were starving and keeping quiet, stuffing themselves.

Jim and Sarah did most of the talking, telling Nadia story after story about Kayla's many accomplishments.

Everyone seemed to have a great time talking, laughing, and getting to know each other. Kayla was so pleased with how smoothly everything was going.

She noticed Jim and Dana's curious expressions at times during the meal but was pleased overall with the dinner Ciara had prepared.

"She wasn't sure what everything was called that she had cooked, but it all tasted delicious," she thought as everyone finished and headed back to the den for another glass of wine.

She noticed Sarah and Silas had quickly snuck out of the kitchen door into the backyard.

Hoping there was nothing to be alarmed about, she tried to act as though she did not notice.

"It has been so nice to get to know all of you," Nadia said as she filled their glasses.

"None for me," Jim said. "I'm the designated driver."

"Kayla, would you like to show me around your property?" he asked in his next breath.

"Sure, I'd love to," she answered, seriously wanting to check up on Sarah and Silas.

Before they reached the steps of the front porch, he stopped, looked her in the eye, and took a deep breath.

"Are you O.K.?" she asked.

"I'm fine. Would you go out with me sometime?" he asked. "I have wanted to ask you for a while now, but I wasn't sure how you would feel about it."

"Like on a date?" she asked.

"If you don't want to, I understand," he quickly answered.

"I do. I would love to. I'm just surprised you asked me. I thought you did not do dates."

"I think it would be nice, as friends. Yes, as friends, I could."

He could not move or speak. He was so happy. They both were such dedicated workers. Neither of them had allowed themselves to have a social life for a long time. Friends wasn't exactly what he had in mind, but it would be a good place to start, he thought.

"Aren't you going to say anything?" she asked.

"I am speechless," he answered. "I am so thrilled you said yes. I could… kiss you."

"What...?" Before she could finish her words, Jim took her in his arms and kissed her.

"Wow, I am very impressed," she thought as they walked quietly. After a few steps, she finally spoke. "I thought you understood I said as friends, Jim," she said.

Jim didn't comment. He wasn't sure how to react.

As they reached the side of the house toward the backyard, they saw Silas pushing Sarah in the tire swing.

"There you guys are," Kayla said.

"This is great," Sarah replied.

"You are really going to miss this place," Silas announced before Kayla could stop him. "I mean, I am going to miss this place," he corrected himself, realizing what he had said.

"Jim, it is getting late. We have to work tomorrow," Sarah said.

"I guess we should get going," he answered.

"Kayla, thank you so much for having us for dinner. I had a wonderful time."

"I'm so glad you came. We'll talk later," she smiled as she opened the back door, heading inside to tell Kaci and Dani they were leaving.

Silas and Sarah walked around the front, meeting the others in the car.

"I hope I get to see you again before I leave. I have enjoyed this evening so much, Sarah," he said with a hug.

"I will make it a point to see you again," she replied, with a sweet kiss on the cheek followed by her beautiful smile.

"We need to talk, girl," she said, giving Kayla a hug goodbye.

"Thank you all so much for coming," Nadia said.

"Kayla, you have great friends," she said as they drove away.

"I do not believe that guy kissed my mom," Koda blurted out. "Why did she let him do that? Did my dad know?"

"You must remember, Koda, your mom and dad were not yet together. Besides, he surprised Kayla. She had no idea he was going to do that," I explained.

Chapter Nineteen — Trillian's Fate

At The Caves of Ka'ron...

"Sorry about the kiss, sir," Ikan said on the way into the council room.

"It was totally unexpected, my king!" he insisted.

"Ikan, it appears my daughter cares more for you than you know. This is a… good thing! She knows nothing of my plans, my dreams for her life with you. She has taken notice of you from her own heart. It is good."

"I could not be more pleased!" I replied.

"I must admit, I was quite pleased myself, sir."

When they entered the council room, all the warriors and guards were patiently waiting for the messengers to return from their search of the Draconians.

"Sir Meinkard, Sir Eckhard, and all our faithful warriors and guards, I have news of great distress," I said as we interrupted the meeting already in progress.

"It is true. We have an informant in our midst. One of my own, I must sadly share with you. I received word of this only moments before my return."

"In my hands, I hold a black pad taken from the room of Talisha… very disturbing words indeed."

"Forgive me, Ren, for not discussing this matter with you privately, as it concerns your family, but I must make this known to all."

A loud mumbling swept across the room at the mention of Talisha's name in connection with this evil.

"Quiet, please," I sadly insisted.

"In summary, the words from this pad prove Talisha has been planning for years to give her daughter, Yara, unto Ciar, following the sacrifice he has planned for my daughter. Through these evil doings, they had hoped Ciar and Yara together would produce the strongest of evil children. If that were not enough, these writings prove Talisha has been helping Trillian and Ciar for a time now, planning the destruction of our lands."

"This must be how they knew when to plan the invasion and capture of our women and children and the Ceairan Queen. She also writes of her promise to inform Trillian of all secrets and powers of our lands. Written on the final page, she offers him and his followers the use of what few powers she and Yara have within them to help in the destruction of our world as we know it."

"We know not how much she has learned of us over these years. She has been Nadia's best friend since she arrived here, in our home, as a stranger from a faraway land. I am certain she has much information to share with these evil ones. Not only did they plan for Ciar to receive Kayla's great powers, knowledge, and abilities through her sacrifice unto him, but it is possible Yara could have gained powers from her birth father, unlike anything we have known. Talisha could have kept these powers hidden from us over the years for this evil plan."

"We must remember Yara is not of our blood. Aaron was not her father. Talisha is also not of our lands. Aaron brought her to us from an adventure to lands beyond our world. We truly know nothing of her before that time."

"We must find Trillian and the Draconians for our future and the future of all that is good in our lands. We must annihilate them once and for all!"

"I know this is against all we stand for, but the future of each and every one of us depends on this. We must not allow these things he has planned to take place. If you do not agree, I must know now, and I will face them alone."

"For me and my men, all Draconians must be destroyed!" Eckhard shouted. "We must rid our land of this evil. We must protect our families and our homes."

"If we must destroy them to keep the good in our lands, then we must."

"We are all in!" Meinkard shouted in return.

"Trillian's evil must be stopped once and for all!"

"Peace in our land must be returned!"

"We are one!" he yelled.

"I will be forever grateful to you, one and all, my dear friends," Neree cried.

Malachi barged through the doors in the midst of the shouting, very pleased to hear the last words.

"Attention, my friends, I must interrupt!" he said loudly.

"The Draconians are deep in the caves of Ka'ron. Talisha, sir… She led the way for the evil ones. She is one of them, my king. She planned to reveal unto him the shrine of Kayla, sir."

"Shrine…? What shrine?" I demanded.

"It matters no more, sir! By luck, Sly and Silas knew of this. They gathered all that was of her… took all things with them on their journey to the Small's farm… to leave with Nadia in Kayla's world, for safety, away from the hands of Trillian, sir."

"The cave was empty when the Draconians arrived."

"The sight of Trillian's face… it was most frightening, sir."

"He instantly spun into a rage, most angry with Talisha, when his eyes glared inside the empty cave. He, giving her no chance to explain, tore into her like a beast ripping apart its prey, sir. He was certain she had lied… to trick him. He killed her, sir, giving her no chance for words."

"My eyes saw the most frightening evil man, sir. He killed her like an animal. He walked away… a grin stretched across his face… it was a pleasure to him. He is truly an evil, cold-blooded man, sir… the worst known to any lands."

"He must be stopped."

"What of Yara?" Ren sadly asked.

"I overheard her cries to her mother. Much fear in her shallow voice, as her tiny body trembled with fear, sir. The screams… over and over, pouring from her lips. 'Why had she done this to her… How could she?' Over and over, she cried the words."

"I am certain that she knew nothing of this. It was Talisha, my friend. It was all Talisha. Yara is safe for the moment."

"Ren, I had words with Yara before this tragedy took place. She loves you, my friend. From all I saw and heard, she knew nothing of this. She is most sad and fearful among these evil beings. She fears they plan to harm her, sir… as do I."

"She asked that I tell you, one and all, she only wants to come home to her husband. She wants to be near her family and friends."

"Ren, she is with child, sir. She had planned to speak of it with you after the war."

"We must save her before they find out, sir."

"They will surely kill her and your unborn child. We must return quickly. We must save her and your new life inside her."

"Two of our best stayed behind to watch out for her in hopes of a chance to sneak her out of the caves, sir."

"There are eleven warriors, large creatures of Jadar's kind, Trillian, Ciar, and Yara."

"We must go in haste, my friends! The fate of Yara and Ren's unborn child depends on our actions!"

All the warriors gathered together with much determination to make their way to the caves of Ka'ron and end this senseless battle at once. They numbered in hundreds to conquer only twelve evil Draconian warriors and their leader, Trillian.

"La-too, gather two hundred Ceairans, Komodo, and Litoran men to stay behind in each of their own lands. We must have this extra protection for all the women and children during our absence. We must leave them well guarded in case of another plan of invasion. I do not want to take any more chances with the lives of our families," I ordered.

"Eckhard, Ikan, and I, along with a hundred men, will travel ahead to the hills of Ka'ron to get a closer look and form a plan of attack. Meinkard and the rest of the warriors will travel on horseback to keep an eye out along the way in case of a trap or escape of the evil beings. We must be sure the Draconians do not get away from us again and cause more destruction."

"Everything is much too calm and quiet," I whispered as Malachi quickly appeared as a small frog and entered the cave to learn the exact location of the Draconians, Talisha's body, and the location of Yara.

"A rider ahead… moving at a very fast pace!" sir Meinkard yelled.

"There, sir, the direction of the caves. It appears a man — with a woman, sir!" Miki yelled, rushing quickly from his lookout point at the top of a tall tree.

"There!" he said, pointing in the direction of the man on horseback. "Just ahead of the others, traveling this way, as fast as his horse can move."

"Warriors, prepare for danger!" Meinkard ordered as the rider approached.

Ren jumped off his horse and ran to the stranger.

"Yara!" he cried.

"Oh Ren, I am so glad to see you," she whispered, much too exhausted to speak.

"I am unharmed, thanks to Ciar," she said faintly, falling off the horse into Ren's arms.

"Ciar!" Meinkard yelled.

"Take her home immediately, Ren. Guard her with your life," Meinkard demanded as several guards secured Ciar, with great confusion about what had just taken place before their eyes.

Ciar, the son of Trillian, one of the most evil creatures known in these lands, doing something good for Yara, a Litoran, in defiance of his own father?

"If you are indeed the son of Trillian, why have you done this good deed for one of our kind?"

"This makes no sense to me."

"What of your father?" Meinkard demanded.

"I am certain when Trillian hears of Yara's disappearance and that I have assisted her, I will no longer be called his son."

"Do not expect me to believe you have done this for good for Yara! I am not an idiot!"

"What kind of trickery is this?"

"Sir," Ciar spoke, "I know all that you have known of me. My father is a most evil man."

"Yes, as his son, everyone assumes I am evil. He would hope it to be that way. I have only known of evil doings my entire life. In the midst of all the confusion, just before Talisha freed us, I overheard several of the Draconians discussing the day they stole me from a ship far away from these lands and gave me to my father."

"I am not his flesh and blood… I do not have to be of evil ways. If the good is Talisha and Yara, then it is what should be of this world — not Trillian's ruthless, cold-blooded evil."

"Talisha was forced by my father to do the things she has done. It was of an evil spirit inside her… all of his doing. She had no control over his wishes."

"I fear him with all that is in me!"

"When I saw him kill Talisha, so cold and thoughtless, I knew I had to save Yara and her unborn child from his evil plan. He needed Talisha for the destiny he had planned for my future. She obtained a secret power unknown to all that knew her, sir. This power was Trillian's chance to have his way with these lands and with the Litoran Princess."

"After he killed Talisha, he became enraged, realizing what he had cost himself with his selfish actions. He told me to remove myself from his sight and that I was no longer of use to him. He vowed to kill Yara for pleasure at the next sign of light, simply because he could. He thinks only of himself and the evil he can cause to others."

"I snuck her out in the midst of the planning, sir. I do not know what will take place when he sees she is gone."

"What is to become of me matters not. The importance here is that good is not destroyed in these lands. I am relieved Trillian is not my father. I realize no one should trust my word, but know this: Yara and her baby are safe because of what I have done for her."

"You will never hear from me again if you choose to spare my life. My plan for myself is to disappear as far away from Trillian as possible.

I want to make a life of only good doings with my own family — in another land — as far away as I can take myself from this evil man that I have always known as my father."

"If it be your choice to destroy me, then it shall be. It matters not to me. Anything you do with me is better than the life he has planned. This I have done for Yara. This matters most."

"Know this! I will never be the evil Trillian's son or a Draconian again. I would rather be destroyed, sir. The choice is yours."

"Take him to the dungeon of the Litoran Castle and chain him to the walls!" Meinkard demanded of three of his most trusted guards. "Guard him with your lives!" he screamed sternly. "He must not escape!"

"We will deal with you after this has ended, Ciar," he added. "You must know I cannot release you on your word alone. All I have known of you has been of your evil doings. I cannot trust your word. You must know that only a fool would believe these words you speak."

"I cannot bear to look into his face. Leave with him at once!" he demanded.

As they gathered outside the hills of Ka'ron, Neree listened to the words of Eckhard as he spoke for all the warriors.

"We have the powers and abilities to end this in an instant, sir. I am certain everyone here would agree that this is the way it should be. Enough sadness has disrupted our lives these past few days! Enough lives have been lost. This needs to end right here! Right now!"

"With your order, sir… you must know… our plan will work quickly, with harm only to the Draconians," Eckhard insisted. "May I speak of it?"

"Let us hear," I replied.

"In our natural form, as you well know, all Komodo dragons have the power to shoot a deadly poison from our mouths. This poison is so powerful that it can paralyze or kill our prey on contact, sir. The powerful quantities we could produce inside this cave, with this multitude of warriors among us, would leave no one safe from our attack, sir. The Draconians have never seen our true form. They would think of us as harmless creatures of the land. They would know not what hit them, sir."

"It sounds like the perfect plan, but what of Talisha and Yara? They are of us. I need to understand how they became part of all of this. I cannot believe Talisha could have done these things. Nor can I believe that Yara knew of her mother's plan. Then again, I forget that she is not of our blood."

"We must not take a chance of anyone else being harmed. We need to be sure of all things before we can take a chance like this with their lives."

"Riders are coming!" Ikan interrupted. "Meinkard and our warriors, sir."

Meinkard rushed ahead of the others to give Eckhard and me the news of Yara, Talisha, and Ciar.

"Enough!" I interrupted. The instant I was informed that Talisha had been killed and Yara was safe with Ren, I turned to Eckhard.

"All is clear for your plan," I assured him, giving his shoulder a hard squeeze. "Proceed at once," I insisted.

"Be safe, my friend," I whispered. "I will never forgive myself if something happens to you."

Only seconds passed as Eckhard prepared his warriors for their attack. He demanded that all Ceairans and Litorans move as far back into the brush of the land as possible and remain a safe distance clear of the powerful poisonous fumes.

As they disappeared into the caves, a strong film of cloudiness and a breathtaking odor covered the entranceway. It settled like a thick fog for more than two hours.

"Something must have gone wrong," Ikan demanded. "It should not be taking this long, sir."

"Eckhard knows what he is doing, Ikan," I assured him. "Be patient, my son. We must wait, as he has commanded."

"Son," Ikan thought as he joined the others to wait as I asked.

Eckhard and his men scattered from the caves, weak from the film of poison of their own breath.

"The film is too thick, sir," he said. "We could not find our way to the passage. We must wait for a time. The air must clear. It could take hours. We must not leave before we find all their bodies, sir," Eckhard insisted.

"To the west!" Meinkard shouted. He pointed in the direction of the river. A large whirl of twisting waters rose like a mountain in the center of the river, bursting into splashes of huge blue creatures. The strange water creatures appeared to be heading in the direction of the caves.

Loud sounds of splashing rose with every step as they grew closer. The air felt cool and damp as they passed. The warriors stood in amazement, stunned by the appearance of creatures of water. They had not seen this before in their land. They were unsure of how this could be.

"I call them Splash Dragons," Meinkard said.

"I made up the name myself, long ago, when they appeared to me in the darkness. They saved my life, sir, and the life of my horse. Loud streaks of fire from above struck a tree as we passed the trail in the darkness. It fell on my horse. My body was trapped as the tree burst into flames. I saw death before my eyes. The creatures of water appeared from the river, as they do now, and saved us both, sir. They are of good."

"I told no one of what had taken place. I felt they had always been protecting our lands from these strikes of fire. I thought they should be left at peace, sir."

The Splash Dragons covered the caves inside and out, weakening the power of the poison.

In seconds, Eckhard's men entered the caves and removed the Draconians.

"All accounted for, sir!" he shouted as he stepped from the opening of the caves.

Shouts of cheer roared with the sounds of rolling thunder as they rushed from the entrance, thirteen Draconians in hand. Proudly placing them at the feet of Neree and Meinkard, they yelled, "Trillian and his evil Draconians — defeated at last, sir!"

Loud sloshing steps of blue water slapped the ground in unison as the Splash Dragons headed in the direction of the river.

"We owe you much thanks for your help!" Eckhard yelled as they passed.

Meinkard showed his appreciation once again with a nod of his head. "They are good creatures of the water," he said.

As the Splash Dragons poured into the river, they formed together, rising high into a huge mountain of blue.

"Go in peace, my friends. We will watch over the good in these lands for all time to come!" roared the mountain as they disappeared into the river below.

I found comfort in learning about these water creatures from the rivers.

"We have so much good among us!" I shouted as I turned to my great followers and friends.

"Sir Eckhard, I speak for us all. We owe you a debt impossible to repay. I cannot imagine how to reward you for all you and your warriors have done here today," I praised.

"Listen, all," Eckhard interrupted. "The only reward needed is for our lands to remain peaceful and safe from this day on. Amity, I demand of all that are here. We must agree to always come together and protect each other and our lands from danger of any kind, as we have in this dark time."

"We are three families as one, tied together by a great bond. Today, tomorrow, and for all times to come!" he said as shouts of cheer filled the air for many miles beyond.

Suddenly, a loud splash of the waters rolled across the rivers.

"Our newly found friends agree!" I laughed, waving to the waters in the distance.

Relief and calmness filled all our hearts as we headed for home. I felt a calmness like I had never known.

"I realize we are all exhausted and anxious to return to our families, but we have one more important task at hand before we are finished," Malachi said as he turned to us.

"We must hold a council meeting this very evening. The decision of Ciar's fate cannot wait another moment."

"Agreed," I replied.

"Agreed, then," Meinkard answered with a nod of his head, followed by Eckhard.

I immediately summoned all the council members to the council room once again.

Ikan gave orders for the warriors to assist in the decision before returning to their families.

Malachi opened the meeting, repeating all Ciar and Yara had told him of her safe return. Although Yara was grateful for her return and her unborn child was not harmed, it was unanimous that Ciar should not be trusted to remain in their lands. However, we felt his life should be spared as repayment for Yara's life and the life of her unborn child.

He was released with a promise that he would make his home in a faraway land. He was ordered never to return to Amphibia or the Dracara Mountains.

Ciar agreed and left immediately, promising never to return or bring harm upon their lands. He presented his need to get as far away from the memory of his father as possible. He vowed to begin a search for the parents from whom he was stolen as an infant.

Several guards escorted him outside the boundaries of all our lands. They watched closely as he rode far from their sight.

With a strange feeling about our decision, I thanked everyone again for their victory. I made a vow to myself that we would always come together in this way in times of need.

"Ikan, get a good rest," I smiled. "At the first sign of light, we must travel to the Smalls' farm to bring Kayla and Nadia home at last."

"Yes, sir," he answered with a smile of excitement.

"Kayla, yes, the time has finally come for her to return home," he thought as he quickly headed for his room.

Chapter Twenty — The Talk

"Grandfather, what of my mother and father?" Koda asked.

"I am getting to them, Koda," I assured him.

"I had forgotten how beautiful the evenings are here, Kayla. I am so glad you chose to make this your home," Nadia said as she sat in the porch swing just outside the front door.

"Sit with me for a bit. We need to talk over a few things. We have not spent much time alone together since we arrived," Kayla said.

"Sly and Silas, would you please help Ciara in the kitchen while I spend some time with my daughter?"

"Thank you so much for letting us meet your friends, Kayla," Silas said as he opened the front door, obeying his queen.

Kayla sat on the porch swing and snuggled up next to Nadia. As she laid her head gently on her shoulder, she whispered, "Mother, I am so glad you are here. I know it may seem odd, but I feel as though some part of me has always known you."

"I am so sorry about all of this. I know it is hard for you to understand why your father and I kept our existence from you," Nadia cried.

"Mother, I understand much more than you think I do. I am a very intelligent woman. I know you were trying to protect me from Trillian. I will be honest with you; I do wish I had known of you all these years. We are all young. We have the rest of our lives ahead of us. I am about to take an amazing journey to begin a new life in my father's world.

There is nothing in this world I want more than to be with you and Father. I am very happy, Mother."

"I have spent my entire life dedicated to school and work, trying to make something of myself."

"It all seems so senseless when I think of everything that has taken place this week."

"In the past few days, my entire world has changed. Everything I have always imagined for my life seems very unimportant now. It's as though I am looking back at my past through different eyes."

"I have parents I have never known."

"I have seen an unbelievable new world in a different time and place."

"There's a new life waiting for me that is so different from anything I have ever known. I can't wait to see more."

"I'm a princess of a nation with powers I can't wait to explore."

"I have this chance to experience the most amazing things anyone could dream of in their lifetime. It's all within my reach."

"I have to live every aspect of this to the fullest, Mother. I don't want to miss one thing."

"How do I sort all of this out? Is it real?"

"Am I going to wake up from some dream, and it all go away?"

"How did a family of frogs become human with the unexplainable powers my father has? And what of the other creatures in Father's land, Meinkard's kind and Eckhard's?"

"How is this all possible, Mother? Is it witchcraft… sorcery… magic? What?"

"That is a lot of questions," Nadia answered, pausing for a moment to collect her thoughts.

"Kayla, you are not dreaming. This is very real. The life that awaits you in Litora Falls is going to be an amazing change for you. The most important thing to remember about the powers your father has is that they use their powers only for the good of their land and families."

"Your father is a great man with much intelligence. His family and his people are amazing. They have awaited your arrival for twenty years."

"Kayla, when you were going through your grandmother's things, did you find a white scroll tied with a golden ribbon?"

"Yes, I have it. I haven't read it. I left it in her chest with all of her special things, which I couldn't bear to throw away. It's in the closet, in the far bedroom, at the end of the downstairs hall."

"Take it out before you retire this evening and read it carefully. Your father gave it to her when we left for Litora Falls. It will answer all your questions about the great powers and abilities you may possess and how your father's family came to be creature-like human beings."

"All of your answers will fall into place as you spend time in our kingdom. Our life is usually very simple. You will understand everything very quickly. Just be patient and try to enjoy all that is about to take place in your young life."

"There is one thing that really has me confused. How did my father and so many others learn to speak our language so well? They sound like they are from here… perhaps in a somewhat less intelligent way."

"Your father, his father, and grandfathers before him traveled through the Tunnel of Litora Falls to our world. They all graduated from schools in the nearby areas and lived here… on the Small's Farm. His family name is well-known here."

"I am a school teacher in the kingdom. I hold classes at the castle for all the young in our land. I graduated from college and was taking classes for my master's degree when I met your father, dear."

"Many of our people are intelligent beyond their time. I have introduced them to many things from this world. I taught them our way of speaking — in the simplest form — to help them learn to communicate as quickly as possible. It is complicated."

"I am sure this all came about through some type of early witchcraft or magic. I am not completely certain. I have been researching this with your father's help. We have not discovered exactly what to call the powers they obtain, but we have a lot of information. Our problem is that your father obtains some powers from every type of wizardry, sorcery, or magic we study. Trying to narrow it down to one and give these powers a name is impossible."

"I am not sure if you are going to understand what I am about to tell you, Kayla. Let me try to explain."

"We did not leave your world, Kayla. We left the time you live in for a different time. From the travels I have made, I believe Amphibia was pretty much right off the edge of Africa during the time the theory of Pangaea reads, before the lands broke apart and spread out over the world. As the lands floated away, I believe the land called Africa turned one way, as your father's land floated closer to the center of our country, exactly where we are at this moment. I am not sure if I have come close to being correct. I will continue to research any information I can find on this matter."

Kayla sat there for a few moments, unable to speak.

"Are you saying that Amphibia is here but years in the past? How is that possible, Mother?"

Kayla was silent for a moment, trying to understand the words she had just heard spoken, knowing that it would explain the simplicity of the world of Amphibia.

"The supercontinent you are talking about was only a theory. Am I not correct?"

"I am certain all of the continents are together in your father's world, as explained in the theory. We can travel from one end of the land to the other. As I said, it is complicated."

"These are only my findings. I am sure there is more information we need to study. I just need to keep searching!"

"Do not try to figure this all out now, Kayla," she said softly. "It will all fall into place and make sense to you as we go along. I promise."

"Perhaps someday you can do your own research and find your own answers."

"Alright, Mother... I will try."

"It's just so much at once... so strange... it's hard to imagine it all."

"So… tell me about Ikan," she said, changing the subject.

"When you were born, your grandfather promised Sir Harold Rainie that his firstborn granddaughter (which would be you) would marry his first-born grandson (which would be Ikan). Together, as husband and wife, the two of you would become the future of our world and rule our great land."

"What did you say?" Kayla asked with surprise.

"Ikan is destined to take your father's place in our kingdom, with you as his queen."

"Are you serious?"

"No way," she grinned.

"Yes, dear..."

"Your father never wanted either of you to be told of this promise! His only hope is that you would grow up, fall in love, and be married of your own doing. He wants you to have a happy life with a loving husband — a loving man of your own choice."

"You must follow your heart and do what you feel will make you truly happy. Do not think of what anyone else wants. Follow your own heart. He will never hold you to this promise."

"I really like Ikan, Mother. When I kissed him, I felt something special. I don't know if anything will come of it or not, but he is a wonderful man."

"Tonight, when Jim was leaving, he kissed me. I felt something for him — but different — in a good friend sort of way."

"How do you know when it's love, Mother? How do you know when it's real?"

"I've never had a boyfriend. I may need a lot of advice from you in this department. Do you think you are up for it?" she asked.

"My beautiful blue eyes, I have waited twenty years to be your mother. I will be here to talk with you anytime you need me," she answered.

"I love you, Mother," Kayla cried.

"I better get some sleep. I should go to work tomorrow. It just doesn't seem as important as it did before all of this."

Kayla remembered to grab the scroll from the chest in the far bedroom as she announced to everyone that she would be at work for a few hours the next morning.

"Make yourselves at home until I return," she said as she rushed up the stairs to her room, anxious to read the scroll.

As she untied the ribbon, there was a knock at her bedroom door.

"Come in," she said, assuming it was her mother.

"Sorry to interrupt you, ma'am, but could I have a word with you? I promise not to be long," Silas said.

"Stop calling me ma'am," she insisted.

"Sorry," he answered.

"Is something wrong, Silas?" she asked.

"I… I think I am in love, ma'am. Sorry again."

"I know I am," he said in a very soft, serious voice. "It… it is your friend — Sarah."

"She is the one."

"She makes my heart pound out of my chest."

"She is your best friend, and you know her better than I. Should I make it known to her?"

"Ma'am, if she is in agreement, could we take her home with us? I want her to be my wife! I want a family with her."

"Silas, I know you are serious, but things do not happen this quickly here. There are things to consider!"

"Things! Explain these things to me," he replied.

"There's dating, falling in love, engagement — a wedding. You only met her today. She isn't a pet you can just simply take home with you. You don't even know her," she explained.

"She is everything I want or need. She is the most… I just know. I am sure."

"Then, let me say this, Silas. She has to feel the same. She has to make that decision."

"I will invite her over for dinner again, and I will talk to her. Just… don't get hurt if she doesn't feel the same way."

"Sarah is a very strong and ambitious woman. She hasn't had many relationships. She works very hard, with little time for a social life of any kind, just like me."

"Oh, thank you," he said. "I will leave you now."

"Sarah isn't going to believe all of this," she thought as she picked up the scroll.

Kayla tried to imagine how these events unfolded as she carefully unrolled the scroll, slowly reading every word.

"I feel like I am reading a novel," she thought as she rolled the scroll up tightly and tied the ribbon back in place. She laid it safely in the little drawer of the nightstand beside her bed as she sat in amazement at all she had read.

"For the first time ever, I wish I didn't have to go to work tomorrow," she thought as she fell deep asleep.

Chapter Twenty-One — Sarah Learns Of Litora Falls

The sound of rain outside her slightly opened window woke her hours before her alarm was set to go off.

"Looks like another nice day," she thought as she hopped out of bed and quickly dressed for work. She tried to think of how she should tell Sarah about all of this. It would be great if she could go with us. I would have my best friend to help me understand all of this. We could research my family and figure this all out together.

"Never happen," she thought as she quietly gathered her things before heading for the front door, trying not to disturb the others.

"I'm ready," Silas announced from the porch swing.

"What are you doing out here in the rain?" she asked. "You startled me."

"Where do you think you are going?"

"Where did you get those clothes?"

"In the chest by the bed. Are they not acceptable?" he asked.

"It is amazing how good he makes the old jeans and blue work shirt look," she thought. "Sarah is going to flip."

"You look fine. However, you can't go with me. I have to go to work."

"My King's orders are not to let you out of my sight. If you leave here, ma'am, I must go with you for protection. Those are my orders."

"First, you must stop calling me ma'am."

"I can't possibly take you to work with me. We don't do things that way here, Silas."

"You must think of a way," he said. "If you do not take me with you, I will simply wish myself there. You cannot stop me. I have to follow my orders," he insisted.

"Hop in, then," she said, opening the car door. "Can you change into a frog?" she ordered.

"Kayla, please."

"Just this once, I promise," she smiled. "Think of it this way — you can hear everything Sarah and I discuss without her knowing you are there. My bag is big enough for you to be comfortable. It's the only way. I can't take a strange man to work with me. We just don't do things that way."

The rain stopped just as she pulled into the office parking lot.

"We're here," she said as she turned off the car.

"Where did you go?"

She laughed when she saw his little face peek out of the top of her purse.

"Thank you, Silas. I owe you one."

"Just talk to Sarah for me," he said, ducking his little head deep inside.

"I will do my best, I promise," she answered, amazed by the adorable little frog he had become!

"I wonder if Ikan is as cute," she whispered as she unlocked the office door.

"I would love to see Father as a frog," Elliott laughed.

"We will have to ask them to change for us," Koda joined in.

"Good luck with that," I snickered as I continued.

"You can relax if you would like," she said. "I will probably be the only one here for the next hour. Don't change form, Silas. I don't want anyone to see you. Besides, you are so cute like this," she laughed.

"Thanks, I think," he said, looking about the office. "So… where is Sarah's office?"

"Through that door," she pointed down the hall to the left. "Don't get into anything," she said as he hopped away.

Kayla lost track of time while checking her messages and going over emails from the boss. She didn't notice Sarah arrive.

"Sarah smells good," Silas said as he hopped up on the chair beside Kayla's desk. "So beautiful! Tell her! This waiting is making me ill!"

"Kayla, did you hear…?"

"Silas, I have work to do. Look, I will do this. Let me do it my way."

"Hey," she said, walking into Sarah's office.

"Hey, you," Sarah replied. "Welcome back to work. I really enjoyed dinner. Silas is a very interesting man. Don't tell him, but I really like him. He seems different from anyone I have known before."

"You have no idea," Kayla replied.

"How long is he going to be here? I would love to see him again. I can't believe I just said that."

"How about lunch?" Kayla asked. "Just the two of us."

"That would be great. I would love to," Sarah said with a smile.

"Eleven or so, if that's good for you. I will drive, or we can walk down the street to the café."

"Perfect," Sarah answered just as Kayla was paged to the boss's office.

"Remember, you do not know a thing," she smiled.

"She likes me! I knew it!" Silas said, sitting under the edge of Sarah's desk out of sight.

Mr. Perfection himself, Jerry Lane, CEO of Perfection Advertising and Design, made his official announcement: "Kayla Marie Gordon has been promoted to Junior Partner of the Company."

As everyone gathered around to congratulate her, she didn't know how to react. She had worked seventy hours plus a week for two solid years, all in hopes of this position. Now that it had been given to her, she knew in her heart that she should not accept it.

"How can I explain myself if I turn this down? Everyone knows it means everything to me. No one will understand if I tell him to give it to someone else. I really need to get out of here. I need to sort this all out," she thought.

Almost eleven...

"Sarah, time for lunch!" she shouted as she set her bag down for Silas to hop in.

"I will be just a second! Meet you by the elevator door!" she answered.

"Silas, you have to be silent. You can't say a single word while Sarah is with us. You have to promise me."

"Do not worry; I will be most busy listening to the sound of beautiful Sarah's voice."

"Oh my, you have got it bad. I hope this goes the way you want, Silas. I really do."

"Sarah's my best friend. I am really going to miss her. Taking her with us would mean a lot to me."

"Good, you are on my side, then," he said.

"Sorry," Sarah interrupted. "Are you talking to yourself again, Kayla?"

"Yes, I was… I'm just excited, I guess."

"I do it all the time," Sarah said. "Let's get out of here before Mr. Lane thinks of another project he needs my assistance on."

"Is Jake's O.K.? It's usually slow this time of the morning, and it's close," Sarah said.

"Sounds good," Kayla replied as they stepped into the elevator.

Jake's is a large café across the street from the office. It has the best soup, sandwiches, and salads in town.

The server seated them at a private booth in the back corner, perfect for Kayla's plan.

Sarah ordered a Chicken Caesar Salad and iced tea.

"That sounds so good. I think I will have the same," Kayla said with a smile.

"Sarah, I have something very important to tell you. You have to promise this will stay between us."

"I would never repeat anything you ask me not to, Kayla. You sound so serious. Is something wrong?"

"This is serious, Sarah. I'm just not sure how to begin."

"I brought something for you to read first," she said, handing Sarah the Litoran family scroll.

"O.K.," Sarah said as she began to read.

With a confused look on her face, she looked up at Kayla.

"Is this for real?"

"It seems to be very old, Kayla. Where did you get this, and why are you having me read it?"

"It belonged to my grandmother, Sarah. My father gave it to her when he and my mother left for his world. They didn't die, as I had believed. They left me for my grandmother to raise… to keep me safe."

"My father is Neree... the King of all the lands of Amphibia. He is Litoran. His great-grandfather's ancestor was one of the teen frogs mentioned in the scroll."

"I know it sounds crazy, but I know for sure it is real."

"I have been there, Sarah. I have seen it for myself. It is the most amazing place that I have ever seen."

"My mother, Ciara, Silas, and Sly are all from Amphibia. Ciara is my mother's personal maid. Silas and Sly are her personal guards."

Kayla paused for a moment before continuing.

"You don't believe me."

"No… quite the contrary, I think I do. It explains a lot!" She hesitated. "I mean, it seems impossible, but I knew there was something strange about all of this… all of them!"

"Two Chicken Caesar salads," the waiter said, setting their plates in front of them. "Will there be anything else?"

"I think we are fine," Sarah answered.

"I know you, Kayla. I could feel something was going on last night. I just didn't know what… until now."

"Sarah, there's something else."

"Silas is in love with you. I mean, he is really in love with you. He wants you to go with us."

"With you...? With you where? To Litora Falls? Kayla, are you losing it here or what?"

"Sarah, this is no joke. I am serious. It is a long story. When we have more time, I will explain everything that I know to you. I am a princess there. It is my destiny."

"Destiny!" Sarah yelled.

"Go home with me after work today. We'll have dinner and talk all night."

"That is a good idea. I will be there. I will bring my clothes for work tomorrow. This can't wait. I need to know everything… NOW," she said. "No, this definitely can't wait. It's so amazing."

"About Silas… I felt something for him, too," she added.

"Now… I don't know, Kayla. This is a lot to grasp at once. I am very confused about what I think and how I feel. This is way too fast. I... would... like to see him again. Yes... I think I would. Spending the night at your place tonight? Um, that's a very good idea. This can't wait!"

"Actually, the more I think about it, this is very exciting. I can't wait to hear more. It might be good for us to shake up our lives a bit. All we have ever done is work. But what a ride it could be!"

"Let's see if we can get away from the office early," Kayla said. "It is slow today. I'm sure the boss will not mind."

Suddenly, Sarah's cell phone rang, interrupting the conversation.

"That is great!" she screamed in excitement.

"Perfect timing," she smiled. "We don't have to go back to the office. The main fuse box that feeds the building blew out. It seems we won't have electricity for at least two days."

"That's perfect," Kayla smiled as she looked inside her purse and saw the guilty grin on Silas's face. "We'll finish this conversation at the house."

"This one's on me," Sarah said, picking up the check.

"I will be there as soon as I can. I need to go by my apartment and pick up a few things."

"You certainly were quiet on the way home," Kayla said as they pulled up in the driveway. "By the way, the fuse box — I don't suppose you had anything to do with that?"

"Of course not," Silas said with a guilty smirk. "I will sit in the porch swing for a bit if that is good with you," he grinned as Kayla continued inside, very pleased with his actions.

"Something smells good in here!" Kayla yelled from the front door.

"We are in the kitchen. Come join us," Nadia replied. "Did you have a nice day, dear?"

"Yes, it's official. Your daughter is now a Junior Partner of the firm. Until a few days ago, it was the one thing I wanted most in this world."

"Now? Now it's like nothing to me. All I want is to know everything about you, my dad, and your world, Mom," she said.

"I'm going to take a quick shower. Oh! Sarah is coming for dinner and staying the night. We don't have to go to the office tomorrow — some electrical problem in the building."

"That is wonderful. Dinner will be ready in about an hour," Nadia replied.

"Perfect," Kayla said as she headed to her room.

On the way up the stairs, she thought she heard a car pull up. She looked out her bedroom window just in time to see Sarah give Silas a big hug as she joined him on the porch swing.

"This is going to work out so well. I just know it," she thought.

Kayla couldn't help but notice that all through dinner, Sarah and Silas couldn't take their eyes off each other.

"Let's go for a walk," she said just as they finished their last bit of dessert. "We need to walk off some of this good food we just pigged out on."

"You kids go along," Nadia said. "Ciara and I will clean up."

"Thanks, Mom," Kayla said as they headed out back.

"She called me Mom," Nadia said.

"Is that not a good thing?" Ciara asked.

"It is a very good thing. It means she is getting more comfortable with all of this," she smiled.

"Let's climb up into the tree house," Kayla said. "We can have a nice private talk up there."

Silas and Kayla took turns explaining everything that had taken place in the past week. He explained, as much as he could, about the world and time he lived in and how much he wanted Sarah to go back with them.

Sarah didn't say a word, making Silas very nervous. After they were finished, she looked at Kayla, then at Silas, and back at Kayla again.

She took Kayla's hand, squeezed it tight for a moment, and then asked her if she would mind leaving her and Silas for a little while so they could talk alone.

Without a word, Kayla climbed down the ladder and quickly went inside.

"I will finish cleaning up. You two sit and rest. You cooked dinner. Now it is my turn," she demanded.

"By the way, where is Sly?"

"He went home to check on things. He will be back by bedtime," Nadia answered. "Go, you two. I'm serious. It's my turn to do the dishes."

"I could get used to this," Ciara said as she and Nadia went into the living room to relax.

Just as Kayla finished the dishes and joined her mom and Ciara, Silas and Sarah entered through the front door.

"We need to talk with you, Nadia," he insisted. "Sarah and I want to be married and live in Litora Falls. Is this possible, ma'am?"

Nadia noticed the glow of happiness beaming off both their faces — something she had not seen in a very long time.

"Yes, I suppose it is possible. You would have to get permission from Neree. I am certain he would agree."

"Sarah, are you sure?" Kayla asked, jumping up from her chair.

"I have never been surer of anything in my life. Besides, I can't let my best friend go traipsing off to another world all alone. You need me," she laughed, giving Kayla a big hug.

"Seriously, I told you I had feelings for Silas before you told me all of this."

"Yeah, I'm sure. Very sure!"

"It is settled then. Welcome to our world," Nadia said, giving Sarah a big hug. "It will be good for Kayla to have her friend close by," she whispered.

Suddenly, Sly appeared.

"Things are going well, ma'am. Sir Neree said we should be prepared to leave for home in the next two or three days. He sends his love, ma'am."

"I am so hungry," he said as he and Ciara disappeared into the kitchen.

"What are we going to tell everyone at work?" Sarah asked.

"Who was next in line for the partnership?" Kayla asked.

"Me," Sarah smiled. "Looks like the job will go to Jim. I overheard the board talking about the three of us. They said you were the most talented young designer they had met in years and that I was a close second."

"They also said they would like to keep Jim around for a long time. They feel he is a great asset to the company and hope he didn't get discouraged by a woman getting this promotion. He will think he was second choice when we both leave."

"That is good. When we leave... Wow, you are sure?"

"Yes, I am," Sarah said with a smile.

"It is settled then," Nadia said as she gathered them in her arms. "Sly, Ciara," Nadia called loudly. "Come for a moment."

As they entered the room, Nadia announced, "You may as well tell them your news."

"Are you sure, ma'am?" Sly said in surprise.

"Yes, Sly, just tell them," she insisted.

"Ciara and I have been seeing each other for two years. We were married in a secret ceremony a few months ago."

"Only the Queen and King Neree know of our happy secret. Our announcement will be made by the King as soon as we return home, as we are expecting our firstborn in the spring. I have been honored with a special position in the kingdom, where we will make our home together."

"Ciara will continue to serve our wonderful Queen as her most honored personal assistant, helping with the continued education of everyone in our kingdom. Her younger sister, Morissa, will take her place as personal maid."

"We are looking forward to our firstborn and our new positions. We are both honored."

"Wow! This has certainly turned out to be quite a night. It seems we are going to be one big happy family," Kayla said, holding up her glass of wine.

"To all of us and the wonderful adventure, we are soon to begin together as friends!"

Everyone joined in with cheers of excitement, joy, and congratulations on the wonderful news of Ciara and Sly and the announcement of Sarah and Silas.

Kayla couldn't help but wish her life were as settled.

"It is odd how suddenly everything can change," she said as she gave her best friend a big hug.

"You will always be my best friend, Sarah. I am so glad you are coming with us. I don't know if I could endure all that is to come without you there with me. I wish you the most wonderfully happy life possible."

"This is not exactly how we thought our lives would turn out," Sarah said.

"Isn't it funny how life suddenly seems to take its own course sometimes?" Nadia interrupted. "I would never have thought that I would marry a frog that became human, but I could not ask for a better man to be my husband. Everything will work out well, you will see. You will have each other. That means a lot to both of you. Welcome to the family, Sarah."

Chapter Twenty-Two — Sarah's Wedding

"Thank you so much for being my daughter's best friend. I will always treat you as our family. I know it will mean so much to Kayla to have you with us."

"Thank you, Nadia," Sarah cried, hugging her tightly.

"I love Kayla like a sister. She has been my family for a while now, and I, hers."

"It feels right," she said.

"My Queen, could you marry us now? You marry ones in our kingdom."

"Yes, I could, but I am sure Sarah would like to have a ceremony with her family."

"Actually, Mother, Sarah has no family," Kayla interrupted.

"Is it fine with you, Sarah?" Silas asked.

"Why should we wait? We have no idea how long it will be before we can leave. I would love to be married to you as soon as possible. I don't need a big wedding," Sarah replied.

"I will do it under one condition," Nadia said.

"Anything, ma'am," Silas answered.

"You have to agree to a big ceremony once things are settled after we return home," Nadia insisted.

"Agreed," he said.

"I have the perfect dress," Kayla said, dragging Sarah upstairs to prepare her for her wedding.

Kayla handed Sarah the dress she had worn to her college graduation. It was a beautiful white gown with a simple touch of elegance.

"It's perfect," Sarah said. "I love it."

"Are you sure you want this?" Kayla asked.

"I have never been more sure of anything in my life," she replied.

"Let's get you ready then," Kayla smiled.

"Kayla, will you stand up for me? Will you be my maid of honor?"

"Of course I will," she said.

"Ready to go?" Kayla said as she hurried downstairs to tell her mother. She was amazed at how quickly Ciara and Nadia had prepared the den.

"It is beautiful, Mother," she said.

"You have to remember that Silas is of your father's kind. He has many powers. He can make things happen very quickly."

"You look great, Silas," Kayla said as she hurried back up the stairs.

Silas was beaming with joy when his eyes met Sarah as she made her way down the stairs to stand beside him.

"You look beautiful," he whispered.

She smiled as Nadia began.

When Nadia said the words, "I now pronounce you husband and wife," Silas grabbed Sarah up in his arms and spun her around in circles with excitement.

Everyone laughed as he collected himself.

"I love her!" he screamed. "She is my wife! I am excited!"

"I will make you the happiest woman in the world, I promise," he said.

"You already have," she cried.

Ciara had a nice dinner prepared for the celebration.

"How did you make a cake so fast?" Kayla asked.

"Ask Silas; that was his doing."

"Sarah, I have never seen you look so happy," Kayla said.

"I am happy for the first time in my life. This feels right. I can't wait until we can leave for your home," Sarah said.

"We are going to have a good life, Sarah. It will be simple but wonderful. I am so happy for you," Kayla said.

She thought of Ikan as they celebrated Silas and Sarah's special evening. She wished once again that things in her life were as settled.

Chapter Twenty-Three — Dark Shadow Of Evil

Ikan anxiously waited in his upstairs loft for dawn to end his sleepless night. At the first sparkle of daylight, he flew down the stairs like a herd of horses, searching for me.

I quietly sat in the dining room with Dubkan, enjoying my morning breakfast, amused by Ikan's sudden nervousness. We laughed as he rushed about the castle halls, from one end to the other, searching for us.

"Join us, my friend," I yelled into the halls as Ikan passed.

Pleased to hear the sound of my voice, Ikan entered the main eating room and took a seat at the end of the table.

"Good morning, my friends," he said.

"Good morning, Ikan," I replied. "You were up with the birds this morning. Having trouble sleeping… or something?" I could not hold back my emotions. I tried to pretend that I did not know why Ikan was searching for me before the light of day.

Picking through his plate, too nervous to eat a bite, Ikan did not know how much longer he could hold his tongue. He stared at me, then at Dubkan, and then at me again.

I could not stand it any longer. "Ikan, is something wrong?" I asked.

"I was just waiting, sir."

"And what would it be you are waiting for, my son?" I asked as he grinned at Dubkan while I continued to eat my meal.

"Sir, excuse me for interrupting your meal!"

"Yes," I replied, trying, once again, to disguise my pleasure in teasing my friend.

"Are we not going to the farm to bring the Queen home today, sir?"

"The Queen? Are you sure you do not mean Princess Kayla?"

"I know how much you have missed the Queen's presence in the castle, sir. Last night, you said we would be bringing her home this morning. I could have misunderstood your words, sir."

"Yes, Kayla too… all of them… Sir."

Noticing us quietly giggling, Ikan felt his blood rush through his body like fire in the wood stove. Unable to hold his feelings a moment more, he suddenly jumped from his seat, slamming his hands on the table.

"You are right!" he screamed. "I cannot wait to see Princess Kayla again. I want her home. I want to get to know her and spend time with her. I have feelings for Princess Kayla. I think she has feelings for me. I need to find out how she feels."

"There, I said it! Can we go now?"

Dubkan was relieved. "Finally," he said.

"What?" Ikan yelled, hitting him with his napkin.

It felt good for me to hear Ikan admit he wanted to get to know Kayla and finally acknowledge he had feelings for her. Nothing would make me happier than giving my daughter away to such a wonderful man.

Ikan and Dubkan exchanged friendly smiles, calming the air a bit. We finished our meal and prepared for our trip.

Within minutes, we were at the farm. The house was quiet and peaceful. Ikan built a warm fire in the fireplace. We tried to relax while waiting for everyone to awaken for the day.

"Neree!" Nadia yelled as she ran down the stairs, throwing herself into my arms. "I have missed you so," she said.

Nadia's excitement woke everyone in the house. I gave Nadia a harsh glare when I noticed Silas and Sarah entering the den from the downstairs guest room.

"It's okay," she smiled. "They are married."

"Married! What do you mean, married?"

"I have a lot to tell you, dear," she said. "Everything is fine. You will just have to trust me on this one."

Ikan waited anxiously for Kayla to join the others.

"What is going on?" she said as she looked over the rail at the top of the stairs.

"Father!" she screamed, quickly running to my arms. "I missed you so much," she cried.

"Kayla," Ikan yelled softly from the other end of the room.

"Ikan, you came," she said, looking toward him. She was unsure how she should react in my presence.

I quickly gave her a soft push and a nod of approval. As soon as she realized that I approved, she ran to Ikan.

"I missed you, Ikan. I am so glad you came with Father."

She buried herself in his strong arms before he had a chance to say a word.

"You are going to think I am crazy, but I love you, Ikan," she whispered.

"I love you too," he whispered. "I never want you to go away again."

Ikan took Kayla's face in his hands and stared at her for a moment.

"Will you be my wife?" he asked.

"Yes," she said.

"Mother… Father… It would appear you have a wedding to plan," she announced, holding Ikan close.

I looked at Ikan with much surprise.

"With your permission, sir," Ikan quickly added.

"Yes, my son," I answered. "You may marry my daughter — with my blessing."

"Quickly gather your things, everyone. We must return to Litora Falls. We have a lot of plans to make."

Halfway up the stairs, Kayla suddenly stopped.

"Sarah!" she yelled.

"What is wrong, Kayla?" she yelled from her room.

"Work, Sarah… We forgot about the office. We can't just leave without telling someone. They will call out the army searching for us. We can't just disappear."

"What are we going to do?"

Together, they approached Nadia and me to explain the situation.

"Father, we need to go to the office and let our boss know we won't be back. I'm not sure how much we should tell him. We can't just leave without a word. It wouldn't be right. We owe him and our friends an explanation of some kind. We don't want them to think something happened to us. It wouldn't be right."

"Go to your office quickly. We will wait for you here. Once you return, we will leave for home," I said.

"How much should we tell him? What should we tell him? I don't know how to explain both of us leaving. They are never going to believe us."

"Tell them the truth," I said softly, trying to calm her down a bit. "Sarah, tell them you were secretly married and must move far away to be with your husband. They have no need of knowing more."

"Kayla, simply tell them you met your parents, whom you have never known, and want to live near them. Tell him you need to spend time with us and get to know us. Both of you are about to experience an amazing journey into a world unknown to this time. Your new lifestyle will give you a peace within yourself you have never known. It is a wonderful experience. Your lives will never be the same."

"Our world is simple in ways you will not believe. You will never want to come back here to live as you do now once you have lived as a Litoran. I am certain of that," I explained.

"One more thing you must remember: you must tell no one of our homes," I demanded.

"I know, Father, don't worry," Kayla said.

It was a beautiful morning drive into the city. The time passed quickly as Sarah and Kayla prepared their stories along the way.

"It's settled. We know what to say," Kayla said as she pulled into the parking lot of their office building for the last time.

As they walked through the office door, they noticed the light in Mr. Lane's office.

"That's very strange. He never arrives this early," Kayla said. "I wonder what's going on."

Without another word, they softly knocked on his office door.

"Yes… come in," he said, looking through the glass door. "My, aren't we the early birds this morning? Hmm... What are you two up to? You look so serious!"

"Good morning, sir," Kayla said.

"Good morning," Sarah followed.

"I am afraid we are serious, sir. We need to talk with you if you have a few moments," Kayla said.

"I have a feeling I'm not going to like this. Have a seat. Please continue," he replied.

"I'm afraid I have some news... um, you may not be pleased with, sir. For me, it is good news. I was married yesterday in a secret ceremony. My husband's home is very far away. We will be leaving today. I know this is sudden, and you will not understand, but I know I am doing the right thing… for me," Sarah explained.

"Sarah, I don't know what to say. This is such a surprise. I am at a loss for words. I... I would never have expected this of you."

"I am so sorry, sir."

"Is that everything?" he asked, with a sound of anger in his voice.

"I'm afraid there's more, sir," Kayla added. "Today, sir."

"Since I was old enough to understand life, I have been told my parents died when I was a baby. I have just learned they are very much alive. This weekend, I met them. They also live very far away and will be returning home this morning. They have arranged for me to leave with them. I have to go, sir. I need to live near them and get to know them. I'm so sorry, sir. This situation has changed my life. They are the only thing important to me now. I spent my entire life wishing I had known them. Now, I have this chance. I need to take advantage of it — in every way. I'm very sorry, sir."

"I have to say that I am very disappointed in both of you. You are my best designers. This isn't how I wanted my day to begin. I don't know what to say. I am angry, hurt, disappointed, but, at the same time, happy for you both. I understand your reasons for leaving. I hate the thought of losing you — both of you — at the same time. This is quite a loss for the company and for me personally," he explained.

"There is good news," Kayla said. "My parents employ Sarah's husband, Silas. We will be living in the same area. We will have each other to get through this change in our lives."

"That is good news for you and probably some other firm," he said.

"We won't be looking for jobs. It's complicated to explain, sir. Just know we will be very happy."

"It sounds to me as though you both have found the kind of happiness that doesn't come around often. I hope it is everything it seems to be for you both. I wish you the best of luck," he said.

"Thank you, sir," Sarah said.

"I am very sorry to leave so suddenly, sir. I want to tell you how much I appreciate your understanding," Kayla said.

"Just be as happy as you seem at this moment," he said as he gave them both a hug.

They left a goodbye note on Jim, Kaci, and Dana's desks. They both felt everything had gone well as they returned to the farm.

"How did it go at the office?" I asked.

"Just as you had said it would, sir," Kayla replied.

At once, we gathered our things and returned to Litora Falls.

"This is the most amazing place I have ever seen," Sarah said, holding Silas tightly.

Entering the gates of the castle, I gathered my family in my arms. "We are home," I said softly. "My family is finally home."

While Ikan and Silas gave Kayla and Sarah a complete tour of the castle, Ciara prepared a late-morning breakfast.

"We have a surprise for you two," Ikan said as they finished their meal.

Kayla and Sarah curiously looked at each other as they followed him to the far end of the stables.

Four winged horses, saddled and ready for a tour of their new world, stood next to the fence post at the far edge of the back lawn.

"Horseback riding!" Kayla smiled. "I love horses."

"More like horseback flying," Ikan quickly explained.

"I have to admit, I have never been on a horse in my life," Sarah said. "I wouldn't know how to begin."

"We can ride together," Silas quickly offered. "We want to show you all three regions of Amphibia. They are closely connected, but there is not enough time to travel on foot in one day. Our lands are wonderful. I do not want you to miss a thing."

They began their tour at the edge of the Great Falls of the south and followed a shortcut northwest, along the Varanus path, to the Varanus Desert. After introducing them to Sir Eckhard and his family, they rode north, along Trundra Springs, to Litora Pond.

Sarah was a little frightened at first. She had not been warned of their creature-like appearance. Quickly, she realized what wonderful beings they had become.

Ikan surprised them with a delicious picnic snack. They rested for about an hour, talking, laughing, and eating. The beautiful view and weather were so breathtaking that they wanted to relax and enjoy as much as possible.

At the north edge of the pond, Silas stopped. He pointed to the dark mountains at the northern end of the land.

"Ahead of us are the Dracara Mountains. Much evil has come from the caves on the dark side of these hills. We know not if it is safe. Never go there under any circumstances," he insisted as they flew past.

They followed the path southeast to the Gibbon Forest.

Sir Meinkard met them at the gate with open arms. "Kayla, you have returned."

"I would like you to meet my best friend, Sarah," she said.

"She is my new wife," Silas added.

Looking a little confused, Meinkard welcomed Sarah and gave his congratulations to Silas. After introducing them to his family and visiting for a time, they continued along Gibbon Springs. They stopped at a small pond that was located in the direct path to the castle.

"This is Kayla Pond," Ikan said while helping Kayla from her horse. "If I have the story right, it was named on the day of your birth by Sir Meinkard."

"Wow!" Kayla said. "It's so beautiful."

After a few moments, they traveled along Kayla's path to the back of the stables, where they had begun many hours earlier.

"Next time, we will travel the outer edges. We will show you all of the beautiful springs, mountains, caves, and waterfalls," Ikan said. "It is a much more time-consuming trip than traveling the center edges of the lands, as we did today. We would have to arrange an overnight stay."

"Everything is beautiful. I am so glad to be here. I never want to leave again. The city has nothing on this place. It is so peaceful and simple. I love it here!" she yelled.

"I feel the same way," Sarah said. "This is so much more amazing than I had imagined. I love you and your home so much, Silas," she said as he slid her from the horse and held her tightly in his arms.

"What was that?" Kayla asked. She caught a glimpse of a dark shadow flash across the trees northwest of the stables.

"What?" Ikan asked.

"Nothing," she said. "I thought I saw something. Just my imagination, ya know…"

They laughed as they left the horses with the stable boy, Taran, and headed for the castle.

"I have another surprise for you, Kayla," Ikan said as they reached the grounds — just beyond the castle door.

"We will return soon, Silas. Tell the King I will take good care of his princess," Ikan said as he and Kayla walked away from the castle — toward the hills to the south.

"What is going on, Ikan? You are acting very mysterious," Kayla said as she walked close beside him.

"There is someone I cannot wait another moment for you to meet," he said, with his eyebrows raised and a smirked grin on his face. "Just trust me, Kayla; you will love her."

"Her? Her who?" she asked, now more curious than ever.

Once out of sight of the castle, Ikan made the sound of a strange whistling noise.

"What are you doing?" Kayla asked.

"Just watch… She will come," he said as he continued to smile.

"She who?" she asked again, with frustration.

"The love of my life… Trust me, you will love her. She is beautiful, soft, loving, and kind. She has been with me for many years, and I love her more than anyone or anything in our world. She will arrive soon," he answered, realizing Kayla was acting a little jealous.

"There she is," he said, pointing to the south sky.

"Is it a bird?" she asked.

"It is Shanauh," he replied.

Shanauh, a white Bengal tiger with beautiful white wings, flew to the ground a few yards beyond the small hill in front of Kayla. She and Mundi, a male white tiger, were found by Ikan alone and sick as young cubs. A group of large dark creatures invaded their home and killed their families. Shanauh and Ikan quickly became soul mates. Ikan protected them both until they were old enough to live on their own.

Kayla was overcome by her beauty and her ability to fly. "She is so beautiful, Ikan," she said as Shanauh slowly walked closer and closer toward her.

"You must be Princess Kayla," she said with a soft yet strange voice.

"Was that… you talk…? Ikan, she talks," Kayla said.

"I am pleased to meet you, Princess Kayla. I have waited many years for your arrival," Shanauh said.

"I…I am pleased to meet you, too. You have to forgive me, Shanauh. Where I come from, animals don't speak. Animals of your kind don't have wings or fly. I'm sorry if I seem a little startled. I have never seen anything like you before. That's not a bad thing," Kayla explained as excitement rushed through her mind. "I'm just not sure what to think. I am so amazed by your beauty and intelligence."

"I know we are going to be great friends one day, Kayla," Shanauh said as she closed her eyes with a slight nod of her head. "I will always be here to protect you, my princess."

"It is getting dark, Shanauh. We must start back," Ikan interrupted. "I wanted Kayla to meet you before we retire. We will come again soon," he said as he put his arms around her and hugged her softly.

"Hop on. I will give you both a ride back to the castle," she said as she lowered her wings to make room for them.

Kayla was a little reluctant to sit on Shanauh's back at first. She couldn't believe she was standing before a white Bengal tiger that could fly and speak. With a little coaching from Shanauh and Ikan, and the fact that she didn't want to walk home alone in the dark, she carefully climbed on Shanauh's back, followed by Ikan. They peacefully flew slowly toward the castle.

"This is wonderful," Kayla said. "I can see the entire castle grounds. It's amazing, Ikan." With the wind blowing through her hair, gliding slowly through the soft clouds, and landing just beyond the front gates of the castle, Kayla had a wonderful feeling about her new world and her new life. No one at home would believe that I rode on a flying horse and a flying tiger... that speaks for me. "Amazing!"

"Shanauh, you are wonderful. Thank you so much for bringing us home. I hope to see you again soon," Kayla said.

"Bring Kayla to meet the cubs soon," she demanded as she flew away.

Ikan stood behind Kayla, wrapping his arms softly around her as they stood quietly watching Shanauh disappear from sight.

"She has cubs," Kayla said.

"A boy and a girl. Wait until you see them. They are the cutest and most mischievous little ones I have ever seen," he replied.

"Kayla, few of us know of them. I only visit them at night. I have kept them hidden for many years for their safety."

"I understand, Ikan. I won't tell anyone."

"Thank you," he said, squeezing her tightly. "We had better go inside. It is late. Your father will have my head."

As Kayla turned toward the castle gate, she saw a flash of dark shadows sweep around the corner of the far wall.

"What was that?" she asked.

"What?" Ikan replied.

"Oh, it must be my imagination," she said as they continued through the gates. Kayla didn't want to worry Ikan with thoughts of something she was not sure she had seen. She looked at the trees with unsettling curiosity as she closed the castle door.

"Sorry we are so late, sir," Ikan said as they joined the others at the dinner table.

"We had a wonderful tour of the lands," Sarah said.

"I love it here, sir."

"Father, I have one question. Am I safe from Trillian?"

"Elliott, Koda, I think it is time we should take a break. The next part of this story is intense. We are all very tired. We should get some lunch before I continue."

"Grandfather, please finish this story first. Just a little longer. I have a feeling something is going to happen to Mother. She keeps seeing something."

"Please!" Elliott begged.

"Yes, I will finish this story... then a break."

"Where is your silver pendant?" I demanded, noticing Kayla was not wearing it.

"Oh, Father, I must have left it on the bathroom counter at the farm when I took a shower. We left in such a rush. I am so sorry, Father."

"How could you have forgotten?" I yelled.

"I told you more than once you must never take it off!"

"I am on it, sir," Ikan said as he and Silas disappeared into the night.

Kayla ran upstairs to her room, upset with herself for her mistake. "I am so embarrassed," she thought. "How could I have forgotten to put it back on after I showered? How could I be so careless?" She yelled, throwing herself into the pillow. "Father must wish he had never come for me," she said as she sobbed.

"Kayla, I am sorry I yelled at you," I said as I entered her room. "You do not know how important the green stone is to you. You must wear it for protection until you have developed the powers within yourself."

"I am not angry with you. I am afraid for your life. I never should have yelled at you in the presence of others. I would never forgive myself if something happened to you, Kayla," I cried. "I have waited twenty years to bring you home. If something happened to you here, I would never forgive myself."

Kayla rose up from the bed and buried herself in my arms. "I don't know how I could have forgotten, Father. Please forgive me."

"I love you so much, Father. I didn't mean to be disrespectful."

"In answer to your question, Kayla, Trillian was killed at the caves of Ka'ron. Ciar saved Yara's life at the risk of losing his own. For that reason, we spared his life. We sent him far away, to another land, with his promise that he would never return to our lands. It appears he was stolen as a baby and is not Trillian's blood. I am a little uneasy about our decision, but it was the right thing to do. I am not sure that I trust him. There's just something about his story. It just did not sit well with me. I just cannot be sure. We cannot be too careful. I must know you are protected at all times. No harm will come to you as long as you wear the pendant. The green stone has the power to keep you safe from all evil. When Ikan returns, he must explain the powers of the pendant and stone to you. He must take you to the training room soon."

"Training room?" she said.

"Soon enough, my child. You must rest now, my princess. Ikan should return soon."

As I shut the door, a dark shadow flashed across the window, sending a chill of fear through Kayla's body.

"What was that? I know I saw something. Just my imagination…" she thought once again.

"I must be more tired than I thought," she sighed. "Father's right. I need to rest," she said as she cuddled once again into her pillow.

Just as Kayla dozed off, there was a knock on her door.

"Come in," she said.

"Kayla, I know that it is late, but there are some visitors anxious to meet you," Ciara said.

"It's okay; I would love to meet them."

Ren and Yara quietly entered the room.

"Kayla, this is Yara and her husband Ren."

"I'm happy to finally meet you both. I'm so glad you are safe, Yara. My father told me about your ordeal. I'm sorry for your loss. Ren, I'm told that you are a very brave and strong defender. I'm very pleased to meet you."

"The pleasure is ours, my princess," he said.

Suddenly, a dark shadow appeared through the open bedroom window.

"What is that?" Kayla screamed as Ren jumped in front of her and Yara for protection.

"Show yourself!" he demanded, drawing his sword.

As he stepped closer, the creature flipped back his hood, showing his face in the shadows.

"Ciar!" Yara screamed with fear.

"I knew you were not to be trusted," Ren said. "Why have you come here?"

"For my sacrifice!" he demanded.

"You fools!" he screamed. "You fools believed all my lies! I saved Yara only for my good, while I awaited your return… my princess… my life! Yara's life means nothing! I will have my sacrifice! My evil will rise above all that is good in these lands! I am proud to be the son of Trillian! My father was a great man!"

"I will never let that happen," Ikan said, bursting through the door after overhearing the voices from the hall.

"Kayla, Yara, leave us!" he demanded, tossing Kayla her pendant.

Kayla quickly put the silver chain around her neck and placed the stone over her heart as she grabbed Yara's hand and wished to see her father.

"Father!" she screamed from the top of the stairs. "Ciar! My room! Quickly, Father! Ikan… Ren…" Kayla could barely continue.

"Go to the visiting room and inform your mother," I said as I ran to Kayla's room.

"Ah, the king himself," Ciar said as he threw a blade, striking me in my shoulder. Screams of my pain echoed through the castle walls.

"Neree!" Nadia cried as she ran up the stairs, followed closely by Yara and Kayla.

Kayla and Yara stood frozen in the doorway. Nadia knelt beside me, lying on the floor in a pool of blood.

"I will be okay," I assured her as she held me in her arms.

"Now!" Ikan ordered. Ren and Ikan attacked Ciar from both sides at once with sharp blades.

Ciar fought fiercely, holding them off with a blade in each hand for several minutes.

Suddenly, Ren had a clear path, jabbing his blade deep into Ciar's heart, followed by two perfect blades thrown from Ikan's hands.

Dark gray smoke instantly filled the room. The smoke blocked the view of a black spirit of evil as it lifted from Ciar's body.

Yara screamed in pain as she doubled over on the floor, grabbing her stomach. Ciar's evil spirit sharply entered her body. It swarmed painfully through her organs and finally settled in the soul of her unborn son.

Strangely, the dark gray cloud left the room as instantly as it had appeared.

Ren ran to Yara. He swept her up in his arms and softly laid her comfortably in the bed across the hall, wanting her out of sight of the tragedy that had taken place in Kayla's room.

"Yara, are you okay?" he asked, softly sweeping her hair from her eyes.

"Sharp pains in my stomach. It hurt deeply. It frightened me so," she cried. "I am good now; it was only fear, Ren. Could be the baby," she said. "It is much too soon."

"What of Ciar?" she asked. "He spoke again of evil!"

"He saved me from this attack on Kayla! Not of good for you or me… but for himself!"

"He… he is evil!"

"He was not truthful!"

"What of the king? Was he harmed? Is he…?"

"He is strong," Ren said. "His wound is deep in his shoulder. He will need time to heal… He will live."

"Good," she said with a sigh of relief.

Ikan carried me to my bed to give Nadia time to attend to my wound. He and Ren personally cremated Ciar's body immediately in the wood-burning stove at the far end of the dungeon.

"With his own eyes, Ikan needed to see this evil man destroyed once and for all!"

"He had no idea, at the time, that his evil spirit had entered the body of Yara's unborn child!"

"I knew something was going to happen. Father is so brave," Elliott announced.

"Yes, he is, Elliott… but now it is time for lunch. We all need a little break," I insisted.

Chapter Twenty-Four — Eckhard's Discovery

At the Dracara Mountains…

The boys did not give me much time to relax. As quickly as they had eaten their lunch, they were ready for another story.

"My next story may be a little more disturbing. Prepare yourselves. I do not want to frighten you."

"We are very brave, Grandfather. Have you not noticed?" Koda asked.

"Yes… Yes, indeed, I have noticed," I assured him. "I will continue."

Unaware of the battle that had taken place in the castle earlier that evening nor of Ciar's death, Eckhard accompanied three dozen of his strongest warriors to the dark side of the Dracara Mountains to explore the Draconian Caves.

A few hours earlier, he had been awakened from a frightening dream. Loud sounds of splashing water and eerie screams filled his room in the darkness. In his dream, Trillian had appeared from the dead, destroying all of Amphibia, with his son, Ciar, by his side in the form of a cloud-like black spirit. He had seen the strange black spirit floating over a pool of black, bubbling water inside a deep, dark cave.

Eckhard awoke haunted, feeling that releasing Ciar without punishment had been a terrible mistake. He sensed that something evil was about to sweep across the lands like never before. His clothes were drenched in sweat, and chills ran through him. The mysterious caves of the Dracara Mountains flashed in his mind.

"Something is happening," he thought. "Something very evil is about to invade our lands."

He quickly woke his trusted warriors and quietly left the Varanus Desert before the first light touched the lands. They rode their strongest winged horses, flying swiftly through the night, deep into the forests of the far northwest corner of the land.

They split into three groups, searching every cave in the mountains to their deepest ends. For hours, they combed through the darkness, hunting for any signs of Ciar or any Draconian that may have survived.

Finally, all the Komodo Dragons gathered at the entrance of a cave.

"We have searched every known cave to its deepest ends," Shawn reported.

"As have we," Modoc added.

Eckhard sighed, disappointed. "Return home to your families," he ordered. "Perhaps my dream was only that — a dream."

As they passed the west side of the mountain, Modoc suddenly stopped.

"Sir Eckhard," Modoc said, "do you hear that?" He pointed toward a black hill, oddly shaped and nestled high in the mountain's center. "Sounds, sir… I hear them coming from there."

Eckhard listened closely. "Yes," he whispered. "Very strange sounds indeed. I hear them now."

He ordered his tired warriors to rest while he and Modoc climbed toward the black hill, hoping to discover what was happening.

The eerie screeching sounds filled Eckhard with fear as they climbed closer to the blackness above them. In the corner of the black hill, they saw a cloudy mass floating, the very presence of evil radiating from the mountain walls.

Eckhard's dream flashed before his eyes.

"This… This is what I saw," Eckhard whispered. "The spirit of evil is here… in the air… I must enter."

"I will go with you, sir," Modoc said firmly. "You must not go alone. It is too dangerous."

Eckhard smiled, impressed by the bravery of his young warrior. "Very well. It is decided, my brave friend."

The two instantly transformed into small lizards for protection and disguise, crawling carefully through the dark, cloudy opening in the mountain. The screeching sounds grew louder and more terrifying with every step.

"There, ahead," Modoc whispered, pointing to a glimmer of fading light that sparkled through an arch-like opening.

They reached a narrow ledge, forty feet above a deep open space that stretched across the width of the mountain. From their vantage point, they could see the mountains connecting in a complete circle.

In the center of the circle, far below them, was a pool of black, bubbling water. Dark clouds floated eerily above the pool.

"My dream…" Eckhard whispered.

"What does it mean?" Modoc asked. "The smell… it's like death."

"Evil," Eckhard replied grimly. "Evil spirits, I'm afraid. We must send for Neree and Meinkard immediately. They must see this with their own eyes!"

"Wait, sir," Modoc said. "I hear voices."

Peering into the darkness, they saw creatures wearing black robes. Their hoods hung loosely on their backs, revealing their faces in the dim light.

"Trillian," Eckhard whispered. "I knew he was alive — and the Draconians and Jadar's followers. There are dozens of them. We thought we had destroyed them all. How did he trick us? How could this be?"

"We must send word to Neree and Meinkard," Eckhard muttered urgently. "Trillian… Trillian lives! The king must be told."

Suddenly, soft shuffling sounds came from the entrance of the cave.

"Someone's coming, sir," Modoc whispered.

"Sir Eckhard," a familiar voice called softly. "It is only us."

It was Lowell and a group of warriors. "We feared you might need our help, sir. Forgive us for disobeying your orders, but you must see what's happening outside. Dark shadows are floating from the black hill, spreading over the mountains. The sky… You must come, sir!"

Eckhard's heart sank. "The entrance is closing," Lowell warned. "We are trapped inside. What do we do, sir?"

"We must find a way out," Eckhard said urgently. "King Neree must be warned! Change to your smallest forms — now!"

In an instant, they all transformed into tiny lizards and scurried through the cave, searching desperately for an escape. As they moved, Eckhard and Modoc listened closely to Trillian and his warriors.

"Soon, our time will come," Trillian declared. "All Litorans and their allies will pay for my son's death. His spirit will live among them, and I will guide him as he grows. I will have my revenge."

"Fools!" Trillian sneered. "Neree knows not that my twin — the evil being — was destroyed in the caves of Ka'ron. The day will come when I appear before him. He knows not that I live. My powers will rule over all lands!"

Trillian raised his flaming staff high above his head. "Evil will overcome all that is good. I will rule this world — and all worlds to come! Neree and his allies will be destroyed. Nothing can stop me! Trillian lives! I am evil above all evil! Destroy them all!"

Laughter and shouts echoed throughout the caves, sending chills through Eckhard and Modoc.

"Something terrible is about to happen," Eckhard whispered. "Something unlike anything we have ever known."

"We must get to Neree," he commanded. "Our king must be warned!"

With renewed urgency, they joined the others, continuing their frantic search for an escape.

"Neree, I have much need of your powers," Eckhard thought as he continued to search for a way out.

"Here!" Shawn shouted, standing in a tiny split in a corner at the south end of the cave.

Quickly, the three Komodo dragons crawled through the tiny opening on the backside of the mountain, leading directly onto the path toward Litora Falls.

"We must hurry," Eckhard said as he glared at the sky above them.

Rolling dark clouds of screaming spirits, streaks of fire, and large dark gray fliers of an unknown kind filled the skies above the Dracara Mountains.

"Evil is among us! A power like we have never known!" Eckhard shouted as they instantly changed into their human-like forms, mounted their horses, and flew off into the strange, thick darkness.

"We must inform King Neree of all the strange things we have seen and heard in this most fearful time of darkness."

"Water and rest the horses," Eckhard commanded as Modoc and Lowell entered the castle unannounced.

"Ikan, I do not mean to intrude, but it is of utmost importance that I speak with the king at once," Eckhard demanded.

"Follow me, sir," Ikan replied. "I can feel from the sound of your voice that something frightening has happened. He is in his room, resting from his injury."

"Injury?" Eckhard shouted. "What has happened here? How and when was King Neree injured? Why was I not told of this?"

"Neree was wounded by the Blade of Ciar in a fierce battle."

"What battle?" Eckhard asked, shocked.

"Princess Kayla was staying in the extra room on the second floor of the castle, in the east corner, for a few days. She had a spat with her father and had retired early. Ciar appeared to her in the night… our thoughts were that he came to kill her, sir."

"He... Who is he? I know not of what you speak!" Eckhard exclaimed. "What has happened here?"

"Ciar, sir. He returned in the night… for Kayla."

"She is safe?" Eckhard demanded.

"Yes, she is safe."

"And what of him?" Eckhard asked.

"Ren and I killed him. We cremated his body in the dungeon's wood burner. Black evil filled the room in the form of smoke the moment he died."

"He was truly Trillian's son. The evil was present. He fooled us all, sir," Ikan answered.

"My king," Eckhard said, entering the room. "I must speak with you if you are up to it. I only learned of your injury and of Ciar just now."

"There is a fear in your eyes that I have never seen before, Sir Eckhard. What has happened?"

"I am afraid I have the most distressing news to add to your pain, my friend. If it were not for the seriousness of the matter, I would not bother you at this most difficult time."

"Just tell me what has happened," I demanded, rising from my bed.

"Sir, you must rest," Ikan said, helping me lie back against the pillows as the healer had ordered.

Ikan and I listened carefully as Eckhard spoke of all he had seen inside the Dracara Mountains.

"Sir!" Dubkan interrupted, rushing into the room. "The baby, sir... Yara... The baby is coming!"

Ikan rushed up the stairs to Ren and Yara's room. Just as he reached the end of the hall, Ciara and Morissa were leaving with a large bundle of laundry.

"It is a healthy boy. Big in size, much like his father," Ciara announced as they passed.

Ikan softly knocked on the door before entering the room.

"Come in, my friend, and meet my son," Ren said proudly.

"He will be called Blade, in honor of the blades that destroyed the evil Ciar on the eve of his birth."

"Much like his father, don't you think? A strong, healthy son and a beautiful wife," Ren boasted. "I am most happy, Ikan. A good time for our lands."

A strange chill rushed through Ikan as his eyes met the eyes of the newborn, held proudly in the arms of his friend.

Ikan could not bear to stay in the room with Blade, sensing the presence of evil within him. "Something is very wrong here," he thought, trying not to show his true feelings.

"I am most happy for you both. I will leave you to be with your wife and son, my friend," Ikan said, returning to my bedside.

"Ren has a strong baby son," he reported. "He will be called Blade. I did not bring the sad news to him. He is most happy, sir. With your permission, we must give him this time."

Ikan kept the odd feelings he had about Blade to himself, thinking it was just a reaction to the battle and Eckhard's disturbing news. He felt it was not his place to judge the child.

"Yes, Yara needs Ren at her side right now. He need not hear the news," I replied.

"What news?" Ren demanded, bursting into my room. "What has happened? You must not keep things from me!"

Once again, Eckhard recounted all he had seen in the Dracara Mountains.

"What must we do?" Ren asked.

"You must stay with your new family," I answered. "They need you safe, my friend."

"Yara has her midwife, Nadia, Kayla, and the other women of the castle. She will understand. I have a duty to my kingdom and my friends. I must protect our home and our families. I will not be left behind, not with Trillian alive," he insisted.

"Go to your wife. Tell her what has happened. Spend time with your son until we leave," I instructed.

"Thank you, sir," Ren replied.

"Ikan, go to the Gibbon Forest. Let Meinkard know all that has taken place. Request his presence at the castle immediately."

"Sir Eckhard, we must call a council meeting," I said. "If the council agrees, invite King Neckatosh to join us. He is a great leader of good and would be most welcome."

"War is upon us once again, I am afraid. Trillian's evil must be stopped for the sake of all that is good."

"Meinkard, Ikan, and I will gather the leaders to your room, sir," Eckhard said.

"That is a very good idea," Nadia insisted as she entered the room. "You are staying right where you are, my husband. I… get to tell you what to do for a change. You have a serious injury, and you are lucky to be alive. It will take at least a few weeks to heal."

"I will gather the council, sir," Eckhard laughed. "I am glad to see you are in good hands," he whispered.

"Neree, you are not well enough to go off on some adventure," Nadia said.

"Nadia, my beautiful queen, Ikan can lead the Litorans. I trust him completely. He has more powers and abilities than any other Litoran."

"I know I do not have the strength to travel. I know I must rest. It would be dangerous for me to go with them. I know how serious my wounds are. I want to get well. My beautiful Nadia, you have my permission to mother me all you want," I said with a smile.

Meinkard, Eckhard, and Ikan will do well."

Within the hour, the council members gathered in my room to discuss the best approach to this troubling matter.

Nadia stood outside the door, quietly listening to Eckhard and Modoc describe the evil apparitions they had seen inside the strange, dark cave. Powers… evil… strange black streaks and flashing streaks of fire… She listened until she could no longer keep silent.

"Excuse me for interrupting, my husband. I don't mean to be rude. May I speak? I have something to tell you that will answer many of your questions," she said.

"Nadia, we agreed," I said softly.

"Neree, it is time."

Chapter Twenty-Five — Nadia's Speaks To The Council

"My friends, as you know, I came from a world many years in the future. During Neree's time with me, we spent many hours researching the powers and abilities many of you possess. It is time you were told more about these things. I have felt for a long time that we should be training each and every one of you to use your great gifts to your full potential. In some of the lands — years from now — there will be many groups of people with different types of magical powers. There will be many names for them. The most common will be called sorcerers, wizards, and witches. They will all possess unique magical and supernatural powers. These powers will be used both for good and for evil through the years. Some will have supernatural powers akin to angels of good. However, many more will wield the powers of demons of evil."

"There will be a great book that speaks of a superior being in the heavens above. It will describe all that is good and name this place *heaven*. It will also speak of an evil being dwelling in the earth below, called *hell*. These evil beings will spread their influence, corrupting the hearts and souls of those who follow them. The world will be divided, and a battle between good and evil will rage for many years. Some people will choose good, while others will embrace evil, seeking to destroy everything virtuous around them. This future mirrors what we face today. We are the good of these lands, and Trillian and his followers are evil. From all the information we gathered, we reached only one possible conclusion. The hot springs — filled with colorful mud and strong-smelling clay — into which your ancestors fell so many years ago were from the future. I believe your teenage ancestors were the first to travel through a time loop into the future, finding themselves in a moment between their time and a future era."

"The waters and clay must have contained magical mixtures brewed by wizards, sorcerers, or other supernatural beings of that future time. After leaving the strange springs, your ancestors must have traveled through another time loop, returning to their original lands at a different point in history. This theory explains the extraordinary powers that each of you has inherited through this incredible chain of events. Some Litorans indeed possess the combined powers of those ancient sorcerers, wizards, and witches. Your abilities are far beyond what anyone could imagine. The reason why the Komodo Dragons and Ceairans have fewer powers is simple: they fell into the waters at different locations. The magic was strongest at its source in the caves, but as the clay's power flowed downstream, it weakened. Those who fell farther downstream received only traces of the magic."

"Every one of you possesses some form of power. With proper training, even the weakest gifts can be developed into incredible strengths. Neree and I plan to expand the training classes, hoping to unlock the full potential in each of you. These classes will also emphasize the importance of using your powers for the good of our lands. Neree fears, however, that some of you might use your powers for evil once they are fully developed. Therefore, we will begin the intense training with the most trusted members of each family. Our research was completed just before the invasion of Litora Falls. The events since that day delayed this announcement, but it is time for you to know our findings and plans. After years of research, we are certain of our conclusions. This is good news for us all. Yet, from what I've heard about the caves, it is clear that Trillian possesses great evil. This will be a tremendous challenge. I do not know the origin of these evil spirits, but when the time of danger comes, look deep within yourselves. Powers you are unaware of will give you strength. Believe in yourselves with all your soul."

For a moment, a great silence filled the room. All the leaders sat in stunned amazement at Nadia's words, unable to speak.

"This is a lot to absorb," Ikan said. "But this is great news for us all!"

Cheers of excitement erupted as many voices praised Nadia for her incredible revelation.

"Silence!" Eckhard shouted. "Thank you, Nadia, for all you have done for us."

He turned to the others. "We must now gather our horses and travel once more to the Dracara Mountains. We must reach the dark hill before the darkness fades. My king, do not worry. Rest and heal your wounds. Meinkard, Ikan, Neckatosh, and I will lead our warriors, guided by your teachings. We will return victorious for the sake of all that is good in these lands."

After Ren left for the meeting, Yara quickly fell asleep, her newborn son resting in a cradle beside her.

Suddenly, a black shadow appeared over the cradle in the room's darkness.

"Spirit of my son, consume the body of Ren's newborn child. Rise from his soul. The dark spirit of our evil awaits you in the cave of the black hill. Rise at once."

The shadow vanished into the darkness just as Ren entered the room for a final farewell.

"I will miss you, my precious Blade. Stay safe until I return," Ren whispered, gazing down at the cradle with pride and hope for his son's future.

As he turned to leave, a chill ran down his spine. He hesitated at the door, glancing back at his sleeping wife and son. A sense of foreboding crept over him, filling him with the fear that he might not return.

"I must survive for my family," he thought as he stepped out of the room and joined the others for the most dangerous journey of his life.

Chapter Twenty-Six — The Disappearance Of Blade

Soon after Ren left the castle, Nadia ensured I was comfortable for the night. She felt saddened that Yara had been left alone so soon after giving birth. Quietly, she went upstairs to check on Yara and the baby before retiring herself.

Yara seemed to be resting peacefully, with Blade's cradle snuggled close to her bed. Trying not to wake her, Nadia carefully slipped past the foot of the bed and approached the cradle.

"That is odd," she whispered, leaning closer to find the cradle empty.

Panic began to rise. Nadia quickly checked the baby's room, hoping Asiya might have placed him in his crib. Asiya was Baldasarre's assistant, and after delivering Blade, Baldasarre had asked her to stay for a while to help care for them.

The crib was also empty. A terrible feeling gripped Nadia — something was very wrong. She stepped into the hallway to call for help, and just then, she saw Asiya approaching.

"Where is the baby?" Nadia demanded.

"In his cradle, beside his mother," Asiya replied.

"The cradle is empty! Someone has taken him!" Nadia insisted. "Why weren't you watching them? Where have you been?"

"I am sorry, my Queen," Asiya said. "I hadn't eaten all day, so I went to get dinner while they were asleep. The baby was still in his cradle when I left. I was only gone for a moment."

"Forgive me, Asiya. I was worried, and I should not have snapped at you," Nadia said. "It has been a long day for you. Please, forgive me."

"Thank you, ma'am. I understand," Asiya said. "But we must wake Yara."

At that moment, Yara stirred, disturbed by the sound of their voices.

"What's going on?" she asked, sitting up slowly.

"Yara, where is the baby?" Nadia asked urgently.

"In his cradle," Yara answered groggily, leaning over to look. A moment later, her eyes widened in horror.

"Where is my baby?" she screamed. "Who has taken my baby? Please, you must find him!"

"Ren!" she cried out. "Where is my husband? I want my baby!" She sobbed uncontrollably.

Unable to console her, Nadia turned to Asiya. "Stay with her. I'll get help," she said, hurrying toward the hall.

Silas appeared from his room across the hall. "What's going on?" he asked. "Sarah and I were awakened by the shouting."

"It's the baby!" Nadia cried. "He's gone! Someone must have taken him!"

"I'll go for help," Silas said.

"Silas, the warriors went with Eckhard to the Dracara Mountains," Nadia reminded him.

"Tell me everything," Silas said, his expression darkening.

Nadia quickly explained what had happened.

"I'll fetch Ren!" Silas declared. "Why was I not informed of any of this earlier?"

"I'll send Baldasarre to assist Asiya with Yara. Go to our room and explain everything to Sarah. Tell her I'll be back soon."

He dashed up the stairs to the loft to find Sly. Together, they swiftly prepared for their journey. Within minutes, they mounted their horses.

"Dubkan!" Silas called out, pounding on the door of the small cottage beside the castle tower.

Dubkan opened the door, startled. "Yes, Silas?"

"Go inside the castle immediately and find Nadia. She'll explain what has happened. Wake all the guards — secure the castle at once!" Silas ordered.

"Yes, Silas," Dubkan replied before hurrying away.

Silas and Sly rode through the night, racing toward the Dracara Mountains. When they arrived, they found Ren and his group of warriors just outside the cave entrance.

"What are you doing here?" Ren shouted, sensing that something was terribly wrong from the urgency of their arrival.

"Ren," Silas said grimly, "it's the baby. He's gone. Someone took him from his cradle."

Ren's face drained of color. "What has happened?"

"We don't know," Silas answered. "Yara is devastated, and we thought it best to bring you back to her."

"Who is guarding the castle?" Ikan asked. "Who is watching over the women and the king?"

"I woke Dubkan and the castle guards before we left," Silas assured him. "I'll return as soon as possible, sir."

"Go at once, Ren," Ikan commanded. "I will inform the others."

"Thank you, Ikan," Ren said, already mounting his horse. With Silas and Sly by his side, they rode away into the dark night.

As Ikan turned back toward the cave entrance, his determination hardened. Finding Trillian was now more important than ever — for Ren and his son.

He moved toward the caves, and out of the corner of his eye, he saw something unusual — a faint black shadow shifting over the mountain's surface.

"Eckhard!" Ikan called out. "I see something!"

Eckhard hurried over. "There! At the top... Is that the black hill?"

"It's starting to form," Ikan said. "Look! The cloudy circle at the entrance... We must hurry before it closes."

Eckhard nodded. "We'll need to transform into our smallest forms for safety. The area above the bubbling black waters is highly exposed."

"Neckatosh, you're in charge," Eckhard said. "If we don't return before daylight, send for help."

Eckhard, Ikan, and Meinkard began climbing the mountain toward the black hill. They carefully crawled through the swirling black mist that marked the entrance to the cliff above the waters.

"The evil here is thick in the air," Ikan whispered, shivering at the malevolent energy surrounding them.

Dark spirits flew in chaotic circles above the bubbling waters, their eerie screeches filling the air. Shadows flickered across the walls, reflecting strange, unsettling shapes.

A faint beam of light sliced through the cracks in the cavern, casting fear across the eerie chamber.

Ikan, Meinkard, and Eckhard stood silently on the edge of the cliff, their tiny forms trembling in the presence of the overwhelming evil.

"This must be the demons Nadia spoke of in her research," Ikan murmured.

"Trillian's power is far stronger than we expected," Eckhard added grimly.

They gazed down at the bubbling black waters, knowing the true battle had only just begun.

"How do we battle against such evil, unknown to us?" "How can we achieve victory over this?" Meinkard asked, his voice filled with concern.

"I can no longer keep silent. I must tell you our secret," Ikan replied solemnly. "Neree and I have been training for months now."

He paused, glancing between his companions. "I have orders not to speak of this, but between us, we've developed many of my powers."

From their research, Nadia explained that I possess the strongest powers of all. I can do many great things — things you've never known."

"In the time of wizards and magic, they used wands and words to cast spells. But I have the ability to think of what I want, and with a simple swish of my hand or the force of my thought, it becomes reality in an instant."

Ikan's expression darkened slightly. "I was ordered to keep this secret. I'm not supposed to use these abilities until my training is complete. However, when the time comes — I'll do what must be done. You'll see. I'll be more than a match for Trillian. He has no idea what I'm capable of."

He exhaled deeply. "Neree will understand. Yes, he will."

Meinkard and Eckhard exchanged glances, feeling reassured by Ikan's words.

"Voices!" Ikan suddenly hissed. "Someone's coming!"

He pointed toward an opening between two peaks of the mountain below. A figure emerged — Trillian, carrying a tiny baby tightly wrapped in a soft blue blanket. Several Draconians followed him, surrounding the pool of bubbling black water.

"Blade," Ikan whispered urgently. "That must be Blade, Ren's son. Trillian must have stolen him from his cradle!"

"We must be sure, my friend," Eckhard cautioned.

The group fell silent, listening closely to Trillian as he spoke to his warriors.

"Son of the Litoran Ren!" Trillian bellowed, lifting the baby high above the dark waters. "The Litorans must pay for the death of my son through you!"

"Ciar's spirit shall live through your sacrifice!"

He glared down at the pool. "Pool of evil spirits — consume this body and release the spirit of my son!"

Before anyone could react, Ikan appeared on the cliff's edge above the scene.

"Eckhard, Meinkard — leave now before the entrance closes!" Ikan commanded urgently.

With a swish of his hand, a glowing streak of smoke shot across the room like a cloud beneath the baby just as Trillian tossed Blade toward the water.

In an instant, Blade's tiny body floated upward, lifted by the shimmering cloud. He hovered in midair for a heartbeat — and then vanished into Ikan's arms.

"Trillian, you will not destroy this child!" Ikan shouted. "You have no power over me!"

Trillian's face twisted with rage. "Ikan!" he screamed, stunned by the display of power.

He thrust his arms into the air, summoning the skies. Black clouds rolled overhead as a streak of lightning blasted from his hands, striking the cave's entrance.

Ikan acted instantly. With Blade held securely in his arms, he vanished just before the lightning hit the ridge. The impact shattered the rocks, sending a rain of stone and dust to seal the cave opening.

At the base of the mountain, Ikan reappeared with the baby in his arms, where their companions and horses awaited.

"We must return to the castle at once!" Ikan ordered. "You know what to do."

With a thought, Ikan transported them all to the gates of the castle in an instant.

Inside the sealed cave, Trillian seethed with fury.

"Seal all the entrances!" he roared. "No one must enter these caves!"

His voice lowered to a dangerous hiss. "This war has only begun."

Pacing in frustration, he muttered to himself, "I know nothing of the powers of this Litoran. Why was I not informed of Ikan's abilities?"

Trillian's eyes glimmered with malice. "Let him believe he has won — for now."

He sneered. "Let them keep the child for a while. They do not know that Ciar's spirit lives within him."

"They know nothing of the tragedy this child will bring to his family."

"Ciar's spirit will grow stronger as the boy grows among them."

He clenched his fists. "Our day will come. When I return for my son's spirit, we will shake the very foundations of this land!"

His laughter echoed through the caves. "I will win this war in the end! I will destroy the Litorans and all that is good. And my evil will reign for all eternity!"

Trillian and his followers retreated deeper into the heart of the Dracara Mountains, vanishing from sight.

At the castle gates, Eckhard climbed out of the pocket of Ikan's robe.

"Most impressive, Ikan," Eckhard said, brushing off the dust. "I apologize, sir, for disobeying your orders. I slipped into your pocket when the baby appeared in your arms."

Ikan chuckled. "Was it a comfortable ride, my friend?"

Eckhard grinned as he shifted back into his humanoid form.

"All went well, thanks to you," Ikan said. "Soon, the lands will know of these things. I'm just glad you're safe."

Eckhard clapped him on the back. "We must find a name for the incredible powers you possess, my friend."

"Thank you all once again for your help," Ikan said, turning to the others. "I must return Blade to his mother and father at once."

He bowed to Meinkard, Neckatosh, and Eckhard. "I owe you deeply, and I have a plan to repay you. I must first present my thoughts to the King, but I believe you will be pleased if he agrees."

"Call on us anytime, Ikan," Meinkard said warmly. "We stand ready."

"You didn't need us today, my friend," Eckhard added. "You alone saved the child's life."

Ikan smiled. "We are bound by our friendship. None of us should face danger alone."

With that, Ikan entered the castle, carrying the sleeping baby. "Ren and Yara must know that their son is safe," he said.

As the warriors prepared to leave, Meinkard looked back toward the castle. "He will make a great king one day," he said with admiration.

Eckhard, Neckatosh, and the rest of the warriors nodded in agreement as they turned toward their homes.

Chapter Twenty-Seven — Blade

Safe on the Smalls Farm…

Ikan threw open the castle doors and rushed up the stairs to the second floor in search of Ren.

"Blade!" Ren screamed from the doorway of his room as he saw Ikan enter the hall at the top of the stairs. "How did you find him?"

He sprinted toward Ikan and scooped his son from his arms. "You saved my son, Ikan."

"It is a long story," Ikan replied. "Take your baby to his mother and comfort her. I will go to the King and inform him that Blade is safe. Meet me in the dining room in an hour, and I will tell you everything that happened."

Ren hurried to Yara and gently placed Blade in her arms.

"Ikan saved our baby. I owe him my life, Yara. He has given us back our son," he whispered, kissing her forehead. "Keep him close to you. Keep my family safe."

He brushed her cheek softly. "I must see Neree. I need to know everything that has happened. I'll return soon. Try to rest, my wife… my son," he murmured, then disappeared into the hall and down the stairs.

Entering the room quietly, Ren listened to Ikan, who was recounting the events in the dark cave.

"Sir," Ikan began, "I apologize for disobeying your orders. But had I not used my powers, Blade would have been thrown into the black, bubbling pool of evil spirits. I had only a moment to act."

He took a deep breath. "When I heard Trillian's words — that Ciar would be reborn through the sacrifice of Blade — I knew I had to save him. I responded the only way I could overpower such evil."

Neree nodded, his expression thoughtful. "My son, your training is complete. You've proven yourself once again. You are the first true wonder of our world. It's time for us to reveal our secret to the warriors, guards, families, and friends."

He placed a hand on Ikan's shoulder. "We owe you a great debt for your bravery. You made the right choice, my son. Now we must begin training all in our land. Everyone has unique powers of their own, and they must be developed to their full potential."

Neree's voice hardened. "Trillian possesses powers of his own. We must be prepared for his return."

He paused for a moment. "Nadia and I have made a decision. We will arrange your wedding soon. After that, we'll step down as King and Queen and dedicate our time to training others."

He smiled proudly. "You've proven yourself, Ikan. You're ready to become King of our lands."

"But, sir…" Ikan started to protest.

"It is done."

Ikan bowed his head. "Thank you, sir."

Ren stepped forward, emotion welling in his eyes. "Ikan, I know not how to repay you for saving my son."

"Ren," Ikan replied warmly, "you can repay me by accepting the position of Head of the Defenders on the day I am crowned King of Litora Falls."

"I would be honored," Ren said, embracing Ikan gratefully. "Thank you, sir."

Ikan turned to Neree. "With your permission, sir, I'd like to take Ren and his family to the Smalls' Farm for safety. I'll return once they are settled. They'll find peace and rest there for a time. When we learn more about Trillian's plans, I'll bring them back."

Neree nodded. "Trillian may leave our lands, but knowing some of what we are capable of, he will understand our strength. Yara needs this time to recover after everything that's happened. Your plan is perfect. Prepare to leave at once."

Ikan turned to Ren. "Go to Yara and get ready to leave within the hour."

Just then, Kayla entered the room. "Father, may I go with them? I can help guide them through my world and ensure they feel safe. I'll return with Ikan once they're settled."

Neree smiled fondly at his daughter. "Prepare to leave, my princess. When you return, we have a wedding to plan."

Kayla grinned, giving her father a warm hug. "Thank you, Father!"

She glanced at Ikan. "I'll be ready in no time!" she said before dashing upstairs to her room.

Ikan watched her leave, struggling to hide how much her words pleased him.

"She could use the time away to recover from her experience with Ciar," Neree said, observing Ikan.

"Yes, sir," Ikan replied with a smile. "And I wouldn't mind spending time with her, either."

Neree gave him a knowing nod. "She'll be well with you, my son."

Ikan hurried to his room to prepare for the journey.

Meanwhile, Nadia leaned against Neree's shoulder. "I'm happy for Kayla. Ikan will make a wonderful husband for our daughter. And it will be a relief to let them take charge for a while. I'm looking forward to helping you with the training. Together, we'll build a world strong enough to overcome any threat."

Neree smiled warmly at her. "Have I told you how proud I am to have you as my wife?"

"Not in quite some time," Nadia teased. "But I don't mind being reminded now and then."

Just then, Kayla re-entered the room, her excitement evident.

"Mother, I'm leaving with Ikan for a few days. Ren and Yara need time away to recover from all that has happened. Yara can relax at the farm and enjoy time with her newborn without fear or stress."

Nadia embraced her daughter. "You've been through a lot in the last 24 hours, my brave girl. Some time away will do you good. And when you return, we'll plan your wedding, my beautiful blue eyes."

Kayla hugged her mother tightly. "I'll miss you, Mother."

She turned to Neree. "And I'll miss you too, Father," she whispered, giving him one last squeeze. "But I'll be in good hands."

At that moment, Ren and Yara entered the room with baby Blade.

"We're ready," Ren said. "Thank you for giving us this time away."

Nadia embraced them warmly. "Enjoy your time together as a family," she said.

Neree placed a hand on Ikan's shoulder. "Take care of my princess," he instructed.

"Not to worry, sir," Ikan replied.

With a wave of his hand, Ikan transported them all to the Tunnel of Litora Falls.

Chapter Twenty-Eight — The Hidden Scrolls

Nalana proudly welcomed them at the opening.

"Nalana, I am so happy to see you again," Kayla said.

"The pleasure is mine," Nalana replied warmly. "I heard of your troubles. I am so pleased your baby is safe. Ikan, you should be proud. It is good to see you finally embrace your powers and recognize the greatness of your abilities. Have a restful visit to the farm, my friends," she added as they walked through the tunnel to the edge of the Smalls' Farm.

"Amazing," Ren said, admiring the view of the backyard and Kayla's home.

"Beautiful," Yara whispered. "You will be safe here, my son," she murmured as she held Blade tightly in her arms.

"Make yourselves at home. Let's all relax for a bit before I show you around the house and the property," Kayla said, leading them into the living room.

Yara looked around, overwhelmed by the modern surroundings. She stood still for a moment, taking it all in. Like Ciara, she had never been outside of Litora Falls, and everything felt new and unfamiliar.

"I am not feeling well," she sighed softly.

"Is there a place where she could rest?" Ren asked.

"I'll show you to your room," Kayla said. "It might be best if you stay in the downstairs bedroom. Climbing the stairs could be hard for Yara for the next few days."

Kayla led them down the hall, past the kitchen, to a bedroom at the end of the corridor. She quickly explained a few things about the electrical appliances in the room and the adjoining bathroom before leaving them to rest.

"Ikan, thank you for bringing us here," Ren said with a grateful nod.

"Relax and enjoy this peaceful farm with your family. You're safe here, Ren. If you need anything, we'll be around the house. Just call, and we'll hear you. Have a good rest," Ikan replied before heading back to the living room to join Kayla.

They sat together on the couch in front of the fireplace, discussing their wedding plans and future.

"Ikan, I have an idea," Kayla said, her eyes twinkling. "Let's go shopping while we're here."

"Shopping?" Ikan asked, raising an eyebrow.

"I need a wedding dress," she said as she cuddled closer to him.

"Your mother would love to help you pick out your dress," Ikan noted.

"You don't want to go with me?" she asked, a little concerned.

"I'd love to, but what about Nadia? I heard her say how much she missed out on with you and how she wants to make up for it. She told your father how excited she was to bring you here and help you pick out a dress right after we announced our plans to marry. I wouldn't want to take that away from her."

Ikan's voice softened. "Since I've known her, she's carried sadness for you. This would mean a lot to her."

Kayla sighed, realizing the truth in his words. "You're right. I'll ask her to come with us. What about my father?"

"She could come just for the day. The stores stay open late," Kayla said. "She could have Baldasarre, the healer from Varanus, check on him. Ciara and Sarah can look after him while she's away. He'll understand — it's only for today."

Kayla smiled hopefully. "Please, Ikan. It's the perfect time. Let's at least give her the choice to come. I wouldn't want to leave her out after everything you told me."

Ikan nodded. "I'll go for her. I'll be back soon."

Kayla hugged him softly before he vanished from her sight.

"I really need to get used to this," she thought with a small smile.

She walked to the desk on the far side of the room, searching for paper and a pen to make a list of things needed for the wedding.

"There must be some paper here somewhere," she muttered as she opened a cabinet door in the bottom right corner. She pulled out stacks of papers and books but found nothing useful.

"What a mess," she sighed, sitting on the floor to organize the papers before putting them back.

As she rearranged the clutter, she noticed an oddly shaped drawer at the back of the cabinet. It seemed locked, but with some effort, she pried it open and pulled it onto the floor.

"Wow!" she whispered as she rummaged through the old papers and scrolls inside. "This is amazing."

The drawer contained ancient maps and diagrams of her property, the town of Eureka Springs, the healing waters and springs, and the lands of Amphibia. At the bottom were several old documents.

As she carefully unfolded them, Kayla realized she had found floor plans of the castle, the Litoran family tree, and three ancient scrolls.

The first scroll she unrolled was titled *The Destiny of the Litorans: The Tunnel of Litora Falls*. It was too long and complex to read immediately, so she skimmed through it, making a mental note to study it later.

Carefully placing everything back in the drawer, she organized the shelves to hide the opening and ensure nothing looked disturbed.

"I'll take the papers and scroll back to Litora Falls when I return," she thought. "I'll ask Sarah to help me study them."

Satisfied with her plan, Kayla went upstairs to shower and change for the shopping trip.

When she came back downstairs, she heard voices in the kitchen.

"Mother, you came!" Kayla exclaimed happily.

"Thank you, Ikan," Nadia said warmly. "I wouldn't miss this shopping trip for anything."

"I know it's a bit late in the morning, but breakfast is ready," she added cheerfully.

"We should eat before we leave," Ikan suggested.

"Good morning, Yara. I hope you're feeling better," Kayla said as Ren and Yara entered the room.

"I feel much better, thank you," Yara replied, settling into a small rocker in the corner. "I must thank you, Ikan, for saving my son and bringing us to this wonderful place."

Ren noticed Nadia and bowed slightly. "My Queen, I didn't realize you were here. How is the King?"

"He'll be fine. He just needs a few weeks of rest," Nadia answered. "Thank you for asking, Ren. I'll be going on a shopping trip with my daughter to find her wedding dress. I'll return in the morning."

"Ah yes, the royal wedding," Ren said, shaking Ikan's hand in approval.

Ikan smiled. "Ren, it would mean a lot if you would be my best man."

"Best man?" Ren asked, puzzled.

"A best man is a close friend who stands beside the groom during the wedding ceremony," Ikan explained. "Kayla told me how she wants the wedding to be, and I must choose a best man. It would be an honor if it were you."

Ren smiled warmly. "Thank you, my friend. I'd be proud."

"It's settled, then," Ikan said as they all sat down to enjoy breakfast.

After they finished, Kayla and Nadia cleaned the kitchen and prepared for their trip.

"Ren, make yourself at home and enjoy this time with your family. We should be back before nightfall," Kayla said as she and Nadia left for the city.

Chapter Twenty-Nine —
Shopping Trip

After spending most of the morning at the bridal shop, Kayla had found the perfect dress — a simple white gown with a lifted collar and slightly flared sleeves. A rhinestone-covered ribbon at the waist enhanced the beauty of the smooth, flared skirt. The veil, made of soft, sheer material that flowed down her back, was attached to a simple rhinestone and leaf crown — perfect for a Litoran Princess.

Luckily, the dress fit Kayla perfectly.

"Mother, I would like to scatter a few tiny rhinestones along the trim just to pretty it up a bit. I want it simple but a little more elegant."

"I only plan on getting married once. I want it to be special."

Ikan smiled at Kayla's words just as the bridal clerk interrupted.

"We would be able to add rhinestones, ma'am. It's a slow day. I could have it ready by five o'clock."

"Perfect," Kayla said. "I'll take it. Thank you."

While Nadia browsed the shop, picking out dresses for herself and one for Sarah, Kayla sketched how she imagined her dress with the added rhinestones.

"Nadia, this gives you much pleasure, doesn't it?" Ikan asked.

"Oh, Ikan, you have no idea," Nadia replied with a smile.

"It's only two o'clock, Kayla. It's a long time to wait. We could come back for the dress this evening if you'd like," Nadia suggested.

"Mother, if you don't want to wait, you can take the car home. That is if you remember how to drive," Kayla teased with a laugh.

"There's a good movie showing at the theater. I'd like to take Ikan to see it if he's interested. I've read the book, and it was excellent. I'm not sure how the movie compares, but I think it'll be exciting. Ikan has never seen a movie theater, much less a movie, so this could be a fun experience. We'll be home in time for dinner."

"Perfect idea," Nadia said. "Enjoy yourselves. And, of course, I remember how to drive," she added with a giggle.

At the ticket window of the theater, Kayla stopped and turned to Ikan.

"Before we go inside, I want to explain something to you," she said. "A movie is based on a book or someone's imagination. It's just a story — someone's thoughts on how events could unfold. None of it is real. It's made only for entertainment. Do you understand, Ikan?"

"Kayla, your mother taught me many things over the years — about books, television, and movies. I understand how these things work. Now that I've met you and we're planning to marry, it all makes sense. This is how it was meant to be. Don't worry… I get it. Now, about that movie... I'd love to see it."

During the film, Ikan sat on the edge of his seat, completely captivated. His face was filled with excitement.

"That was the most amazing thing I've ever seen," he exclaimed as they left the theater and crossed the street to a coffee shop near the bridal shop.

"So, I take it you liked the movie?" Kayla asked, amused.

"Kayla, I loved it! It was an incredible story. I'd like to know how they make movies. How do they create something like that?"

"Maybe someday we can visit my world and tour a movie studio. You could see how it's all done. I'll see what I can arrange, Ikan."

Ikan grinned. "And maybe, someday, someone will make a movie about our life — our world."

"That would make a good movie, wouldn't it?" Kayla said with a serious look.

"It's almost four-thirty," Kayla noted. "The dress might be ready early. We should head back soon — Mother will have dinner ready."

"Kayla, I'm so glad she came with us."

"Me too, Ikan. I can't wait for our wedding," she said as they returned to the farm.

After dinner, Kayla smiled and said, "Mother, I'll show you my dress. It's so beautiful."

"She made me wait outside the shop when we picked it up," Ikan complained playfully. "She said I have to wait until the wedding to see the finished version."

"Ikan, it's bad luck for the groom to see the wedding dress before the wedding," Nadia reminded him with a grin.

Nadia then turned to Kayla, her voice soft. "Thank you for including me in everything, Kayla."

Kayla reached for her mother's hand. "Mother, I want you to be part of everything in my life from now on."

A little while later, Ikan asked, "Kayla, may I speak with you for a moment? Would you take a walk with me before we retire for the night?"

Kayla nodded, and they stepped out into the backyard.

"I spent the afternoon showing Ren how things work in a modern home and on the farm," Ikan said as they walked. "They'll stay here for a while and enjoy their time with their son."

"We'll return to Litora Falls early in the morning," Nadia had mentioned earlier.

"Yes, ma'am," Ikan had replied courteously.

Now, in the quiet of the evening, Ikan took Kayla's hand. "Kayla, there are some things your father spoke of this morning before we came here. I need to share them with you."

"After our wedding, your mother and father are going to crown us King and Queen of Litora Falls and all of Amphibia."

"So soon? They are young. Why?" Kayla asked.

"They plan to run the training school. They want to develop the powers of all the Litorans to their fullest. It's a good thing, Kayla. It's time. We've suppressed our great powers long enough."

"Yes, it is time," Kayla said, though a bit confused. "It's just so sudden. I don't know enough. I don't know if I'm ready to be Queen. What if I don't do a good job?"

"Kayla, you will be a wonderful Queen. You just need to relax," Ikan assured her. "There's something else. I'd like to change how things are run a little. I plan to talk with your father as soon as we return home. But I want your opinion first."

"What, Ikan?" Kayla asked, uncertain if she wanted to hear his answer.

"I would like Sir Eckhard and Sir Meinkard to share the responsibility of the King. They could be Kings of their own lands, with full control. We could keep the council as it is. They've earned the right to this honor, and it would make them feel more valued. The Litoran King would still hold full control over Litora Falls and lead the council, but Sir Eckhard, Sir Meinkard, and King Neckatosh would stand by his side."

"That's a wonderful idea, Ikan. Talk to my father — he'll understand. They've done so much for him, and I'm sure he'll agree," Kayla said warmly.

"Thank you, Kayla, for agreeing with me."

They sat together on the glider swing on the back porch, gazing at the stars and making plans for their wedding, unaware that I knew everything they discussed.

Before they realized it, they had drifted off, peacefully falling asleep in the cool night air.

At the crack of dawn, Nadia's voice broke the quiet. "Wake up, you two! We must leave for home."

Ikan gave Kayla a gentle shake. "Wake up, sleepyhead," he whispered with a smile.

"Good morning, Mother. I'm so sorry — we must have fallen asleep," Kayla said groggily.

Ikan and Kayla quickly showered and dressed, preparing for the journey home.

Just as they were about to leave, Kayla remembered the maps and papers she had discovered in the hidden drawer.

"I can't leave this information behind," she thought, slipping the documents into her bag.

In a blink, they were back home.

"I'm going to check in with the guards," Ikan said. "I'll return soon."

"Mother, I'll go with you to check on Father. I hope he's feeling better this morning," Kayla said as they walked through the entrance hall and into the visiting room.

They arrived just in time to see me standing, moving about the room.

"Father!" Kayla exclaimed sternly. "You're supposed to be resting!"

Nadia shook her head. "Obviously, your father didn't expect us to return so early. I can't leave you for one day! Here you are, up and about the house. You know you're supposed to be taking it easy. What am I going to do with you?" she said, guiding me back to bed.

"Stay by my side and take care of me," I replied with a grin.

"Has there been any news of Trillian, Father?" Kayla asked.

"No, my daughter. It's as if he and all his followers have vanished."

Ikan entered the room, his expression serious. "I believe Trillian sealed himself and the remaining Draconians in the deep cave of evil spirits. But I also believe he'll reappear when we least expect it, sir. He has a plan — be certain of that. He won't forget what he saw of me on the edge of that cliff."

"Trillian will seek revenge, especially against me. I feel it with every part of me, my King."

"We must be prepared," I said. "The training classes must begin. But first, we have a wedding to plan — and a new King and Queen to crown."

Elliott, who had been standing quietly, finally spoke. "Grandfather, there's something strange about Blade. I've always felt it. Maybe it wasn't a good idea to send him to the Small's farm. What if the evil spirit was inside him when he was there?"

I interrupted gently. "I know, Elliott. I've thought about that many times since then. Time will tell, my child... Time will tell."

Chapter Thirty — Wedding Plans

"I can't wait to show Sarah her dress," Kayla said excitedly as she rushed up the stairs to Sarah's room.

"You're back!" Sarah exclaimed, jumping up from the edge of the bed. "I missed you, Kayla," she whispered, hugging her tightly.

"I brought you something, Sarah. I hope it fits. I hope you like it."

"It must be my dress for your wedding," Sarah said, recognizing the bag from the bridal store in the city.

She quickly pulled the dress from the bag and held it up in front of her, glancing at herself in the mirror.

"It's perfect. It's so… pretty, Kayla! I love it. It's the perfect size — I'm sure it will fit just fine."

Spinning in a circle, her light blue dress flowed around her like her long hair in a soft spring breeze. "Simple yet elegant — exactly the kind of dress I imagined you picking out," she said, pleased. "So, have you set a date?"

"We haven't told my parents yet, but we're hoping to have everything ready by this Sunday."

"In four days?" Sarah asked with concern.

"I know… it's short notice. Do you think we can pull it all together in four days, Sarah?"

"We can do anything," Sarah replied confidently. "We'll spend the rest of today and the evening together, making plans. We'll just stay up until it's done. We've always been the best at rushing deadlines."

"You're right," Kayla said with a laugh. "This is what we do best. We'll sketch everything out today. There's plenty of staff to help pull it together quickly."

Sarah paused, giving Kayla a curious look.

"What?" Kayla asked.

"Do you ever miss home, Kayla?"

Kayla thought for a moment. "Sometimes I miss the modern world, but I'd rather have my mother and father. Most of all, I'd rather have Ikan — more than anything I left behind. Besides, we can visit anytime we want."

"Yeah, you're right. Nothing I left behind could replace Silas. I have my own family now — and I have you, my dear friend."

Sarah studied Kayla's expression. "What's that look for? Did I say something wrong?"

Kayla hesitated, then spoke slowly. "I found something, Sarah. Something important… I need your help to research it. I want to show you, but… there's no time. It'll have to wait — until after the wedding."

"Kayla! You can't leave me hanging like that! If it's serious, you won't enjoy your wedding day with it on your mind. You'll drive me crazy if I don't know what's going on."

She crossed her arms. "Spill it. Now."

Reluctantly, Kayla opened her bag and pulled out the papers, maps, and three scrolls.

"I found these in a hidden drawer at the farm just before we left," she said. "I'm not sure what they are. Read the inscriptions on the scrolls."

Sarah carefully examined the scrolls. "The Destiny of the Litorans, Scroll One: *The Tunnel of Litora Falls.*

Scroll Two: *The Evil Returns.*

Scroll Three: *The New World.*"

She looked at Kayla in amazement. "Wow, Kayla… these are old. It's like a trilogy of the destiny of these lands and your father's kingdom."

"The future of this world could be written in these scrolls," Kayla said, her voice low.

"I don't know if we should even read these," Sarah whispered.

"This is my world, Sarah. Neree and Nadia are my parents. I need to know everything I can about this land — about the place my father's people call home. These scrolls could hold the answers to questions I've had all my life. I need your help."

"Please, Sarah. We have to keep this between us."

Sarah hesitated. "I have a bad feeling about this, Kayla. But I'll help you. Let's finish the wedding plans first and show them to your mother. After that, we can spend the rest of the week going through these papers. Then we'll decide if anyone else needs to know."

"Thank you, Sarah. I love you like a sister."

Kayla smiled and went downstairs to invite her mother to join them in their planning session.

After a pleasant lunch, Nadia joined Kayla and Sarah in Kayla's room with many ideas of her own, all of which delighted Kayla. Together, they spent the afternoon discussing flowers, decorations, food, and the wedding cake.

"I want you to have the most beautiful wedding ever," Nadia said warmly.

"Mother, I understand this is a big deal for everyone here, but I want it to be simple. It can still be elegant — but not overdone. I don't like a lot of fuss or stress. I want something nice but easygoing — just like my dress."

"I understand, Kayla," Nadia said kindly. "You seem stressed, though. Is something bothering you?"

Kayla looked down. "It's been an overwhelming few months, Mother. My entire life changed in an instant."

Nadia reached over and gently touched Kayla's hand. "Let me plan the wedding for you. I think I know exactly what you'd like. I have some wonderful ideas."

Kayla looked at Sarah, who gave her a slight nod of approval.

Kayla scooted closer to her mother and snuggled against her. "I've only known you for a short time, but you already know me so well," she whispered.

With tears in her eyes, she softly added, "I'd be honored for you to plan the wedding your way. I trust you. I know I'll love whatever you decide."

Nadia hugged her tightly. "Oh, Kayla, you won't regret this. I promise your wedding will be perfect. Everything will be ready by Sunday afternoon."

Kayla smiled, enjoying the excitement on her mother's face.

"I'll tell Ikan and Silas to give you and Sarah some time alone. Relax and enjoy the rest of the day — and evening."

Nadia rose to her feet with a bright smile. "I have a wedding to plan!" she declared, rushing off to begin her preparations.

Chapter Thirty-One — Kayla, Sarah, And The Scrolls

"I have the most wonderful parents. I wish I could have spent my life with them," Kayla whispered as she locked the door to her room.

"You've just made your mother the happiest woman alive, Kayla."

"Yes, I did. It's good," Kayla replied, spreading the maps, papers, and scrolls across the floor to begin their research.

"There is so much information here. Where should we begin?" Sarah asked.

"We could start by you letting me in on your secret."

"Secret? I don't know what you mean."

"Sure!" Kayla smiled. "I'll let it go for now, but when you're ready, I'm here to listen."

"I will go over the scrolls while you go through the papers and maps," Kayla said. "Once we finish, we'll try to figure out what it all means."

Kayla carefully unrolled Scroll One and slowly began reading: "King Neree traveled through the tunnel to the deep green stone. On the way home, Neree told his daughter he was her… the evil Trillian… the destiny of Ciar… the evil spirit… Ren's son… Talisha's black pad… the bubbling black pool of evil spirits… the royal wedding… the evil Ciar's destruction through his evil spirit in the soul of the Litoran child… What?"

Kayla suddenly stood, shaking, with a look of concern in her eyes that Sarah had never seen before.

"Sarah, this is so frightening. Every word that I have read is everything that has happened to me and to Litora Falls since I opened the little box on my birthday that changed our lives forever. I don't know if I want to know what is in these scrolls. They must hold the information of everything in the past and future of this world. I don't know if we should know these things, Sarah. I don't know if I want to know."

"How could anyone from the past have written the future like this? These are very old, yet everything I have lived in these past few months is reflected in what I just read."

Suddenly, a flash of bright light appeared in the window of Kayla's bedroom.

"It's Nalana!" Kayla shouted as she opened the window to let Nalana enter.

As Nalana flew through the window, she formed into a large cloud of light. Before their eyes, the tiny fairy, Nalana, suddenly became a beautiful four-foot-nine-inch young woman with golden-brown hair and sparkling blue eyes. She wore a glowing white gown with soft, white wings covered in sparkling diamond chips.

Her breathtaking beauty left Kayla and Sarah speechless for a few moments, uncertain of what had just taken place.

"It is I," Nalana said softly as she sat on the floor in front of the papers and scrolls.

"Nalana, you are so beautiful," Kayla said. "I must admit, I am a little overwhelmed. I didn't know you could transform your appearance in this way."

"I've only done this on one other occasion," Nalana replied. "On the day these scrolls were written, my mother was chosen to protect them. She was in the same human form and size as I am before you now. She placed the maps, papers, and the three scrolls in a bag and was preparing to transform back into a tiny fairy. Her plan was to fly through the Tunnel of Litora Falls and hide the bag somewhere on the Small's Farm. I was watching from the dark end of the hills when two evil men in black cloaks appeared in front of her — out of nowhere. The older one threw his hands up and mumbled some odd words. It was all too sudden for her to realize what was happening. A sharp streak of bright smoke and light struck her, and she vanished in an instant — like air forming a thick cloud. It was impossible for me to see exactly what had taken place. All I knew was that my mother had been destroyed and was gone from me forever."

Nalana paused and continued, "I transformed instantly, grabbed her bag from the table, and vanished before the air cleared — before these evil beings realized what had happened to the scrolls. I knew they must be very important if my mother was willing to risk her life to protect them. I flew through the tunnel quickly. They never saw me — never knew what happened to the bag. I created the secret drawer, hid the items deep inside, and locked them away safely. They have been there… all this time…"

"Until I found them," Kayla interrupted. "I was wrong for taking them, wasn't I?"

"I am sorry about your mother and for taking the papers from the drawer, Nalana. I didn't know."

"I am also sorry, but I must take them with me. I am not sure how much you have read, but I cannot let you read anymore — especially in the presence of someone who is not of our world. No one should know what is going to take place in his or her future. It is very dangerous for all that you have spread here before you to be in Litora Falls once again. Many years ago, when I placed these things in the secret drawer of the desk where you found them, I knew I must never let them get into the hands of Trillian."

"You see, Kayla…" She took a deep breath and paused briefly. "…it was Trillian who killed my mother. He must never get his hands on these scrolls and maps. They are no longer safe in your home. I must find a new hiding place for them at once."

"But, Nalana, these scrolls and maps can help me understand everything about who I am — what I am to become — the future of these lands and all of my people," Kayla said, sobbing. "You have to let me read them. You just have to. Please don't do this; don't take them away. Let us read them first. Sarah is one of us now. She became one of us the day she gave up her life in our world and came here to make a life with Silas. She is my best friend. You can trust her, too. Everything we learn from this, we will keep to ourselves. We promise."

"Please, Nalana, I beg you. Just give us tonight. Please!"

"We will never repeat a word of what we read here — not a word!"

Nalana sat in silence, looking at Kayla and Sarah.

Kayla and Sarah sat quietly across from her, nervously awaiting her reply. The time passed slowly as they waited patiently, trying to appear as though they were much calmer than they truly were.

After the longest wait of their lives, Nalana stood up, gave a little shake of her beautiful hair, and softly spoke, "I will make a deal with both of you."

"Anything," Kayla said with hope.

"You must go to dinner with your family. They will be coming for you soon. Give Ikan and Silas some excuse for both of you to spend the night discussing plans. Anything… Just be sure they do not interrupt your research. I will wait here for your return… here in your room, protecting the papers."

"You must agree for me to stay and go through the information with you. I can explain anything you do not understand. I must be sure you understand certain things thoroughly if I am going to let you do this."

"You must promise you will reveal to NO ONE anything we discuss in this room on this night. You are going to learn things you should not know. Most importantly, you must not interfere with the destiny of this world. It does not matter what you learn about the future. You must promise me these things. There could be serious consequences beyond your imagination if you interfere with the happenings written in these scrolls."

"I promise," Sarah said.

"I promise, too," Kayla said. "I don't know how to thank you, Nalana."

"Are you two coming to dinner?" Ikan interrupted, banging on the door of Kayla's room.

"What are you two up to in there?"

"Coming!" Kayla yelled. "We will be there in a few minutes, Ikan."

"You will be here when we return… right?" Kayla said.

"Enjoy your dinner, Kayla. I will be here. You have my word," Nalana replied.

"Come in here, you two!" Nadia yelled from the front sitting room as they reached the bottom of the stairway.

On the long table against the far wall, Nadia had spread out all the plans for the wedding.

"Look them over and tell me what you think, Kayla. If there is anything you want changed, just let me know."

Kayla quickly looked over the sketches and plans her mother had made.

"This is perfect. It is exactly what I wanted. How did you know, Mother?"

"You're my daughter, Kayla. Through my mother, I watched you grow. I learned about the kind of person you are and the things you like and dislike. I have always known you from a distance. You just didn't know me. Someday, I will make it up to you, I promise."

"Mother, I love you. I am so glad I have you now. The past is gone. We can't bring it back. What we can do is make the future brighter," Kayla said as she held her tightly in her arms.

"Now, we must go to dinner before Ikan or Silas break down your door looking for us," Kayla said.

"You did good, Mom," she whispered with a sweet smile of approval.

Nadia's heart filled with joy, knowing how pleased Kayla was with the plans she had made for her wedding. Finally, she had a chance to be a mother to her beautiful daughter. Her time had come.

All through dinner, Ikan and Silas spoke of plans for an early morning journey to visit Sir Meinkard and Sir Eckhard, with personal invitations to the wedding and discussions about training classes for their warriors.

"This is perfect, Sarah. They are going to want to retire early. Let's interrupt and tell them of our plans."

"Silas, excuse me for interrupting, but if you two don't mind, Kayla and I would like to get together after dinner in her room for a few hours, perhaps most of the night. We only have four days until the wedding, and there are so many things to discuss and finalize."

"You girls have fun. You have not spent much time together since we returned home. So much has taken place. You need to spend this time together," Silas said.

"We will stop by your room and let you know when we leave, probably at the first sign of light," Ikan added.

"You two are so special. Thanks for being so understanding, Ikan," Kayla said, giving him a big hug and kiss goodnight.

They rushed up the stairs quickly, hoping Nalana was still there waiting.

"You're still here!" Kayla said with excitement as they entered the room.

"Of course, I am still here; I gave you my word, Kayla."

Kayla nodded and smiled in approval as she and Sarah quickly sat on the floor to continue their research.

Nalana sat quietly for hours, amazed at the intense way they approached the situation.

Suddenly, there was a knock on the door. Kayla quickly hopped up to see who was disturbing them.

"Who is it?" she asked.

"It is I," Ikan said. "Silas and I stopped to tell you we are leaving now. We brought you some coffee."

Sarah ran to the door as Kayla opened it. They slipped out into the hall, closing it quickly behind them.

"We have something you can't see before the wedding," Sarah said with a smile.

"It's not yet daylight," Kayla said. "Why are you leaving so early?"

"Silas could not sleep and would not let me sleep. We decided to get an early start."

"I could not sleep without you by my side, Sarah," he said as he held her tightly in his arms.

"I hope you feel that way after we are married," Kayla said.

"You know I will," Ikan said with a hug as they left for the day.

"Sorry for the interruption, Nalana," Kayla said as she locked the door.

They poured themselves a cup of coffee and continued their research once again.

Light from the skies filled the land as the sun rose over the trees just outside the window of Kayla's bedroom. She finished reading the last words of the third scroll.

"Nalana, am I missing something? Is the end not written within these scrolls or papers somewhere? Will everything I have read here tonight come to pass? Is this real? Is this actually what is going to take place over the years to come?"

It reads of a child among us. It doesn't reveal his name. It reads that Ciar's spirit lives within him, and the tragedies he will cause are not of his own doing but of the spirit of Ciar inside his soul. It reads of a Queen from another world and a King, the most powerful wizard and greatest leader of our lands. It reads they have twins, a boy and a girl. Is this Ikan and myself?

It reads of many in our lands and the powers they develop over the years of the three scrolls. It reads of a friend of the Queen from her world — coming here and marrying a castle guard of high standing. AND... It reads they have two sons, a year or more apart. The oldest of which saves and marries the twin princess. Is this Sarah and Silas?

If these words are true, there will be many wars with the evil ones, many deaths, and many good times. "It reads of great destruction and rebuilding of Litora Falls!"

These scrolls read many things; however, they do not reveal how it all ends. Will all of this come to pass? Will Trillian take over these lands with his evil, or will we be strong enough to overpower him and live as we are… "A Peaceful World of Good?"

"Kayla, come over here," Sarah said. "Look at this."

Sarah had made her own sketches of the map drawings of the Small's farm and the surrounding woods just outside the edges of Eureka Springs. She also sketched a map of Litora Falls and all of the Amphibia lands, including the Dracara Mountains. She cut out the sketch of the lands of Amphibia, laid it on top of the map of the hundreds of acres owned by the Smalls, and turned it slowly, clockwise, several times. "Watch this," she said with a final turn.

Kayla took a loud, deep breath as her eyes shot up to meet Nalana's. "What does this mean?" she demanded.

"You are very clever, Sarah," Nalana said. "I had no idea how intelligent you both are. I will explain this to you as best I can. First, I must be certain you will honor your promise to me — after all you have read."

"We will, I promise," Kayla said. "You can trust us. At least we have each other to confide in. I just need to know, Nalana. You can't leave us confused like this. You said you were here to help us understand things correctly. So… help us, please.”

“These scrolls were written by an old and powerful man of the lands at the beginning of this world. He vanished before finishing the final scroll. As you have read, he was at the very end. My mother knew him well. I only know what I heard him reveal to her. Just before he vanished, he told her that if anything happened to him, she must take the scrolls and hide them beyond these lands. From what I remember, he was unsure of the outcome of the final war between the evil beings and the good beings of our world. His prediction was that if evil takes over these lands — as we know them — they will be destroyed forever. The lands will be covered with black clouds of evil spirits, and the beings of good deeds will be destroyed forever.”

“If we develop our powers and strengths to our fullest potential and pull together all the powers we have as one… If we can overpower this evil and destroy all that follow evil ways, our world — as we know it — and your world will come together… One world… In One time…”

“Let me explain more about these two worlds of yours, Kayla.”

“I think I know exactly what you are going to say,” Sarah interrupted. “My world and this world are the same — in a different time in life — perhaps even millions of years in the past. If I understand these maps correctly, Kayla’s farm and Litora Falls are in the same place, separated only by time. That explains why all of Amphibia is so small. The Tunnel of Litora Falls allows us to venture between these times. Am I correct?”

"Once again, I am amazed by your intelligence," Nalana replied. "So, you are saying if we can destroy Trillian and all of his followers, these two worlds will come together in one time, and we can all live in peace?"

"I am not saying anything. I do not know for sure. I only have my opinion, as you have yours!"

"I just remembered… Mother and I were sitting on my porch swing at the farm. She said something about my father's world being in the past of mine. So much has happened since I met them. I haven't thought of it again." She said I wasn't leaving my world — I was leaving my time in my world — something like that. "She was right, wasn't she?"

"Kayla, you will learn many things as time passes. It is very important that you, and all among you, develop every power you have to your fullest potential. The children must be trained at a very young age. You have learned many things that will come to be. Remember that you must not interfere with this destiny. Put all of your thoughts into developing your powers. Use every ounce of strength you have within you. You and Ikan will be the most powerful leaders for all times to come. Use your gifts wisely, and you will win this war. I must return to the tunnel and find a safe hiding place for this bag. If you ever need me, just think of me, and I will appear to you," she said as she flew away.

"We must keep all we have learned here to ourselves, Sarah."

"I know. I wish I was from this time. I wish I were one of you," Sarah said. "I have something to tell you, Kayla. I think I am going to have a baby."

"Sarah, that's wonderful! Finally! I had a feeling."

“Have you told Silas?”

“When he returns, I hope he is pleased!”

“Kayla, from what I heard you say to Nalana — I will have a son, and he will save and marry your daughter — in a year or two, I will have another son. You will have twins on the same day.”

“Amazing,” Kayla said as she put her arms around Sarah. “We will win this war in the end, I promise you,” she whispered.

“I know where they are, grandfather. The scrolls… I have seen them. Mother showed them to me the last time we visited the Small’s Farm. She told me that if anything happened to her, she wanted me to take care of them for her,” Elliott explained.

“You must tell no one! Keep their location to yourself until the time comes when there is a need for them,” I demanded.

“I will, grandfather; I promise.”

Chapter Thirty-Two — Taran And Black Prince

For the next two days, Kayla managed to put the scrolls out of her mind. She spent most of her time in the training room with Ikan. They were secretly developing her many amazing powers. She quickly became very confident and comfortable with her new life.

On the afternoon before the wedding, she and Ikan took a break from the intense session they had just completed. They sat on the floor in the training room, discussing her accomplishments.

"Your father will be very pleased with all you have accomplished in these past two days," Ikan said, proud of his Princess. "He will be amazed at all that you are capable of doing. We will surprise him when the time is right," he added.

"I never dreamed I would have so many magical abilities and powers, Ikan. I thought, as a man, you would naturally be more powerful than I."

"I have come to realize over the past few days that you will be much more powerful than I am once your training is complete, Kayla. After all, it is written, you will be the most powerful Litoran of all time. Considering the progress of your training, I know well that this is how it was meant to be. We have only begun, Kayla. I am certain we are in for many surprises as we proceed with your training."

"Wow!" she said. "I love it!"

Suddenly, there was a loud muffling of voices and sounds of horses shuffling about the grounds outside the walls of the castle.

"Something has happened," Kayla said. They rushed out the door of the training room. The sounds led them to the stables.

Several guards were gathered around Taran. Taran was a young, stable boy who had been found outside the gates of the castle by Dubkan as an infant sixteen years ago. He was alone, frightened, and hungry. It was never known from where he came. He was taken in and trained to care for the horses by Lin.

It became obvious, at a very young age, that he had a natural talent for the care of animals. By the age of only fourteen, he had become an expert at caring for and training horses. He was honored with the gift of a new colt, Black Prince, for his loyalty and dedication. By the age of fifteen, Lin had appointed him to the position of head trainer of all horses in the royal kingdom.

"What has happened?" Ikan asked.

Lin's son River turned to Ikan as Kayla knelt beside Taran to comfort him.

"I saw, sir. It was the strangest thing. Taran was brushing him," River said, pointing to Black Prince, the tall black horse tied with ropes and held by two stable hands against the fence. "Suddenly, he raised his front legs high — forced Taran to the ground, sir — we could not stop him. Black Prince stomped him many times before we could tie the ropes and pull him away. It was strange… Black Prince loves Taran — he raised him from a colt — it makes no sense, sir."

Looking up with a sigh, Ikan caught a glimpse of Ren walking away from the stables toward the castle.

"River, when did Ren arrive?"

"Only moments before the accident, sir. He and Yara walked up to the stables with their new baby just before Black Prince rose up against Taran, sir."

"Thank you, River. Secure the horse in the stable and inform me of Taran's progress as the evening passes. Black Prince is his property. He alone must decide what should be done."

"I will do as you ask, sir. Taran is hurt, but he will heal. I am sure he will be fine in no time."

"Thank you for helping him," Ikan said as he and Kayla headed for the castle to find Ren and Yara.

"I will check upstairs," Ikan said.

"I am going to check on Father," Kayla said as she slipped into the door of the Royal sleeping room.

"Father, you look wonderful," she said as she walked across the room to his chair. "You are up and dressed. You must be feeling better."

"I am good. Tomorrow is the big day. I must prepare to give my daughter away," he said as a tear rolled down his face.

"Father," Kayla said with a loving hug, "I love you so much. You are not giving me away... You are letting me be married."

"You love Ikan! I know you do!"

"You are not losing me as a daughter; you are gaining the son you already love. Who knows…? Maybe you will have grandchildren someday."

"Now, that will be a great day indeed," he said as he held his daughter tightly in his arms. "Were you told of the accident with Taran and Black Prince?"

"Yes, I do not understand what could have come over Black Prince. It does not make sense that he would turn on Taran in that way. He has always been a calm horse, especially with Taran."

"Ikan is trying to find out what could have happened. We will let you know what he finds out. You get some rest. Don't worry! Ikan will take care of everything while you are ill. Tomorrow is a big day, and you haven't fully recovered yourself."

Ikan entered Ren and Yara's room to find the baby in his cradle. He quietly stepped close enough to look inside the tiny cradle. As his eyes reached Blade's, a chill swept through his body. Their eyes connected for several seconds, giving Ikan a strong feeling of the presence of evil.

"Handsome… do you not agree?" Ren said, breaking the eerie presence surrounding Ikan and Blade.

"Very handsome, just like his father," Ikan said. "When did you arrive?"

"Just before the accident near the stables," Ren replied. "It was so odd… the strangest thing…"

"What happened, Ren? Did you see?"

"I was talking with Dubkan about the wedding. I am afraid my back was turned. I heard the noise. By the time I turned around, Taran was on the ground. The stable hands were pulling the horse away. It happened so quickly."

"Where was Yara? Did she see?"

"She was showing off our little one to Taran. He was brushing Black Prince. She ran to the side when the commotion began. It was very odd. I do not understand what could have come over that horse," Ren said.

"Nor do I," Ikan agreed.

"Get some rest and take care of Blade. I will see you at the wedding," Ikan said.

He glanced into the cradle for a quick look at Blade as he left the loft. He had a very strong feeling that there was something odd going on with Blade.

"Kayla, I need to speak with you," he said. "I will walk you to your room."

"O.K.," she said, "but this is the last time you can see me before the wedding."

"Agreed," he replied. "This must stay between the two of us," he insisted.

"I have the strangest feeling when I am near Blade. There is something very odd about it. I hate to say this, but I feel the presence of evil when I look into his eyes."

"Ikan, how can you say something like that about Ren's son? He would be very hurt to hear you speak of his son in this way."

"I know, but the feeling is so strong… since the day of his birth, Kayla. I cannot explain it."

Suddenly, Kayla remembered reading in the scrolls about Ciar's evil spirit living in the soul of a young Litoran.

"Oh my… no," she said before she could stop herself.

"Kayla, what is it?"

"Oh, Ikan," she said as she turned away from him to hide the tears pouring down her face.

"You know something… What is it, Kayla?"

"Ikan, could you leave me for a few moments? Just wait outside the door. There is something important I must do. Just trust me, please. I will explain. Please… just trust me."

As Ikan left the room, Kayla placed the green stone next to her heart and thought of Nalana, not realizing her powers had become so strong — she no longer needed the help of the stone for things she wished to appear before her.

Instantly, Nalana appeared before her eyes.

"Kayla, I have been following the progress of your training. You must know the amazing strength of powers within you. You no longer need your pendant for protection. You have all the power of the stone and much more than I had imagined for you to have within yourself. Use these powers and abilities with confidence and pride. You have been very blessed, my friend."

"Put your stone safely away and save it for your children or for someone you care about who may need protection."

"Thank you, Nalana. I have something very important I must ask of you. Please, may I explain?"

"What is wrong, Kayla?" she asked.

Kayla quietly explained what had happened and asked permission to explain the scrolls she had found to Ikan.

"Please," she begged, "I can't begin my marriage to Ikan with this secret in my heart."

Nalana opened the door and invited Ikan to join them.

"Nalana, what are you doing here? What is going on?" Ikan asked.

Nalana told him of all Kayla had learned from the scrolls and maps and held him to the same promise she had made with them. She agreed for him and Kayla to share the news with Silas, understanding the problem of secrets among them.

Together, they swore to reveal nothing of these things without her permission. Nalana left with the feeling that she had made the right decision for all concerned. She knew that she could trust their word.

After dinner, Kayla, Sarah, and Ikan met in Kayla's room with Silas. They filled him in on all that had happened. They agreed to keep this disturbing news between them and to keep a close eye on Blade. They knew this was not of his doing; it was of the evil spirit of Ciar living inside this innocent child.

Once they all agreed, they retired for the evening to get a good night's rest. They had a very long day ahead of them. Sarah had not been feeling well and was in much need of rest.

In the deep of the night, the castle dark and quiet, Ren and Yara were fast asleep in their beds. A dark shadow appeared in the moonlight over Blade's tiny cradle.

"Ciar, my son," spoke the voice of Trillian from the form of the dark shadow. "Release your spirit from the body of this child — unto me. I will keep you safe for all time to come. I will make great use of your powerful, evil spirit."

Blade's body began to rise, floating above the cradle on a black cloud. As he sat up and turned his tiny body to face the shadow of Trillian, deep-sounding words spoke from within him.

"I have great plans of destruction… from within the body of this child. My evil spirit will serve you well. In time, we will destroy these lands, and our evil spirits will live on for all time to come. Return to your cave and seal yourself away for a time. Watch the destruction as I grow. Know this… All evil that sweeps across this land will be of me. You will know when the time has come for you to take your place here. Be patient, my father. My evil lives strong in the soul of this child. I can cause great destruction… beyond anything you have ever imagined. You will see."

Ciar's spirit spoke as the black cloud faded away. Blade's body suddenly dropped back into the cradle as he awoke and began to cry. Yara rose from the bed to comfort her baby as Trillian disappeared deep into the dark caves. He sealed himself away once again to patiently watch over the growth of Blade.

Yara fell asleep, holding Blade tightly in her arms. She was unaware of the evil consuming her innocent little son's soul.

Chapter Thirty-Three — Ikan And Kayla's Wedding

The darkness passed quickly as the beautiful sunrise appeared over the trees beyond the castle.

"It is time to wake up, my beautiful blue eyes," Nadia said, standing over Kayla's bed with a breakfast tray fit for a princess.

"Mother, this is so nice of you," Kayla said, sitting up in bed as Nadia placed the tray across her lap.

"It smells wonderful, Mother. Thank you."

"You are getting married in less than five hours. You must eat a good breakfast. There will be no more time for food until the feast this evening. You must stay in your room. We cannot have you running into Ikan this morning. It is bad luck for the groom to see his bride before the ceremony on their wedding day. Everything is prepared… just the way you wish. The sky is clear — a beautiful day for a wedding. The flowers in the garden have all bloomed, and it appears as though all the trees and flowers in the world have come alive for this special day."

"There you are," Nadia said as Sarah entered the room.

"Good morning! I slept in a little," Sarah said. "Are you excited, Kayla?"

"Very," she replied, smiling from ear to ear.

"Your breakfast is on the table by the window," Nadia interrupted. "All of the men are having breakfast downstairs," she continued.

"Sarah, are you feeling all right?" Nadia asked. "You look a little pale this morning."

"I will be fine. I'm just a little tired," she replied.

"Men have it made. We plan the wedding, have much more to do to prepare, bear the children, and have more responsibility in raising them. They seem to sit back, relax, and enjoy it all while we do all the work," Kayla said.

"Normally, that is true; however, I must tell you, Ikan spent a great deal of time the past two days helping me set up the tables and decorations in the garden. He is very handy. He is a very special man indeed."

"He knows how lucky he is to have Kayla," Sarah said.

"The two of them are a perfect match. They are both very lucky to have found each other," Nadia said.

Kayla smiled as she finished her coffee and headed for the shower.

"It is time," Ren said as he entered Ikan's room. "It is your big day, sir. I wish you and Kayla a happy life together, my friend."

"Thank you, Ren. I am ready."

"Good morning, sir," Ikan said as he reached the bottom of the stairs.

I sat quietly in the chair against the wall, waiting to escort my daughter into the garden.

"I know you will be a good husband for Kayla. I only want happiness for her," I said as I stood to embrace Ikan.

"Welcome to our family, my son," I whispered, giving him a final hug. "Go," I said before she came down the stairs. "You must not see her before the ceremony begins."

Ikan and Ren quickly rushed off to the garden and took their place under the arch.

"How did you do that?" Ren asked, referring to the two old trees that appeared to have bent together as if holding on to each other's limbs, forming a beautiful arch covered with leaves and flowers.

"I simply asked them for a little help," Ikan replied with a grin.

"Funny, Ikan," Ren said.

The garden was filled with family and friends from all the lands, waiting for their princess to arrive and take her place beside her prince, unaware they would also be crowned king and queen in a few days.

"Your beauty is breathtaking," I said as Kayla appeared at the bottom of the stairway.

"Are you ready, Father?" Kayla asked as they began their walk into the garden.

"Yes, my princess, I am ready."

Morissa began to play the harp as they slowly walked down the flower-covered path to the arch.

"You look so beautiful," Ikan said as Kayla took her place beside him.

The wedding was as simple yet elegant as Kayla had always dreamed. She glanced at Sarah by her side with a smile.

"Everything is perfect," she whispered.

Nadia performed the ceremony, adding the final touch to make everything perfect.

She began, "This is a most special day for our lands as I perform this ceremony for Ikan and Kayla. I have dreamed for many years of this moment."

The time seemed to pass quickly as Nadia spoke. They exchanged vows and rings and said, "I do."

"I now pronounce you husband and wife, Prince and Princess of Litora Falls. Ikan, my Prince, you may kiss your bride."

Cheers, and the thunder of clapping hands filled the air for miles around, making known the approval of all as Ikan kissed his beautiful princess.

"Friends and family of all our lands, I introduce to you Mr. and Mrs. Ikan Rainie, Prince and Princess of Litora Falls and all of Amphibia. Thank you all for coming and helping us make this a special occasion. Let the feast begin," Nadia announced.

Morissa beautifully played the harp for hours as the feast and dancing continued into the evening.

"Mother, I can't thank you enough. Everything was so beautiful. It couldn't have been more perfect. It was everything I dreamed it would be." After a deep breath and a short pause, Kayla wrapped her arms around her mother and held her softly.

"I love you more than you will ever know, Mother," she whispered.

Nadia could not speak as Kayla turned to find Ikan. She watched her walk away, her heart filled with pride, knowing what a wonderful woman her daughter had become.

"Thank you, Mother. I know you are watching. You did a wonderful job raising her. You can be proud," Nadia whispered, looking at the beautiful rainbow in the sky as she sat next to me.

"You did well, Nadia," I bragged. "Everything was so nice."

"It is official, my King. You now have your son."

"Yes… Yes, indeed. The only thing missing is grandchildren," I said with a smile.

"Soon enough, my husband, soon enough," Nadia said with a soft hug.

"Ikan, I am very happy for you, my friend," Ren said as he glared into the arch. "I must know… how you did this, Ikan. There are no ropes, no tied branches, and no pegs. The trees are curved where there were no curves. I would really like to know how…"

Suddenly, the trees slowly returned to their original shape, stretching their limbs and shaking their leaves.

"Will there be anything else, my friend?" asked a deep, low voice, which seemed to come from inside the slightly taller tree.

"That will be all for now, my friends. Thank you for your help," Ikan said as he winked at Ren.

Ren stood speechless as the trees seemed to raise their limbs in acknowledgment of Ikan's words.

"I told you... I just asked them, and they were happy to help," Ikan whispered as he walked away.

Ren stood in amazement, glaring at the trees for a few moments before he could move to join his family.

"Most amazing," he said as he walked away. "Most amazing."

"There you are, my husband," Kayla said as Ikan wrapped his arms around her shoulders from behind.

"Imagine," he said, "we are married."

"Yes, we are," she said as she wrapped her arms around his.

Everything was perfect. The weather, the flowers, the ceremony, the food, the music… everything. "It has been the perfect day for our wedding."

"That is because you are here, Kayla. You have no idea how special you are to these lands. You make everything so perfect. Your presence here makes all the difference. Let's have children right away," Ikan said.

"We have not talked of children, Ikan."

"You do not want any?" he replied.

"Yes, of course I do," Kayla answered. "We just haven't talked about it, that's all. What happens — happens. We will just have to wait and see. I would love to have children... as soon as possible. I know my father can't wait to be a grandfather. He has never raised a child. He will be a good grandfather."

"Yes, yes, he will," Ikan said.

"Ikan, you must not tell Silas — Sarah is pregnant."

"That is wonderful! Now, if we have a child right away, they can grow up together."

"Imagine little Kayla and little Sarah running around the castle," Kayla said.

"It could be a little Ikan and little Silas," Ikan argued.

"We are going to have a good life, Ikan. That is if…"

"If what?"

"Never mind."

"You are thinking of Trillian and of Blade."

"Yes."

"Let's not think of this today."

"You're right. This is a good day. I don't want to spoil it."

"I love you so much, Ikan. We're going to have a wonderful life here in Litora Falls."

"I've never been happier," she said as they enjoyed the view of the beautiful garden and all their friends and family. The sky grew dim as the beautiful sun set behind the trees, giving their special day… a perfect ending.

Chapter Thirty-Four — Litoran Twins

And Little Danny…

Time passed quickly in the days following the royal wedding. All the lands were peaceful and calm. The training classes had gone well, with final testing for graduation day approaching for many Litorans, Ceairans, and Komodo dragons.

Ikan and Kayla were happily enjoying their new lives. Having been crowned King and Queen of Litora Falls and expecting their first child in a few days, they felt very blessed.

As Ikan's first order of business, he announced his plan to honor Meinkard and Eckhard in a special ceremony, crowning Sir Meinkard King of Gibbon Forest and Sir Eckhard King of Varanus Desert. They were given full control over the business of their land, families, and homes. They were proudly honored as equals to the Litorans with a royal feast.

Ikan remained head of the council but was King only of Litora Falls, allowing himself more free time to spend with his family. As King of the Taltons, Neckatosh was officially welcomed into the Litoran council, and his kingdom was recognized as part of our family of lands.

The three brave and powerful kings vowed to join King Ikan to protect our peaceful world from all that is evil for all time to come as they shared the leadership and responsibilities of our peaceful world.

Meinkard, Eckhard, and Neckatosh vowed to honor Ikan as the head of the council and always come together — as one — to help and protect each other at any time of need.

Silas and Sarah's son, Koda, was walking about, looking much like his father... at a little over a year old. Sarah had quickly adjusted to the lifestyle of Litora Falls and was expecting their second child in a few weeks.

Sly and Ciara's daughter, Bri, seemed to be growing up quickly. At only twenty-two months, she was showing signs of being an extremely bright little girl. She amazed her parents, speaking clearly and understanding many things years beyond her young age of one year.

Nadia was impressed by her potential. She began teaching her to read simple words and sentences at only fifteen months of age. Bri quickly advanced, showing signs of genius. Nadia had never before seen such intelligence in such a young child. She knew in her heart that Bri had a very bright future, and the time would come for her to live at the Small's farm to continue her education.

Ren had become the proud leader of the Litoran Defenders. He moved his family into the little cottage beyond the castle, taking advantage of the peacefulness of the lands by spending much of his time at home with Yara, raising their young son, Blade. He appeared to be growing up happy and normal.

Ikan continued his close watch over Blade's development. Knowing there had been no signs of Ciar's evil spirit since the evening of the wedding and that all had been quiet and peaceful in the lands of Litora Falls for many months, he decided to give peace to his friends and Kayla. He convinced them that he finally had peace in his heart about the evil spirit. He admitted it must have been sealed inside the Mountains with Trillian and his Draconians for all time.

Blade was free to live as a normal little boy, with no signs of the evil that had once lived inside his small body. With the help of Ikan's positive words, Kayla, Sarah, and Silas managed to push their fears deep inside their minds and peacefully concentrate on their families and the time at hand. They had not spoken of the scrolls since the evening Nalana had appeared to them and taken them away.

Ikan continued to secretly keep a close eye on Blade as he grew. He visited him daily. They had become good friends. Although he had seen no signs of evil in Blade's eyes for a very long time, he could not shake the feeling that there was still something very odd about his friend's son. Something in his eyes that Ikan could not understand.

It was a beautiful evening, with a light mist of rain falling over the trees. In the deep of the night, Kayla suddenly woke from a frightening dream in which a dark cloud covered the sky over the lands of Litora Falls as she gave birth to her firstborn child. It was a son — no, a daughter — no, a son. The healer could not make up his mind.

Suddenly, the dark cloud covered the baby before her eyes. She followed the cloud... just out of her reach... screaming for her baby... as it mysteriously vanished into the dark of the night. Black spirits circled the land from where her baby had disappeared. She woke trembling with fear. As she gathered her thoughts, she quickly realized that she was in labor.

"Ikan, wake Mother. Please. Bring her to me quickly; something is wrong!" she screamed.

"Is it the baby?" he asked.

"Hurry, Ikan, please!"

Ikan threw on his robe and rushed up the stairs to their room. After news of Kayla's pregnancy, I insisted that Kayla and Ikan switch rooms with me and move into the downstairs royal sleeping room. I felt it would become too difficult, as time went on, for Kayla to climb up and down the stairs.

"Forgive me for intruding — it is Kayla — something is wrong. Please hurry, ma'am. I think it is the baby!"

Without a word, Nadia rushed to our daughter's bedside.

"Mother, I must go to our world to have my baby — something bad is going to happen. I had a dream — I have a terrible feeling, Mother — I just know something isn't right. Please, Mother, I must go as soon as possible. I don't want anything to happen to my baby."

"We will go at once!" I shouted as I entered the room, overhearing Kayla's cry for help. "I agree. Your world is a wonderful place to have a baby born, especially if there is a problem."

"What is happening?" Silas asked, coming from the hallway. "I have been looking for you, Neree. Sarah said the baby was coming. It is much too soon, sir. She is afraid something could go wrong. She wants to go home to have the baby in the hospital, sir. She does not want to take any chances. If something should happen... it is much too early... the modern facilities... She is very insistent, sir."

"We must take her with us, Father," Kayla interrupted. "It is much too soon for her baby to be born. If it is born now, she needs to be at the Woman's Center to get proper care for him… or her. Remember, she had a miscarriage just before she became pregnant with this child. Something could be wrong. I love Doctor Baldasmere, but he doesn't have the knowledge. He is too... too out of date. He doesn't know about special things... please, Father."

"Silas, prepare your family to leave immediately," I agreed.

"Oh, thank you, Father," Kayla cried.

Quickly, they gathered their things and, within minutes, appeared in the waiting room at the Eureka Springs Woman's Center, a special facility connected to the hospital that specializes in the delivery of babies and newborn trauma.

I traveled ahead of the others through the Tunnel of Litora Falls, informing Nalana that the babies were about to be born. I quickly left their things at the small farm and took my checkbook from my hidden safe to cover all of the expenses. I arrived at the Women's Center only a few moments behind them.

Kayla and Sarah were admitted quickly and placed in connecting birthing rooms at their request. Luckily, the hospital was having a slow week for the birth of babies, and several rooms were available. The doctor on call had just finished the delivery of a baby a few rooms away, allowing her to see them both within minutes of their arrival.

"Your twins are very anxious to arrive," she said as she completed her examination of Kayla.

"Twins!" Kayla yelled. "Are you sure I am having twins?"

"What doctor have you been seeing? Didn't he or she perform a sonogram and inform you that you are expecting twins?"

"I haven't had a sonogram. My doctor is... It's complicated, I'm afraid."

"You have been seeing a doctor — haven't you?"

"Yes, Dr. Baldasmere. We are from... he is very old... a very secluded community... an old-fashioned family doctor. As I said, it's very complicated," Kayla said.

"Luckily, you are a healthy young woman, and your babies have very strong heartbeats," the doctor replied, very concerned and confused by Kayla's reaction to her question.

"Two babies! That explains a lot of things," Kayla said, trying to change the subject.

"I am going to check your friend now," she said. "From what I see, your babies should make their appearance within the hour."

"You probably should know that we have been seeing the same doctor. We live in the same secluded community. He is the only doctor for many miles."

"Wonderful," Dr. Hinge said, with a slight grin and a soft shake of her head.

"Mother, I didn't know how to answer her question. I couldn't possibly explain where we come from. Baldasmere — how could I possibly explain him to a doctor of this world?"

"You did fine, Kayla. All she needs to know is you have taken very good care of yourself, and that, my dear, is obvious. Everything will be fine. You just need to concentrate on giving birth to those two little lives inside you. Nothing else matters right now."

Nadia held Kayla's hands while looking into her eyes with excitement. "You are going to be a wonderful mother," she whispered.

"Twins… in an hour," Kayla couldn't stop smiling. "What are Father and Ikan going to think?"

"I am so excited, Kayla," Nadia said. "I have been thrilled beyond imagination by the thought of becoming a grandmother. Twins? Wow! You probably should clue Ikan in ahead of time, but let's surprise your father."

"I agree... he is going to be beaming with pride."

"I may need your help with them while they are little, Mother. I haven't been around very many babies. I'll have much to learn from you."

"I want a son and a daughter, Mother — Elliott and Eliza. I heard the name Eliza at college. It's also the name of my father's great-grandmother, Angelique Eliza Small. I love the name Eliza so much."

"I hope he won't mind. What do you think?"

"I think we should wait and see when they are born," Nadia replied. "You may have two boys or two girls."

"I know. I was just thinking how nice it would be to have one of each," Kayla said, looking very pleased.

"Ikan," Kayla said as he entered the room, "I have wonderful news. We are having twins! Imagine two babies at one time. We are going to have our hands full, my husband."

"As it is written, Kayla," he replied, with a pleasing smile. "It will be a boy and a girl. Have you forgotten the words written in the scrolls?"

"The scrolls… you're right. Hmm, I will wait to see for myself," she replied, a little doubtful.

"What scrolls? Written where? What are the two of you talking about?"

"If it's one of each, I would like to name the boy Elliott and the girl Eliza. That's if it pleases you," Kayla said, trying to ignore her mother's questions.

"Kayla, anything that pleases you will certainly please me. Eliza and Elliott," he said, placing his hand softly on her stomach. "I love the name Kayla. I cannot wait until they arrive."

"Ikan, call the nurse!" she screamed. "I don't think you are going to have to wait much longer. It seems the time has come!"

The nurse rushed into the room to examine Kayla, immediately paging Dr. Hinge. Within seconds, she arrived — just in time to deliver Elliott, the firstborn of the twins.

"A very strong, healthy boy," she announced, handing him to the nurse.

Ikan felt light-headed at the amazement of the birth of his son. Leaning against the bedside, tears of joy rolled down his face.

"This is the most amazing thing I have ever seen," he said as Kayla squeezed his hand tightly.

Two minutes later, Eliza arrived.

"Much smaller in size but equally as healthy," she announced, handing her to the second assistant.

"You are amazing," Ikan said, carefully brushing Kayla's hair from her face with his hand as he softly kissed her forehead. "They are so beautiful."

"Wonderful job, my dear," the doctor announced. "You should be very proud parents. You have beautiful, healthy twins."

"Thank you so much," Ikan said as she finished with Kayla and quickly left the room to check on Sarah.

Nadia rushed to the waiting room to tell me the wonderful news about my two grandchildren.

"Twins!" I shouted loudly, jumping from my chair with excitement.

Once I collected myself, we proudly returned to Kayla's room just as the nurse handed the babies to Ikan and Kayla.

"They are so beautiful," Nadia said. "May I hold one of them?" she asked, very anxious to feel her grandchild in her arms.

"His name is Elliott," Ikan said, carefully handing his son to his grandmother.

"Father, I have given him the name Elliott after your father and grandfathers before him," Kayla said. "Her name will be Eliza, the middle name of your great-grandmother, Angelique. I hope you are pleased."

"She is so beautiful... like her mother. It is like looking at you, once again, on the day you were born," I said, tears of happiness rolling down my face. "Only…"

"Only what, Father?"

"Only this time we get to take her, both of them, home with us to Litora Falls and watch them grow up."

"Father, you now have the chance to experience all of the things you missed with me through your grandchildren. Would you like to hold your granddaughter?" she asked.

I proudly took Eliza in my arms, overcome with joy.

"Eliza, hmm... a beautiful name for a beautiful little princess. It is amazing how very much you can love someone that you have only just met. We have been waiting a long time for you, my child. You are going to be grandfather's little girl, Eliza," I whispered.

"We will always be here for you and your family, Kayla. We will never leave you... or them. You will never know how much love you bring to my heart. I have been blessed with the most wonderful family... and now... two little angels... This is a good day for our family," I said, looking at Elliott, sleeping quietly in Nadia's arms. "You look much like your father, my little Prince," I added, with pride glowing from my eyes.

"It is a boy," Silas interrupted, entering Kayla's room. "He is very small — just a little over four pounds. A bit too early, the doctor said. They must keep him for a few days, it seems. His lungs are a little underdeveloped or something. Dr. Hinge said he should be fine with a little time. Looks much like his mother," he said proudly, "unlike this little guy, a copy of me," he insisted, referring to Koda.

"The twins are very healthy-looking, indeed. Two at one time. I cannot imagine."

"Congratulations, my friends," he said, holding Koda high in his arms to see his new little friends.

"Before long, they will all be running about the castle, getting into everything, bringing a lot of joy to all of us," Nadia said.

"A beautiful thought," I insisted. "I cannot wait for that moment. A new generation for our kingdom... a wonderful day indeed... for all of us."

"Neree, we should go to the farm. It is getting very late. Kayla needs to rest. Ikan and Silas can stay here through the night with Kayla and Sarah. It is much different from twenty years ago when Kayla was born in the old part of the hospital. The healthy babies stay here in the room with their mothers now. If the fathers want to stay overnight, they have cots to sleep in and feed them meals."

"Amazing," I replied. "I remember sleeping in the waiting room when Kayla was born."

"Silas, we will take Koda to the farm with us. He will be more comfortable there, playing about the house. There is not much for him to do here at the hospital. He will rest better in a comfortable bed."

"Thank you, ma'am. It is very nice of you. Danny will be in the nursery for several days. The machines... and tubes..."

"Do not worry about Koda. He will be fine," Nadia said. "Danny will be fine as well, Silas. He is in good hands here."

"I remember! I remember," Koda interrupted. "I remember the farm!"

Elliott laughed as I continued.

"He is so small; he must survive," Silas replied sadly. "Danny, a very different name. I like it," Nadia said.

"My father's name was Harold Danahee Taylor. We will give him the name Danahee Silas Taylor. Danny is short... for Koda to speak. Danahee… a lot for this little guy."

"It is a good, strong name," I said. "We will stop by the nursery to see little Danny, then be off to the farm."

"Do not worry about Koda. He will be fine."

"Try to get some rest. I am so proud of you," Nadia whispered, hugging Kayla softly.

"Thank you, Mother. I love you so much."

"Silas, you and Ikan need not concern yourselves with the hospital bills. It has been taken care of," I said as we headed for the nursery.

"Bills? What are bills? I do not understand," Silas said.

"Not to worry, my friend," I laughed. "This world is much more complicated than Litora Falls. Neree will see to things. Take this time to enjoy your family. I will have Neree explain once everyone is well and home," Ikan explained.

"I must check on Sarah. I will leave you now, my friends," Silas said, a bit confused by the ways of this world.

"Nadia, I have a very strong feeling we should return home for the evening. Something does not feel right," I said with much concern.

"Neree, I cannot leave… not even for the night. What of Koda? Danahee is not out of danger as long as he has these tubes and monitors. Look at how small he is. You never know for sure about these things… even here in this wonderful facility, something could go wrong. I need to be close. No, I cannot leave," she insisted. "We are Sarah's family now. She has no other. I must be close… to her… in case something happens. I promised Sarah I would always be here… for her. I have to keep that promise. Please understand, Neree, I must stay."

"Yes… I will send Yara…"

"No, Neree… not Yara. Please send Ciara instead. She can bring Bri to play with Koda."

"Ciara, it will be then," I said, concerned at the reaction to the mention of Yara's name.

"Thank you," she replied. "Little Bri and Koda will have a very good time together on the farm."

"As you wish," I replied.

"Ikan, I would like to see Sarah," Kayla insisted. "Would you ask for a wheelchair at the desk and take me to her room before they bring the babies back for the night?"

"Very good idea," he said, heading for the desk at the nurses' station.

When he returned to Kayla's room, she was sitting on the edge of the bed, anxious to see her friend Sarah. Ikan carefully helped her into the wheelchair and pushed her down the hall.

"This is fun," he said, passing Sarah's room.

"Where are we going?" Kayla asked. "I want to see Sarah."

"Yes, I know, but first, you need to see her son."

He stopped in front of the nursery window and pointed to the incubator against the back wall.

"There, Kayla. The little guy with all the tubes and monitors… he is Danny, Sarah's little son."

"Oh, Ikan, my heart breaks for him. He is so tiny. I hope he makes it. My poor friend… I can't imagine how she must feel to see him like this," she said, tears of sadness flowing down her face. "He is so tiny and helpless."

"Now, you need something to cheer you up."

He quickly moved her wheelchair across the hall to the nursery window, parking in front of their beautiful twins.

"Look at them, Ikan. We're so fortunate they were born healthy and strong. I can't wait until they wake up and the nurse brings them back to me."

"We can get them now if you want."

"As much as I would love to hold them, I need to see Sarah first, Ikan. It wouldn't be good to show them off to her just yet," she said sadly.

"Sarah, it is," he said as he pushed her wheelchair into her room.

"Kayla… Ikan… come in," Silas said, shaking Ikan's hand. "Sarah, how are you feeling? You look great."

"So do you, Kayla. Eliza and Elliott are beautiful."

"You saw them?"

"Silas took me to the nursery to see Danny and the twins a few moments ago."

"We just saw Danny. He looks just like you, Sarah. He is going to be just fine. I can't believe our babies were born on the same day," she said, trying to cheer up her friend.

"Kayla, don't you remember the writings?" Sarah whispered.

"I remember! Now I know they are true," Kayla whispered in return.

"I cannot thank you enough for bringing us with you so that our son could be born in this unbelievable facility," Silas said. "If he had been born in Litora Falls… without the knowledge of these nurses and doctors and the equipment of this hospital, he surely would not have survived. I have seen the amazing care he has received here. This is a wonderful world you are from, my friend."

"Yes, it is," Kayla replied. "Yes, it is indeed."

"It was a good thing for Danny to be born in mother's world, grandfather."

"Yes, yes, it was, Koda. One more story, boys. We must take a break for a time," I insisted as I continued with my final story for now.

Chapter Thirty-Five — Ikan's Vow

It was late evening, and darkness had settled over the land when I arrived at the castle. Sly was entering the sitting room from the north stairway just as I appeared through the south entrance.

I quickly explained the situation regarding Silas and Sarah. I told him about Nadia's need for Morissa and Ciara's help and their company. I asked him to prepare to leave as soon as possible and briefly instructed him to guide them on their journey to the farm and help them get settled.

"Sir, before I go to Ciara with your request, there is something you must know. A meeting is taking place in the council room as we speak. Kings Meinkard, Eckhard, and Neckatosh have arrived — only moments ahead of you, sir. It is the darkness… Blade and Yara… so much confusion has come upon us. They will know better how to explain all that has taken place here, sir."

"Prepare your family for their journey with haste, my friend. Nadia must not be left alone on the farm any longer than necessary. When you feel your family has settled in, you must return at once," I demanded as I entered the council room.

"Sir Neree, what of Kayla, Sarah… and the newborn?" Meinkard asked. "Did all go well?"

"Two beautiful grandchildren, Elliott and Eliza," I proudly announced. "They are strong and healthy. Kayla was amazing. All are doing quite well… Thank you for asking, my friend."

Cheers of approval roared across the room as I continued, "Silas and Sarah have a son, Danny. Making his entrance into the world much too early, I am afraid. He was born a bit too small and will need much care for some time before they can return to Litora Falls. He will become strong and healthy with the care he is receiving in Kayla's world."

"Sarah is well, with much concern for her young son. Silas is a proud father once again."

"Twins!" Ren said with excitement. "Ikan must be proud."

"Indeed! Yes, very proud indeed."

"What has happened in our lands?" I demanded, changing the subject to the concerns at hand.

"The darkness, sir," Eckhard replied. "Hanging over our lands… Circles of flying shadows… Evil spirits… Over the Drakara Mountains... Very strange — eerie sounds… sir."

"We have not seen the light since you made your journey with Kayla and Sarah. This is not the usual darkness that covers our lands at the time of rest. It is a terrifying darkness that we cannot explain, sir. Something very evil, I am afraid. We know not what is happening… We know not where the light has gone or why the darkness covers the lands in this strange way!"

"Blade is… something very odd, sir. You must see with your own eyes. I know not how to explain all that has taken place in your absence, sir!"

"Sly!" I yelled as I caught a glimpse of him passing the door of the council room. "Go to the hospital before you return to us. Ikan must be told of the situation. We must not keep this from him. He must return with you. My daughter will understand… Nadia, Morissa, and Ciara will be there for her and for Sarah. The women must stay as they are — safe from this dark time, for now. Ikan's place is here… We have much need of his powers and his wisdom. Go with haste, my friend. Return as quickly as possible… with your King."

"As you pass the tunnel, please inform Nalana of all that has taken place. Express our wishes for her to stay near the tunnel. We may have much need of her assistance for passage soon."

"As you wish, sir," Sly replied as he quickly continued on his way.

"Ren, where is Blade? What has happened to your son?" I asked, anxious to know everything.

"He is…" Ren paused sadly. The pain in his heart from the last sight of his son was too much for any father to bear. "He is in the cottage, sir. Dubkan stayed behind to watch over him. I did not wish to leave him… Dubkan would not take no for an answer, sir. He demanded I call the meeting of the council and inform the Kings of all that has taken place here since the darkness fell upon us. It is much too difficult to explain… you must see."

"For what reason is his mother not with him? What is going on, my friend?" I demanded.

"Follow me, sir. I cannot... I do not have the answers you wish, sir. You must see with your own eyes... in my home."

As Ren opened the door to his cottage, fear rushed through my body. The sight of the evil presence surrounding young Blade was horrifying! In the center of the sitting room, dark clouds of evil spirits were hanging in the air, floating softly above us.

Young Blade was sitting in the center of the blackest cloud. He seemed to be unaware of his surroundings. He appeared as though asleep — yet awake, in a trance or… under some kind of strange spell. No sound… His eyes… open… glaring… frozen with no movement…

"This is most strange! How is this possible? How did this begin?" I demanded.

"I found him floating over his bed… in this way… when I woke at the beginning of the day, sir. In an instant, dark spirits, eerie sounds, and evil smells appeared over the land. I felt this presence of evil as you began your journey with the Princess in the darkness, sir. Yara was gone from our bed. I rose to see what was happening. I could not find her. I heard voices outside the castle. As I looked out the door, you suddenly vanished from sight. The clouds of spirits under my son were floating from his room. They settled where you now see him, sir. What could be happening to him… to our lands? I do not understand any of this."

"I can answer your questions, Ren," Ikan said, suddenly appearing before them!

"An evil spirit, my friend… the evil spirit of Ciar…"

"On the night we killed him…" Ikan paused.

"What, Ikan? If you know what is happening, you must tell us at once," I demanded.

"On the night that Ren and I took Ciar's life, his evil spirit entered Yara's body. It settled inside the tiny body of your unborn son, my friend!"

"The sky's filled with darkness, much like the darkness before us."

"I saw," Eckhard said. "The darkness was as eerie as the evil presence that now fills the land."

"Kayla's room darkened with shadows of eerie clouds the moment the blades pierced Ciar's body!"

"Yara instantly fell to the floor in pain," Ikan continued.

"Yes," Ren interrupted, "I remember clearly. The darkness… much like dark shadows of clouds under Blade… I carried Yara out of the room. She was in much pain… Oh, Ikan, this cannot be true!"

"I have seen this evil spirit in Blade since my eyes first met his on the day of his birth," Ikan added, with great sadness.

"In fear of being wrong, I chose not to speak of this. I wanted it to be a dream. I did not want it to be real!"

"It is not of him, my friend. It is the evil spirit of Ciar inside of him, trying to consume his soul!"

"It is not your son he wants, my friend. It is you and I… We took his life from him. This is his revenge… and... only the beginning, I am afraid," Ikan replied.

"Nothing this evil causes to take place is the fault of this child. He is not in control of these things!"

"Blade is an innocent child. No blame shall be placed upon him," Ikan explained.

"You must be wrong!" Ren cried. "This cannot be what is happening to him. He is my only son… He is my life…"

"I heard Trillian speak of this — in the caves — the day I rescued Blade from him and returned him home to you," Ikan argued. "Ciar's voice spoke from the mouth of Blade… before my eyes. He sat on a cloud of evil spirits… as he does now."

"I thought the spirit left him when I disturbed the spell and raised him to my arms. I thought Ciar's evil was sealed in the caves with Trillian… until…" He paused.

"Until what? Ikan, we must know everything!" I demanded.

"Until the night before my wedding… I felt in my heart… it was Ciar's evil spirit…"

Ikan paused, taking a deep breath and looking up at Blade.

"What, Ikan?" I insisted. "You must tell us everything!"

"I knew then that the evil spirit was inside of Blade. I was certain this evil caused Black Prince to turn on Taran!"

"Yara was at the stables, sir. She was showing Blade to Taran when Black Prince rose against him. It is the only possible explanation," he insisted. "He raised Black Prince from a colt. The horse loves him, sir. He would never have turned on Taran if this were not so!"

"Is this true, Ren?" I asked.

"Yes," Ren answered, suddenly realizing Ikan's words must be true. He felt it in his heart. "The spirit of Ciar must live inside his innocent son!"

"When I went to Ren's room, I saw the evil in Blade's eyes once again," Ikan added. "Much time has passed. All has been peaceful in our lands… Kayla and I were…"

"Kayla," I interrupted. "My daughter knew of this. Why is it she did not inform me of something this important?"

"We were certain the spirit had left him, as Trillian and his warriors were sealed inside the caves. I have had no thoughts of this since a few days after the accident. Everything has been peaceful in our lands since that day, sir. Blade has shown no signs of this evil presence. We have watched him closely. If I had thought that there was any reason for fear, I would have told you at once."

Ikan paused for a moment, realizing I was upset with him.

"Yes, Neree, Kayla has known everything. We did not want to bring this worry to you, sir. We promised Nalana," Ikan continued.

"Nalana… Nalana also knew of this! How is it that so many knew of these things, and I was not told? Why have you kept these things from me?" I demanded.

"Kayla insisted we not worry you, sir. We thought it had passed. That it was gone from him!"

"We thought the decision became our responsibility the day I was crowned King."

"Ren, I am most sorry, my friend," Ikan said, giving me no chance to respond to his statement. "You must remember… this is not of your son. He is an innocent young child. The fault of this lies only in the evil spirit trying to consume his soul."

"We must find a way to stop this. We must save my son!" Ren cried.

"Ren, what of Yara?" I asked. "Please do not tell me something has happened to her."

"We have searched everywhere for her, sir. We cannot find her. I had thoughts — hopes — that you had need of her with you, with no time to let me know, sir. We know not what has happened to her. I am so frightened for her, sir," Ren replied.

"Please, we must save my family! I love Yara more than my own life!"

"Blade… he is just an innocent little child," Ren cried. "Please, my friends, help me save my family. I cannot lose them. I know not how I could go on without them," he said, collapsing to the floor, sobbing.

Kneeling to comfort his friend, Ikan felt a presence of hatred inside his own heart that he had not known before. Trillian had brought evil to his land.

Suddenly, remembering the words of the scrolls, Ikan secretly feared that his world, as he now knew it, could be lost forever. He knew he must find a way to destroy this evil spirit and save this child.

Suddenly, everything that had taken place flashed through his mind. He quickly rose to his feet, shouting, "Trillian may have survived! My friends, you must know war may be upon us once again. A war against an evil power we know nothing of how to destroy. We must find a way to rid Blade of this evil spirit inside his innocent body... without harm to him. We must find Yara. And… We must know, once and for all, if we have been wrong about Trillian. We must. I need to be sure in my own heart that he did not survive — as it appeared! We cannot allow this evil to destroy our world!"

"The child!" Dubkan yelled with fear.

"The cloud lifted from Blade's body as it continued to float higher in the air above us. As it circled about the room, sweeping past our heads, it suddenly left Blade floating in midair and settled above him."

"The eerie sounds from Blade echoed off the walls around him."

"Leave my son alone," Ren shouted as he stood, raising his fist to the spirit floating above his son.

Chills of fear filled our bodies as we heard the deep sound of frightening words shouting from within Blade, as the cloud slowly formed into the image of Ciar.

"You know not the destruction awaiting you and all in your lands, King Ikan… and you, Ren. You will never destroy my evil! You will never save this child… he now is mine. Your powers mean nothing to me! I will destroy your world! My evil will win this war…"

Ignoring the words of Ciar's spirit as it continued to speak, I whispered my own words to Ikan as he turned toward Ren.

Ikan quickly raised his hands toward the spirit of Ciar.

In an instant, streaks of lightning and fire shot across the room into the black spirit, accompanied by loud sounds of crashing thunder. Smoke instantly filled the spirit with sparks of fire.

Stunned by the power of Ikan, the spirit Ciar was frozen, unable to react for a few seconds… confused about what was happening, paralyzed by the great powers of Ikan!

In that second of confusion, I rose into the air beside Blade, grabbing him from the cloud as I lowered myself to the floor. I carefully placed him in Ren's arms. Before anyone knew what was happening, I managed to vanish through the tunnel with Ren and Blade.

Knowing they were safe at the Small Farm, far away from Ciar's evil spirit, I instantly returned to the cottage.

I raised my hands to assist Ikan as Eckhard covered the spirit with poison.

Screeching sounds… cries of pain… screamed from the black spirit as powerful streaks of fire and smoke began to fill the room.

Ikan, Eckhard, and I were much too powerful for the spirit of Ciar to escape its fate.

"Meinkard, everyone must make their way beyond the cottage as quickly as possible!" I yelled.

Within seconds, the spirit burst into flames.

"LEAVE NOW!" I screamed as all in the room rushed to the ground. "Fire quickly spread, consuming the small cottage!"

Standing together, we watched as the little cottage burned to the ground.

Through the flames, terrifying faces of evil spirits screamed with cries of pain as they were all destroyed.

We, four great kings and all of our warriors, stood calmly, watching the flames disappear into the darkness. Only ashes remained where the home of Ren and his family had stood.

The darkness quickly lifted from the lands. The sky sparkled as the sun began to rise over the trees.

Once again, you could feel the peace of the land in the air.

An amazing calmness, like never before, swept across the fields of Litora Falls. There was no doubt that Ciar's evil spirit was put to rest at last.

"Is it over, my King?" Dubkan asked.

"For Blade and for Ciar, it is over. Blade is safe from harm and free of the evil spirit… And Ciar's spirit is finally gone from our world!"

"Yara? I know not… We must find her. If only someone had seen…"

"If it were Ciar's spirit…"

Ren appeared before their eyes, his heart very pleased that his son had been saved.

"Why have you returned? You should be with your son," I demanded.

"Nadia and Ciara are with him, sir. He is fast asleep. He is at peace!"

"Blade remembered something of importance, sir. I must share his words. I had to come. He saw the evil spirit take his mother to the dungeon. He spoke of chains on the floor, against the wall in a corner… rags in her mouth… oh yes… big logs, barrels, and things, in front of her… hiding her from his eyes… hearing her cries…"

"Please, we must find her before it is too late."

"We must split up into groups. Search every inch of the dungeon as swiftly as possible," Ikan demanded.

"Here!" yelled Neckatosh from the darkest end of the largest area in the dungeon.

Several Taltons removed the heavy logs and barrels blocking the corner.

Ren squeezed through the opening, much too anxious to wait.

He rushed to the corner as he saw Yara chained to the floor like an animal — trembling and cold, near death!

He threw himself onto the floor beside her as Ikan raised his hand to shatter the chains, releasing her into his arms.

Without a moment to waste, I grabbed Ren and Yara and vanished once again to the Small Farm for safety and care!

I had peace, knowing Nadia would know exactly what to do to save her. Nadia and Ciara quickly began to bathe and care for Yara.

"She will be fine," Nadia assured Ren. "She is exhausted, terrified, and very hungry but unharmed. She wishes to see her son... and you, my friend."

Ren took Blade in his arms and carried him to his mother. He softly laid him beside her for warmth and comfort. He stood over the bed, smiling at his beautiful family, safe from the evil spirits at last.

Ikan stood on the grounds of the castle, looking toward the Dracara Mountains, amazed by the beauty of the green rolling hills and trees and the return of the colorful flowers across the lands.

The evil darkness had faded from the lands as far as his eyes could see.

Ikan's heart warmed with the sounds of the birds, the animals rustling about the grounds, the peaceful sounds of the flowing streams, and the wonderful cascading sounds of the waterfalls that surrounded his beautiful lands in the distance.

"This is how it should be," he thought.

Suddenly, hearing a shuffling of sounds in the grass, Ikan looked to the south.

"Shanauh," he shouted as he ran to her.

She rubbed her soft head on his side, like a kitten, showing her affection for her dear friend.

Side by side, they stood staring at the new beauty of their world, which sparkled before them.

"I feel, with everything inside of me, that you are sealed away somewhere deep inside your mountain, Trillian," he whispered, glaring into the Dracara Mountains.

"I alone can feel your presence. I am no fool."

"For now, this will remain between us," Shanauh said.

"I know when the time comes, he will return to face me once again. I can feel him as though he were standing before me. I will be here, waiting for his return. He now knows of the great powers that we all possess."

"Our day will come! I fear him no longer!"

"I vow, personally, to rid my land of him and all of his evil. The destiny of the Litorans will be fulfilled."

"I must leave for Kayla's world for a few days, Shanauh. When I return with her, she must meet your family, and you must meet ours."

"Go in peace, my friend! I know in my heart, our world will survive through you. I will wait for your return."

"I will always be here for you," Shanauh promised.

"Thank you, my friend!" Ikan said as he put his arms around her.

He stood, his fist high in the air, glaring in the direction of the Dracara Mountains.

"THIS IS MY WORLD," he yelled. His voice echoed across the lands.

Shanauh closed her wings and kneeled before Ikan. He knew well it was her way of letting him know that she wanted to accompany him to the tunnel.

It was a peaceful flight across the land — just enough light to enjoy the view. They arrived at the waterfall as the sky began to darken for the night.

Nalana was waiting, with the entranceway open. She yelled frantically for them to continue through the tunnel, giving them no time to question her intentions.

The opening instantly closed behind them as they passed.

Nalana followed them through to the end. She explained her feeling of an evil presence covering the land as they flew across — a feeling she could not explain.

"Go, Ikan… Go to your family in peace. I will see to the matter at hand and come to you in the morning. Hide Shanauh in the trees near the pond. She will be safe there until she can return home. I will see to her cubs."

Ikan left Shanauh hidden deep in the thick trees and continued to the farm home. He had complete faith in Nalana; she had always protected their family.

When he arrived, the house was quiet, with a warm light glowing from the fireplace. It seemed as though everyone was sleeping. A smile filled his face as he entered the den. Kayla was sitting in the rocking chair beside the fireplace, her arms full of the twins.

The moment completely consumed him. It was, without a doubt, the most wonderful feeling he had experienced in his lifetime. All he could do was stand there and stare at them. He did not want the feeling to go away.

Kayla quickly noticed his presence. "Well, it seems your father has finally come for us," she whispered.

Kayla appeared a little weak and pale.

Ikan took the babies from her arms and followed her to their room so she could get some rest. He sat in the chair beside the bed, enjoying his new family while their mother slept beside them. His life had never felt so peaceful and complete.

Nalana returned before sunrise to inform Ikan that all was peaceful in the land. The time had finally come to take his family home.

He felt in his heart that he now had the power to keep them safe.

Ikan chose to return home instantly, as he could not wait for all his friends and family to meet their newborn prince and princess.

All the while, he felt sadness for his friend Silas, with hopes he could soon return home with his family.

One of the most precious memories of my lifetime was the days, weeks, and months following the birth of you and your sister, Elliott. Before I knew it, you were toddlers running about the castle — getting into pretty much everything, I laughed.

I enjoyed nothing more than holding you both snuggled up next to me, so tiny and innocent, feeling that I must keep you safe forever. But I let you down, I let everyone down. I did not keep Eliza safe.

"Grandfather, what happened? I know she disappeared just as we began to walk about, but I was never told how it happened. I was asleep, and Mother would never tell me more than she was gone. I would really like to know how it happened. Please tell me," Elliott cried.

"I would like to know, Grandfather Neree. Please tell us the story. We are old enough… are we not?" Koda added.

"Yes… Yes, you are old enough. It is just so hard," I replied. "I will tell you the story. I must ask your mother's and father's permission."

"That will be enough for today, Father," Kayla interrupted. "Grandfather is very tired and needs his rest. You two run off to dinner and then to bed. It has been a long day."

"Mother, we are not tired. We want to hear more. We love Grandfather's stories. Please, just a little longer," Elliott begged.

"Your mother is right. It is late. I am starving. We must stop for today. I have many stories… Another time!"

To be continued...

"The Destiny of the Litorans"

Two

The Evil Returns (to Litora Falls)

9 798894 063768